Taken by Love

The Bradens

Love in Bloom Series

Melissa Foster

ISBN-13: 978-1-941480-00-7
ISBN-10: 1941480004

This is a work of fiction. The events and characters described herein are imaginary and are not intended to refer to specific places or living persons. The opinions expressed in this manuscript are solely the opinions of the author and do not represent the opinions or thoughts of the publisher. The author has represented and warranted full ownership and/or legal right to publish all the materials in this book.

Cover Design: Natasha Brown

WORLD LITERARY PRESS
PRINTED IN THE UNITED STATES OF AMERICA

A Note to Readers

When I finished writing the first six Braden books, the demand for more lovable Bradens was overwhelming. Thank you for reaching out and pushing me to bring the Braden cousins to life. Luke Braden is the youngest child of Catherine Braden, Hal Braden's sister. If you loved the first six Bradens, hold on to your hat, because these Bradens are a little edgier, and of course, fiercely loyal, wickedly sexy, and yes, a tad naughty. In *Taken by Love* you will meet Daisy Honey. She's smart and beautiful and has spent her years learning to be strong—and pining over Luke.

Taken by Love is the seventh book in *The Bradens*, and the fifteenth book in the Love in Bloom series. While it may be read as a stand-alone novel, for even more enjoyment, you may want to read the rest of the *Love in Bloom* novels (Snow Sisters, The Bradens, and The Remingtons).

Melissa Foster

For my readers, for pushing me to give you more

PRAISE FOR MELISSA FOSTER

"Contemporary romance at its hottest. Each Braden sibling left me craving the next. Sensual, sexy, and satisfying, the Braden series is a captivating blend of the dance between lust, love, and life."
—Bestselling author Keri Nola, LMHC
(on The Bradens)

"[LOVERS AT HEART] Foster's tale of stubborn yet persistent love takes us on a heartbreaking and soul-searing journey."
—Reader's Favorite

"Smart, uplifting, and beautifully layered. I couldn't put it down!"
—National bestselling author Jane Porter
(on SISTERS IN LOVE*)*

"Steamy love scenes, emotionally charged drama, and a family-driven story make this the perfect story for any romance reader."
—Midwest Book Review (on SISTERS IN BLOOM*)*

"HAVE NO SHAME is a powerful testimony to love and the progressive, logical evolution of social consciousness, with an outcome that readers will find engrossing, unexpected, and ultimately eye-opening."
—Midwest Book Review

"TRACES OF KARA is psychological suspense at its best, weaving a tight-knit plot, unrelenting action, and tense moments that don't let up and ending in a fiery, unpredictable revelation."
—*Midwest Book Review*

"[MEGAN'S WAY] A wonderful, warm, and thought-provoking story...a deep and moving book that speaks to men as well as women, and I urge you all to put it on your reading list."
—*Mensa Bulletin*

"[CHASING AMANDA] Secrets make this tale outstanding."
—*Hagerstown* magazine

"COME BACK TO ME is a hauntingly beautiful love story set against the backdrop of betrayal in a broken world."
—*Bestselling author Sue Harrison*

Chapter One

DAISY HONEY JUGGLED a cup of coffee, a cake she'd bought for her mother, a bag of two chocolate-dipped doughnuts—because a girl's gotta have something sweet in her life, and this was about all the sweetness she had time for at the moment—and her keys.

"You sure you got that, sugar?" Margie Holmes had worked at the Town Diner for as long as Daisy could remember. With her outdated feathered hairstyle and old-fashioned, pink waitress uniform, Margie was as much a landmark in Trusty, Colorado, as the backdrop of the Colorado Mountains and the miles and miles of farms and ranches. Trusty was a far cry from Philly, where Daisy had just completed her medical residency in family practice, and it was the last place she wanted to be.

Daisy glanced at the clock. She had ten minutes to get to work. *Work*. If she could call working as a temporary doctor at the Trusty Urgent Care Clinic *work*. She'd worked damn hard to obtain her medical degree with the hopes of leaving the Podunk town behind, but the idea of relocating had been delayed when her father fell off the tractor and injured his back. She'd never turn her back on her family, even if she'd rather be starting her career elsewhere. She supposed it was good timing—if there was such a thing. Daisy had been offered permanent positions in Chicago and New York, and she had four weeks to accept or decline the offers. She hoped by then her father would either have hired someone to manage the farm or decided if he was going to sell—an idea she was having a difficult time stomaching, since the farm had been in her family for generations. Since the closest hospital or family physician was forty-five minutes away and the urgent care clinic picked up the slack in the small town, Daisy was happy to have found temporary employment in her field even if it wasn't ideal.

"Yeah, I've got it. Thanks for the cake, Margie. Mom will love it." She pushed the door open with her butt—*thank you, doughnuts*—just as someone tugged it open, causing her to stumble. As if in slow motion, the cake tipped to the side. Daisy slammed her eyes shut to avoid seeing the beautiful triple-layer chocolate-almond cake crash to the ground.

There was no telltale *clunk!* of the box hitting the floor. She opened one eye and was met with a pair of muscled pecs attached to broad shoulders and six foot something of unadulterated male beefcake oozing pure male sexuality—and he was holding her mother's cake in one large hand, safe and sound.

She swallowed hard against the sizzling heat

radiating off of Luke Braden, one of only two men in Trusty who had ever stood up for her—and the man whose face she pictured on lonely nights. When she'd decided to come back to Trusty, her mind had immediately raced back to Luke. She'd wondered—maybe even hoped—she'd run into him. Residency had been all-consuming and exhausting, with working right through thirty-six-hour shifts. She hadn't had time to even think about dating, much less had time for actual dating. Her body tingled in places that hadn't been touched by a man in a very long time.

"I think it's okay." With smoldering dark eyes and a wickedly naughty grin, he eyed the cake.

His deep voice shuddered through her. *Okay, Daisy. Get ahold of yourself. He might have saved you in high school, but that was eleven years ago.* He was no longer the cute boy with long bangs that covered perpetually hungry eyes. No, Luke Braden was anything but a boy, and by the look on his face, he had no recollection of who she was, making the torch she'd carried for him all these years heavy as lead.

"Thank you." She reached for the cake, and he pulled it just out of reach as his eyes took a slow stroll down her body, which was enough to weaken her knees *and* wake her up. She'd left Trusty after high school and had purposely found work near her college and med school during summers and breaks, so her memory of the people she'd gone to school with was sketchy at best after eleven years, but his was a face she'd never forget.

"You've got your hands full. Why don't I carry it to your car?" His dark hair was cut short on the sides.

The top was longer, thick and windblown in that sexy way that only happened in magazines. His square jaw was peppered with rough stubble, and Daisy had the urge to reach out and stroke it. *His stubble, that is.*

Luke looked like one of those guys who took what they wanted and left a trail of women craving more in their wake, and in high school his reputation had been just that. *Carry the cake to my car? Like that won't end up with you trying to carry me to your bed?* The idea sent another little shudder through her. It was exactly what she'd been hoping—and waiting—for.

He had been two years ahead of Daisy in school, and because she'd spent her high school years fighting a reputation she didn't deserve, she'd kept a low profile. She'd darkened her hair in medical school to combat the stereotypical harassment that went along with having blond hair, blue eyes, and a body that she took care of. Now, thanks to a six-dollar box of dye every few weeks, it was a medium shade of brown. She'd never forget the time in her sophomore year when Luke had stood up for her. She'd carried a fantasy of him thinking of her for all these years. *Was I really that invisible to you?* Apparently, she was, because by the look on his face, he didn't recognize her. It stung like salt in a wound.

Her eyes caught on a flash of silver on his arm. Duct tape? She squinted to be sure. Yes. The wide strip of silver on his bulging biceps was indeed duct tape, and there was blood dripping from beneath it.

He followed her gaze to his arm with a shrug. "Scraped it on some wire at my ranch."

She should take her cake and walk right out the

door, but the medical professional in her took over—and the hurt woman in her refused to believe he could have forgotten her that easily. She took a step back into the diner. "Margie, can I borrow your first-aid kit?"

Luke's brows knitted together as he followed her inside. "If that's for me, I don't need it. Really."

Margie handed Daisy the first-aid kit from beneath the counter. "Here you go, sugar." She eyed the tall, dark man, and her green eyes warmed. "Luke, are you causing trouble again?"

He arched a thick, dark brow. "Hardly. I'm meeting Emily here, but I'm a little early."

"Good, because the last thing you need is more trouble." Margie gave him a stern look as she came around the counter, and he flashed a warm smile, the kind a person reserved for those he cared about.

Daisy felt a stab of jealousy and quickly chided herself for it. She'd been back in town for only two weeks, and she had kept as far away from gossip as she could, but she couldn't help wondering what type of trouble Luke had gotten into. Her life was crazy enough without a guy in it. Especially a guy with enticing eyes and a sexy smile who deserved the reputation she didn't. She focused on his arm and slipped into doctor mode, which she was, thankfully, very good at. In doctor mode she could separate the injured patient from the hot guy.

Luke shot a look at Daisy, then back to Margie. "Can't believe everything you hear."

I bet.

"Glad to hear that." Margie touched his arm like

she might her son. "I have to help the customers, but it's good to see you, Luke."

He flashed that killer smile again, then shifted his eyes back to Daisy, who was armed and ready with antiseptic. "I don't allow strangers to undress my wounds." He held out a hand. "Luke."

"You really don't remember me." Even though she'd seen it in his eyes, it still burned. "Daisy Honey?"

His sexy smile morphed into an amused one, and that amusement reached his eyes. "Was that Daisy, honey, or Daisy Honey, as in your full name?"

She bit back the ache of reality that he didn't even remember her name and passed it off with an eye roll. She turned his arm so she could inspect his duct-tape bandage. "Daisy Honey, as in my given name."

He laughed at that, a deep, hearty, friendly laugh.

She ripped the tape off fast, exposing a nasty gash in his upper arm.

"Hey." He wrenched his arm away. "With a name like Daisy Honey, I thought you'd be sweet."

She blinked several times, and in her sweetest voice, she said, "With a name like Luke Braden, I thought you'd be more manly." *Shit. I can't believe I said that.*

"Ouch. You don't mince words, do you?" He rubbed his arm. "I was kidding. I know who you are. I get my hay from your dad. I just didn't recognize you. The last time I saw you, your hair was blond." He ran his eyes down her body again, and damn if it didn't make her hot all over. "And you sure as hell didn't look like that."

You do remember me! She ignored Luke's

comment about her looks, secretly tucking it away with delight, and went to work cleaning his cut. "How'd you do this, anyway?" She felt his eyes on her as she swabbed the dried blood from his skin.

"I was walking past a fence and didn't see the wire sticking out. Tore right through my shirt." He rolled down the edge of his torn sleeve just above his cut.

"Barbed wire, like your tattoo?" *Your hot, sexy, badass tattoo that wraps around your incredibly hard muscle?*

He eyed his tattoo with a half-cocked smile. "Regular fence wire."

"Was it rusty?" She tried to ignore the heat of his assessing gaze.

He shrugged again, which seemed to be a common answer for him.

"When was your last tetanus shot?" She finished cleaning the cut and placed a fresh bandage over it before wrapping the dirty swabs in a napkin.

He shrugged. "I'm fine."

"You won't be if you get tetanus. You should stop by the medical clinic for a shot. Any of the nurses can administer it for you." She tucked her hair behind her ear and checked the time. She was definitely late, and he was definitely checking her out. Her stomach did a little flip.

"Are you a nurse?" He rolled up his torn sleeve again.

"Doctor, actually," she said with pride. She wondered if seeing her helping *him* stirred the memory of when he stood up for her all those years ago. By the look in his eyes, she doubted it. He had that first-meeting look, the one that read, *I wonder if I have a shot,* rather than the look of, *You're that girl everyone said was a slut.*

He nodded, and his eyes turned serious. "Well, thank you, Dr. Daisy Honey. I appreciate the care and attention you've given to my flesh."

He said *my flesh* with a sensual and evocative tone that tripped her up. She opened her mouth to respond and no words came.

Margie returned to the counter. "Can I get you something, Luke?"

Thankful for the distraction, Daisy pushed the first-aid kit across the counter, then gathered her things. "Thanks, Margie."

"I'd love coffee and two eggs over easy with toast," Luke said.

Daisy felt his eyes on her as she struggled to handle the cake, bag, and coffee again.

"Coming right up, sugar." Margie disappeared into the kitchen, and Daisy headed for the door.

He touched her arm and batted his long, dark lashes. "You're just going to dress my wound and leave? I feel so cheap."

Despite herself, she had to laugh. "That was actually kind of cute."

He narrowed his eyes, and it about stole her breath. "Cute? Not at all what I was going for."

Then you hit your mark, because it wasn't cute that's making my pulse race.

He held the door open for her. "I hope to see you around, Daisy, honey."

"Tetanus isn't fun. You should get the shot." She

forced her legs to carry her away from his heated gaze.

LUKE THOUGHT ABOUT Daisy as he sat in a booth drinking coffee and waiting for his sister to arrive. Luke bought hay from Daisy's father, and he'd known David Honey's daughter was coming back into town for a few weeks, but he'd never have put the Daisy Honey he met today with her entrancing blue eyes and way-too-sexy body as the white-blond girl who used to walk through the halls of school with her head down, trying desperately to be invisible. Daisy's eyes were sharper and wiser than they'd been all those years ago, and there was something else about this new, grown-up Daisy that had captivated him. When she touched him, the air between them sizzled. She'd done everything possible to keep him from seeing that she'd felt it, too, and for some strange reason, that intrigued him.

He was still thinking about her when Emily slapped an armful of drawings and folders down on the table.

"You are such a pain. I can't believe that after I asked you a dozen times if you were sure you wanted the bed and bath separate, and I begged you—*begged you*—not to do it that way, now you want to change it." She tossed her straight dark hair over her shoulder and straightened her white silk blouse and black pencil skirt before sitting down. Emily was an architect and owned a design build company. She was also becoming an expert in the field of sustainable energy. "This would have been much easier if you'd listened to me at the beginning—but..." She narrowed her eyes and pointed a finger at him. "Then again, if you had listened to me, I could have built you a passive house, and you could have saved seventy percent on your energy bills—"

"Okay, okay. I get it. Sit down and chill." Emily was fourteen months older than Luke, and at the moment she was giving him the same narrow-eyed, knitted-brow stare he'd seen too many times growing up. "Maybe you should skip the coffee this morning."

"Ha-ha." She flagged down Margie and ordered coffee. Black. Emily had always been feisty, and Luke supposed she'd had to be, growing up with five brothers. "So, are we just modifying the bed and bath in the apartment above the barn, or did you decide to move the kitchen to the other side of the apartment as well?"

He knew moving the plumbing and the framing was going to be a pain in the ass for Emily and her staff. He'd never ask another builder to move the plumbing; he'd have left it as it was originally designed. But just as Emily had no issue calling him at three a.m. to discuss a dream she'd had or to show up unannounced with a bottle of wine when she needed to vent with someone she trusted, he knew she probably had expected his changes and was relieved he'd made them before the walls were erected.

She ran her eyes down his arm. "Hey, what happened?"

Margie brought Emily her coffee as Wes walked into the diner. "And then there were three."

"Hey, Margie." Wes slid into the booth beside Emily. Each of the Bradens were blessed with thick, dark hair, though Emily's was straight and shiny, Luke's was coarse and wavy, and Wes's was a shade lighter and he kept it cropped much shorter than his brothers'. His cargo shorts and tank top were streaked with dirt, as was his forehead.

"Hey, sugar. I'll bring your usual over in just a sec." With her hand on her hip, she looked Wes over and shook her head. "Were you out on the trails already today?"

Wes raised his hand. "Guilty as charged. Checking out new trails. Tough life, but someone has to do it." Wes ran a dude ranch and spent his days teaching well-paying clients how to rope and run cattle, ride horses, skeet shoot, and fish and many evenings taking them on overnight pioneering adventures. Wes eyed Luke and Emily, then the pile of drawings on the table. "Did I miss anything?"

"What are you doing here?" Luke had recently helped Wes on a pioneering trip with a group of clients. He'd wound up going head-to-head with one of them and was arrested for assault. Even though the charges against Luke had been dropped, Luke was still dealing with what it said about him. He'd been thinking of nothing but ever since.

"Em said she was meeting you for breakfast." Wes shrugged. "I was hungry."

"I was just asking Luke what happened to his arm." Emily arched a finely manicured brow.

Luke shrugged. "It's nothing. I cut it on a fence, but I did just run into Daisy Honey, who cleaned it up for me. You guys remember her?" He thought of the way she'd ripped the tape from his arm and her snarky comment. She was feisty, and he liked it.

"Isn't she the girl who had that horrible rep about sleeping around in high school?" Emily drank her coffee and opened one of her folders. "God, I felt so bad for her." Trusty was like any other small town, where gossip spread faster than weeds.

"Hot little blond number?" Wes asked.

"Not anymore. I mean, hot, yes, but she dyed her hair darker. I guess she got tired of dealing with all the crap, and just for the record, I don't think those rumors were true." Luke could relate to dealing with crap, and a memory was snaking its way into his mind. He couldn't quite grasp it, but he had the distinct feeling that it had something to do with Daisy.

"I see that look in your eye, Luke. Careful. You're the last thing a woman dodging a prickly past needs." Wes held his gaze a beat too long. One of his key employees, Ray Mulligan, had quit a few weeks earlier, leaving Wes and his business partner, Chip, to lead every group that came to the ranch. Wes had been snappy and short-tempered ever since.

Luke was all too aware of his own reputation, and the arrest didn't help much. He wasn't big on lasting relationships. Or rather, he didn't connect well on deeper levels with people. Give him a horse and he could practically tell what they were thinking, but people? Women? Whole different ball game. It was only recently that he'd begun to wonder why that was.

"Dude, what's that supposed to mean?" Luke held his brother's gaze. Having been raised by their mother after their father, Buddy Walsh, took off with a dime-store clerk from another town while their mother was still pregnant with Luke, all of his siblings were protective of one another. Luke was the same, and usually their fierce family loyalty served them well, but at times like this, the last thing he needed was to be judged by Wes.

"She's had enough of a bad rep. She doesn't need yours following her around."

"Shit, Wes. You know damn well that arrest wasn't my fault. You saw what went down." The muscles in his jaw twitched.

"I wasn't talking about the arrest."

Emily slid a folder across the table to Luke; then she unfurled a set of architectural drawings, her eyes darting between them. "Can we not play Neanderthal today? Please? I have client meetings to attend to."

Margie brought Luke and Wes their breakfasts, and Emily slid the drawings to the side. "There you are, boys. Em? You want anything else?"

"No, thanks, Margie. I'm good." Emily watched Luke skim the file. "Want me to explain it?"

Luke set the file down. "Nope. I just want you to do it. I don't need to decipher the details. I want the bathroom and bedroom attached. It was shortsighted of me not to do that in the first place. I just didn't like the idea of there not being a guest bath."

Wes shook his head.

"What?" He knew damn well what Wes was thinking. His brother was a planner. He mulled over every detail of his life, which was a good thing in his profession, and he thought Luke was impetuous, that he didn't think things through. The truth was, Luke was a pantser—hard and fast. He ran from planning too far ahead or in too much detail like a rebellious teenager. Most of the time, his gut instincts were right, but sometimes, where they might have been right at the time, after he thought things through, he realized that the next idea he had was better.

In Luke's eyes, those changes would have come after his decision was made even if he'd planned things out first, like Wes did. That thought process was so far from Wes's that they often butted heads.

"Don't you want to go over the specifications?" Wes asked.

"Hell no. What I want is to get home and check on my new foal. I trust Emily's judgment, and she knows my budget. She's banging out a few walls, moving some plumbing around."

"Hey. Nice to know you value my job so much, you ass." Emily took a piece of toast from his plate and bit it, then smirked at him. "It's a one-bedroom apartment for a ranch hand. Why on earth would it need a guest bath? If you'd only listened..."

"Sorry, Em. You know I value what you do, and yeah, maybe I should have listened." Luke shoveled his food into his mouth and lifted his chin in Wes's direction. "Don't you have a playdate?"

"Yeah," Wes said with a sly grin. "With a petite little brunette and a set of books."

"Clarissa?" Emily pointed at Wes. "I knew you two would hook up."

"She's my bookkeeper, not my girlfriend, and we've never hooked up." He put his arm around Emily with a sigh. "If you put as much energy into your own love life as you do mine, maybe you wouldn't be alone."

"I'm not alone. I'm dating." She scrunched her nose. "Sort of. I think. Ugh. Do you have any idea how hard it is to date in this town?"

Luke and Wes both laughed, deep, loud, knowing laughs.

"Right. I guess you do, but it's easier for guys. You guys have dated half the women in Trusty and it just makes the women you haven't dated want you more. It's not like that for girls."

"It sure as hell better not be," Luke said. He might be her younger brother, but he'd learned from the best four older brothers a guy could have how to protect his sister. Part of protecting her meant making sure she didn't put herself in a position to become the talk of the town. That was better suited for the men in the Braden family—or at least it had been. Luke had changed. He'd always been restless, and that included being unable to settle down with just one woman, but since buying the ranch two years ago, that restless itch had calmed, and he'd become far more focused. He liked working with his hands, being around animals, and not being told what to do. The ranch was a perfect fit, and he was finally ready to make changes in his personal life, too. He wanted to be with one woman, a woman who would understand him, love him for who he was—his inability to plan and all. Someone who valued family, loved animals, and wasn't looking for something more than he could give. But that took opening himself in ways he didn't even understand, and he had no clue how to go about any of it.

Wes finished his food and locked his eyes on Luke.

"I've got to run. Bro, just tread carefully with Daisy, that's all. You know what she's been through."

Twenty minutes later, Luke climbed onto his Harley and headed back toward his ranch, thinking about Daisy and what she'd gone through in high school. Maybe they weren't so different after all.

Chapter Two

DAISY HAD JUST finished extracting an enormous splinter from a child's foot when she was pulled into the next examination room to check a two-year-old for an ear infection. Trusty had been without a doctor since Dr. Waxman retired two years earlier and migrated south to enjoy warmer weather. He had been the town physician for more than forty years, and no one had stepped up to the plate to replace him and care for Trusty's stuffy noses and splinters. Like Daisy, most modern doctors preferred to work in a busy metropolis, in the thick of diverse illnesses and cutting-edge research. She'd get there. *Eventually*.

In the next exam room she found Janice Treelong—one of the girls who had spread awful rumors about her in high school—holding her son, Michael. Daisy gripped the doorknob so tightly that her knuckles flashed white. She froze, unable to move fully into the room. She still saw Janice as the skinny, flat-chested girl who would look her in the eye with a smile and say something like, *I heard you had a great time with so and so last night behind the firehouse. Oh, you don't remember? Don't worry. Everyone else knows, and I'm sure they won't let you forget.*

Daisy took a deep breath and fought the urge to turn and flee.

Michael turned red-rimmed eyes up to her. His nose was crusty and pink, and by the flush of his cheeks, she could tell he was burning with fever. A second glance at Janice showed dark circles beneath her eyes. Her muddy-brown hair was pulled back in a messy ponytail, and her clothing was disheveled. The earmarks of the exhausted mom of a sick two-year-old—and the wife of an asshole. Janice had been one of the worst offenders, perpetuating the stereotypical blond-haired, blue-eyed, easy, sleazy reputation that Daisy had fought so hard to disprove, but it looked like she had changed a lot since high school.

Daisy took a deep breath and shifted her eyes back to Michael. He was just a little guy—a miserably sick little guy. She released the door handle and tried not to flinch when the door clicked shut behind her. She couldn't, wouldn't, let their past influence the medical care she gave Janice's son.

"Hey there, Michael. I hear you're not feeling so well. Would you like me to examine you on Mom's lap?" She tried to smile at Janice but couldn't quite pull it off.

Janice mouthed, *Thank you.* She had married Darren Treelong shortly after high school, and rumor had it that he was drinking again. Daisy felt for Janice, despite their history.

"Has Michael been eating, drinking?"

"Not much. He ate some applesauce, and I'm trying to get him to drink, but he just sips it." She brushed Michael's dark hair from his forehead.

"Okay, let's see what's going on. Do you mind if I stick this funny-looking thing into your ear for a few seconds to check your temperature?"

Michael pushed his nose between his mother's breasts.

"I'm sorry. He's overtired," Janice explained, trying to pull Michael from her chest. "It's okay, honey. She's not going to hurt you."

Daisy blew up a latex glove, which she wasn't really supposed to do because it was wasteful and the clinic worked with limited funds, but some things were more important than a wasted glove. She crouched down so she was eye to eye with Michael. "I'll let you have my special balloon if you let me examine you."

He eyed the hand-shaped balloon before stretching his spindly arm out and taking it from Daisy. While he played with the balloon, Daisy took his temperature and checked his ears. He was so engrossed in the new toy that he allowed her to lay him down and palpate his stomach.

"Well, it looks like he has a fever and an ear infection that we can take care of with antibiotics."

Janice sighed with relief. "I knew he did. Every time he lies down, he screams, and the doctor told me the last time he had a fever that if he did that, it could be an ear infection."

Daisy wrote the prescription and handed it to

Janice. "How long has he had this, Janice? Both ears are red and inflamed."

She shrugged. "Couple days."

"Did you take him to your family doctor?" She knew Janice hadn't. If she had, he would have been treated before his ears became so inflamed. The poor boy had to be in tremendous pain.

Janice sighed. "No. It's so far away, and I thought with Tylenol and Motrin it would go away, but..."

"Janice, ear infections are terribly painful, and fevers exacerbate pain. Next time he has a fever, please take him to see his doctor right away. He could have been treated when the infection first came on, alleviating his pain and your sleepless nights." She didn't like to sound so preachy, but Michael's health was more important than the forty-five-minute drive it took to reach his doctor's office. "The antibiotics should kick in after twenty-four hours. If he's still having pain in three days, take him to your family doctor." Since the clinic was supposed to provide only urgent-care services, and doctors should have full family histories in order to best evaluate and treat their patients, it was Daisy's job to remind patients that seeing their family doctors was important.

Daisy watched her leave. Even though she was adept at tucking away the pain from years of being made to feel cheap simply because of her looks, her chest still tightened when she saw the girls who had given her such a hard time in high school. She was thrown right back to the bullied young girl she used to be. She took a second to breathe deeply and to remind herself that she was no longer that defenseless girl before heading back to the front desk.

The front desk secretary, Kari Long, handed Daisy a file. "The results of Mr. Mace's blood work are here. He's lying down in room two." Kari had moved into Trusty when she married four years earlier. She was thirty-five, three months pregnant, and had twin four-year-olds.

Daisy had known Mr. and Mrs. Mace her whole life, and he, like many other Trusty folks, didn't take very good care of himself. She wasn't surprised to see his blood glucose level was elevated. In the exam room, she greeted them both and quickly assessed his flushed skin and the fear in his wide brown eyes before moving to his side and taking his hand in hers.

"Mr. Mace, this is the second time you've been into the clinic in the last five days. Did you see your family doctor like I advised?"

He huffed a breath. "You know that I don't have time to drive all that way and wait in a doctor's office. I have a farm to run."

She'd heard this from so many patients that she had to stifle the urge to shake some sense into them. "You have type 2 diabetes. This is no joke, Mr. Mace. Your blood glucose is high, and your hemoglobin A1C is high, which means this is a chronic condition. You need to see your doctor and get this under control."

He pushed himself up on one elbow. "If Doc Waxman was still around, he'd take care of it for me. Can't you do whatever needs to be done? You're five minutes from my house."

If she had a dollar for every time she'd been asked that in the past two weeks, she'd have an extra thirty bucks. Enough for a cheap bottle of wine, which right now, sounded damn good.

"This is an urgent-care clinic, not a family practice, and you know that I'm only here temporarily. I'll be off to Chicago or New York in no time."

"But I trust you, Daisy."

Daisy. She'd always be Daisy in Trusty, whether her lab coat read Dr. Honey or not. She wondered if it had been that way for Dr. Waxman when he'd first started out. He'd talked with Daisy about medical school, and he'd prepared her for the difficulties and challenges and encouraged her not to give up, but he'd never prepared her for the lack of respect she'd encounter as a medical professional in Trusty.

"Then trust my advice, and see *your* doctor." She administered a shot of insulin and squeezed his hand, then spoke in a soft, but firm tone to both him and his wife. The worry in Mrs. Mace's eyes mirrored Daisy's. She truly liked Mr. Mace, and she wanted him to be healthy. "Please see your doctor. I know driving there is a pain, and I know you're busy, but left unchecked, this can damage your kidneys and liver."

Helen Mace was fleshy and thick waisted. She and Mr. Mace had three children, and the way she looked at her husband spoke of years of love, even if her tone was harsh. "You know he's as stubborn as a mule, Daisy. He won't let me take him ten minutes away, much less forty-five."

"Mr. Mace?" Daisy shot him what she hoped was a stern look of disapproval. "Promise me you will allow her to take you."

He rolled his eyes.

"See? See what I'm dealing with?" Helen took his hand in hers. "We have a grandchild on the way. I keep telling him to see a doctor so he's around to enjoy the baby when it comes."

"Can't you just treat me here? Please?" Mr. Mace pleaded.

Part of her wanted to say, *Yes, of course,* but she hadn't worked her ass off in medical school to come back to a town where she would treat boo-boos forever. Chicago. New York. Those were places she could have a strong, meaningful career.

She met his gaze and once again felt the tug on her heartstrings. She remembered trick-or-treating at the Maces' house and Mr. Mace dressing up as a mummy, wrapped head to toe in toilet paper, scaring off the kids as they approached the front door, and Mrs. Mace calling them back with promises of candy. Their son, Matt, had helped her fix a flat tire in the rain when she was seventeen and had skidded off the road because she was driving too fast, racing away from the gas station where the girls had teased her, and he'd told her to ignore the *idiots.*

"Mr. Mace, in order for your doctor to properly evaluate and treat your symptoms, he needs to be the one evaluating you on a regular basis. Of course I will make sure that we have this under control today, but promise me you'll follow up with your own doctor."

They deserved good medical care. They deserved to have it close to home.

I deserve a life and a meaningful career.

By the time they left the office with a promise of seeing their family doctor, Daisy was ready to drive him to the doctor's office herself.

Kevin Hague, one of the male nurses and Daisy's lifelong best friend, popped his head into the room. Kevin had been shy and a little nerdy in high school. He was tall and lanky with thick glasses and more interested in academics than sports. He and Daisy made quite a pair, and not a day passed that Daisy wasn't thankful for his friendship. "I know you're heading out in five, but we're way behind. Can you give us an extra fifteen minutes?" He waved three charts.

"Sure. I swear, Kevin, if this town doesn't get a doctor soon, there will be no one left to care for. They'd all rather die than drive forty-five minutes." Daisy had been working extra hours whenever she could to keep from going stir crazy, earn a little extra money, and always with the hope of handling an interesting case—which she knew was a terrible thing to hope for.

"You could fix that, you know. Hang a shingle outside your door. Take over where Doc Waxman left off."

She glared at him.

"Right. No way, no how. Pick a file." He held three files up, then whispered, "Pick the middle one." He flashed a mischievous grin that lit up his dark eyes.

"Okay. The middle one it is, but if this is another drunk guy who needs an IV like last time, you're dead." She snagged the file.

"You'll love me this time. Exam room four."

Daisy buried her nose in the file as she walked into exam room four. "Okay, let's see...Luke Brad—"

Oh God.

"Dr. Honey, I didn't expect to see you here."

She cleared her throat to try to gain control of her racing pulse as the room grew ten degrees hotter. Luke didn't even have to try to look sexy. It was so unfair. Sitting on the exam table in his dangerously low-riding Levi's, tanned and muscled arms practically bursting through his shirt, with a lazy smile and absolutely zero visible signs of discomfort or tension, he looked relaxed as hell, while she could barely think straight.

Bastard.

Sexy bastard.

"The shot?" Luke reminded her.

She closed the file and tried slipping into physician mode again. Not so easy the second time around. "Tetanus. Let me just go get the shot. I'll be right back."

His eyes widened in an amused fashion as she stole out of the door and into the supply room, where she leaned against the door, palms flat on the cold wood, and took several deep breaths. She knew he'd seen how flustered she was at seeing him again. *Oh, come on. No, he didn't.*

"What the hell is wrong with me? Pull it together." She smoothed her lab coat and reminded herself that he was just a patient. *A hot, alluring patient who I want to pull into the stockroom and make out with. Holy moly, Daisy. Pull it together.* She grabbed what she needed to administer the shot, and with one final deep breath, she headed back to the exam room.

Surely he wasn't that hot. She was just used to the

Trusty men, who were, in all fairness, pretty damn hot since they worked on farms and ranches, or were mechanics and used to hard work. But they weren't the smartest tools in the shed, and that was something that Daisy couldn't overlook. She tended to lose interest in those who weren't pushing to better themselves. It was a flaw of hers, and she was aware of it, but she'd never been able to squelch it. She knew Luke was bright. All the Bradens were, and well educated to boot. *Oh boy. Not helping.* She was here for only a few weeks. She didn't need to fall into Luke Braden's bed and become another name on a long list of women he'd conquered, even if he was ten times as hot as she remembered, with a body that she wouldn't mind being pinned beneath and a voice that made her tingle all over. She hesitated as she reached for the doorknob. Wasn't she doing just what she'd spent her life fighting against? Was she judging him based on hearsay? Eleven-year-old hearsay?

Yes, she decided. She was doing just that, and that wasn't fair at all. At least that's what she told herself.

She passed Kevin on the way out of the supply closet and grabbed the back of his scrubs. He turned with a tease in his green eyes.

"Do you love me?" Kevin asked with a conspiratorial grin.

"I'm not sure if I hate you or love you, but right now I can barely remember my name, so I'm leaning toward the hate side."

"That means you owe me one. Brunette, please; stacked is good, too." He sighed. "You do know that you're hotter than him, right? Remember that when you go in there. He should be more nervous than you. Brains and beauty. Killer combo."

God, I love you. Kevin was, without a doubt, the best friend a girl could have, and if there were a nice enough woman around to set him up with, she'd do it in a heartbeat, but right now, she had a shot to give.

With a deep breath, she entered the room. *Yup, still damn hot.* "Okay, you're not afraid of needles, are you?"

"A gorgeous woman wielding a needle? Not a chance."

She felt her cheeks flush despite his cheesy line. She moved his arm away from his lap, feeling his pulse while she was at it. Damn him. He was calm as could be. "I'm just going to clean you up before I give you the shot."

"You seem to spend a lot of time cleaning me up."

Oh...I don't mind. She swabbed the area in preparation for the shot. "Ready?" One look into his eyes had her stomach fluttering.

"Always." He narrowed his eyes and flashed that flirtatious grin again, the one loaded with sensual promise. He held her gaze for a beat longer, sending a shiver down her spine.

She gave him the shot and then forwent the urge to redress his wound in order to prolong their visit. She'd spent years fighting her reputation. She didn't need to kill it in one night.

"Okay. You should be good to go."

He didn't move. A slow smile crept across his lips again. This one was friendly, less flirtatious. He looked down at his hands, and in that moment, he looked...wholesome, which took her by surprise.

"Thanks, Daisy." He hopped off the exam table and stood way too close to her.

Daisy lifted her eyes from his broad chest and shoved her hands into the pockets of her lab coat to keep from reaching out and touching him. That's it. She needed to find someone—or something—to settle her hormones. Someone nonthreatening. Someone who wouldn't talk about it. She swallowed hard, knowing it would be a battery-operated friend or no one at all, and both choices sucked.

"Hey, um...Would you like to have a drink later?" he asked tentatively. It drew her eyes right to his, which held hope rather than flirtation and reeled her right in.

"Drinks?"

He shrugged. "Or dinner? Whatever. I thought maybe we could hang for a while."

Hang for a while. She didn't trust herself to hang for a while with Luke Braden. She was too revved up.

"I...um. I need to visit my dad tonight."

His eyes filled with disappointment, followed by a telltale shrug. "Your dad? You don't have to make up an excuse. You can just say you're not interested."

He reached for the door and she reached for his arm, surprising herself.

"My dad fell off his tractor and hurt his back. I really do have to visit him." Why was she explaining this to him when she should be walking the other way? She was here for only a few more weeks, so nothing could come of it, anyway.

"I'm sorry. I thought...Usually, if a girl's not

interested, she'll make up an excuse like that." He ran his hand over his eyes. "I know your dad. I should have put two and two together. Jesus, I'm sorry."

"I'd just say I'm not interested if I wasn't interested."

"So...You are interested?"

She wasn't ready for this. She'd been waiting for an invitation like this from him for years. She was playing with fire—her own fire that desperately needed tending.

"I...didn't say that either." *Shitshitshit.* She contemplated asking him about Margie's comment, but seeing as her mouth and brain weren't working so well together at the moment, she held back.

"Right." The smile he flashed this time was a genuine one, without a hidden agenda, and she liked it.

She knew she was giving him mixed signals. Hell, she was giving herself mixed signals. *Oh, the heck with it.* "I probably won't be with my dad that long. Why don't we go out for drinks after I see him?"

"Yeah?"

"Yeah." Her heart slammed against her chest, as if she'd just won a date with her high school crush. Sadly, she'd been so busy avoiding her rep in high school that she never had time to think about crushing on anyone. She wrote down her phone number and the address of the apartment she'd rented for the next few weeks. Maybe this was what happened when a person spent their life working hard to keep a clean rep and combat a fake one—one day they just went off the deep end and went out with the most gorgeous, troublesome person they could find. She rolled her eyes at her internal thought and glanced at Luke again. This time with clearer judgment, she hoped. She held the paper with her information on it against her chest.

"Wait. The trouble that Margie mentioned? Should I worry? Did you hurt anyone? Run drugs?"

He held her gaze and knitted his brows together. But he didn't appear angry or guilty. He looked annoyed, as if he'd been asked that very question one too many times. Knowing Trusty gossip, he probably had.

Luke sighed. "No, no, and no. Listen, maybe this wasn't such a good idea."

He held her stare for a beat longer, and despite the full-body shudder that ran through her, despite seeing that he looked at her with the same desire she felt humming through her, something told her to trust him. *Oh boy. I'm really playing with fire.* She handed him her number.

"If you're going to buy me drinks, you have to buy me dinner, because after working here all day, I'm starved."

"Dinner it is," he said with a smile, which faded quickly when he continued. "I'm not dangerous, Daisy. At least not in the ways that are running through your mind." He looked at his watch.

"Um, I need at least an hour to see my parents and shower." *And figure out how to stop being so damn nervous.*

"I'm easy. Want to text me when you're ready?"

Why did *I'm easy* make her stomach quiver? "Sure, but I need your number."

He glanced down at the paper, then patted his arm

where she'd given him the shot. "I'll text you so you'll have it. Well, Daisy Honey, thank you for taking care of my needs once again."

Oh shit, I'm in big trouble.

Chapter Three

DAISY BREEZED INTO her parents' house with the cake she'd been thinking about all day. She found her father in his recliner—where, from what she understood, he was spending far too much time since his accident. He wore his signature attire: a pair of Wrangler jeans and a plaid button-down shirt. His light brown hair was thinning on top and graying on the sides, and his blue eyes were as dark as Daisy's and her mother's were bright. He had always been the rock of the family. The provider, the quiet strength that kept them grounded and safe. It saddened her to see how his skin had already lost the sun-kissed glow of working outside from dawn until dusk, and his face was no longer a mask of determination but one of defeat and irritation, which she knew came from the pain he was in. Though the specialists had given him a solid prognosis for recovery, it was unlikely that he'd ever have the ability to go sunup until sundown doing what he loved most—working his hay fields.

"Hi, Dad. I brought you and Mom a cake. Did you get outside today?" Though her father was too prideful to allow Daisy to examine him, she'd seen the MRIs and X-rays. She considered their family lucky that his accident hadn't been worse than a sprain.

"Hello, darlin'." David Honey was adept at avoiding questions he didn't care to answer.

Daisy sat on the couch. "Dad, you're not paralyzed. You fell off the tractor a few weeks ago, and granted, you strained your back and you had pain and swelling, but you didn't break your back. You've been through the worst of it, and it would do you good to get outside and walk. I wish you'd at least try." She'd learned the hard way that in every situation there really was a silver lining, just as the rumors she'd endured in high school had made her stronger, more determined. She wished her father would dig deeper and find the same determination against his injury so he could move forward.

"Daisy, this looks almost too good to eat." Susan, Daisy's mother, joined them in the living room. She and Daisy shared the same natural blond hair, and it felt strange to sit with her mother and know they no longer looked so similar. She reached up and touched the ends of her hair as she took in the dark bags under her mother's eyes and listened to the fatigued sigh at the end of her sentences. Her father hadn't been sleeping well since his accident. Between the pain and the severe change to a sedentary lifestyle, he often spent hours awake at night, which in turn, meant that Susan did, too.

"I've been thinking about this cake all day." That

was a fib. Luke had stolen her thoughts ever since she'd picked up—and dropped—the cake.

Her mother touched her knee. "You'd eat chocolate for breakfast if I let you." She slid her tired eyes to David. "You too. Daisy, did I ever tell you about when you were little and we had leftover cake?"

Daisy smiled. "Only a hundred times."

"I can't tell you how many times I came downstairs to find you wrist deep in cake and beaming like a sunflower. And your father, Mr. Mind-Your-Manners-and-Don't-Talk-Back turned into Mr. Softy when it came to chocolate."

"All I said was that there were worse things in life than eating too much cake, and if that was the worst she ever did, we'd be lucky."

Her mother rolled her eyes. Daisy cringed, because she had left a trail of teenage trouble when she left for college. She'd never done the things the rumors claimed she'd done, but she'd snuck out with Kevin—always with Kevin—tried smoking, drank too much—and got home safely, thanks to Kevin, who never drank or smoked—but in the end, she'd grown up, like kids inevitably did.

"I can't picture Dad even saying that. You were always so strict with me."

Her father dug into his cake. "Were?"

"A girl can dream." Her father had always been strict with her, but he—and the rumors that pushed her to prove herself—were the driving forces behind her 3.9 GPA. When he wasn't working in the fields, he was working in his office. Daisy hadn't realized until she was in medical school how his work ethic had worn off on her.

"Let's not go down that road tonight," her mother said as she touched her father's leg.

"How's it going at the clinic?" her father asked.

"Good. Busy. You know." Daisy was anxious to get to her date. Her father seemed okay, even if tired and disinterested in taking an active part of his recovery. She'd have to work on that.

"And you're doing a good job?" he asked.

Her mother shot him a look that clearly said, *I can't believe you asked her that.*

Daisy sighed. *No. I'm a dolt.* "Of course."

Her father gave her a stern nod.

Nope, there was no way that Daisy could reconcile that serious face with one softening toward a younger Daisy elbow deep in cake. She needed to shift the conversation away from herself.

"Dad, when's John coming to cut the hay? Shouldn't it be done by now?" John Waller owned a farm down the road, and he had been helping her father since his injury.

Her father gazed out the window with a heavy sigh. She knew this was hard on him, not being able to work his own farm and care for his family in the ways he always had.

"He said he'd be here tomorrow." He pressed his lips.

"Should we call him? Just to be sure?" Daisy asked. She caught a stilted shake of her mother's head and knew she'd struck a nerve. She'd brought the cake, hoping to brighten her parents' evening, but she knew that nothing would lift the cloud that loomed above them until by some miracle her father could resume his ability to work—which she feared was never going to happen—or he gave up control and found someone to run the farm.

"*We* aren't going to do anything." Her father turned stern eyes to her. "I will handle this, just like I always have."

"Okay, but I'm here if you need help, and you know I know how to do all the things you need done."

"Of course I do. I taught you." He'd taught Daisy how to do everything from seeding and cutting to baling and selling, and now, as an adult, she looked back and treasured the time she'd spent with him, even if she used to wish she was doing anything other than learning about farming.

Her father's injury made him even more prickly than usual, and Daisy was ready for that drink. She rose to leave, thinking about when she'd peeked out of the clinic window and seen Luke climb onto a big black motorcycle. It had amped up the sexy quotient—not that his sexiness needed amping up. She'd spent her life avoiding men like Luke, but something in his eyes had reeled her right in.

"I've got to go." She kissed her father's cheek. "I love you, Dad. I hope you have a good night's rest tonight, and please, just take one stroll around the yard. Please?"

He mumbled something about there being no sense in it.

"Don't mind him, Daisy," her mother whispered as she walked her to the door. "He's just overtired."

"If you mean cranky, then yeah, he's been

overtired my whole life. I'm used to it. But the injury seems to have made him a little worse, which is to be expected." She searched her mother's eyes. "How are you? Are you okay? This is stressful, and I know you aren't getting out much."

"I need to be here in case your father needs anything."

"I know, but I can come over and sit with him while you go out with a friend, or for a walk, or whatever you want."

Her mother wrapped her arms around Daisy. "You're such a sweetheart. I'm good. I love your father, and I don't mind taking care of him. Lord knows he's cared for us without complaint for years."

"I know, but you know that he's capable of taking walks, and he should be taking them. Not just to strengthen the injured muscles, but for his emotional state, too. Even if he can't work the farm, I think just being out there would help. And if John doesn't show up by the weekend, I'll come cut the hay. I kind of like driving the big machines. It's a great way to alleviate stress."

"Which is exactly why your father loved doing it."

Something in common. Imagine that.

Her mom pushed Daisy's hair from her shoulders. "He's proud of you, you know. Despite his inability to tell you, he is."

She knew, but hearing her mother say it made her tear up a little.

Chapter Four

DAISY TEXTED LUKE as she left her parents' house, and as she neared her apartment, worry stewed in her stomach. She called Kevin as she pulled into her apartment complex. It struck her that even in high school there were a few girls who were nice to her, but Kevin had always been her go-to friend. Her college friends had prodded her to see if there was something more between them, but amazingly, there had never been a time when either of them had wanted their relationship to be anything more than a friendship. As she listened to his voice when he answered the phone, she was glad they'd never tried to force something that wasn't meant to be. She loved him—like a friend.

"Hey, Kev. You would tell me if Luke had done something horrible that I needed to know about, right?" Of course he would.

He laughed. "A little late to ask, isn't it?"

"Shut up. You told me he was arrested in another town and the charges were dropped. That made me feel a little better, but...I've been gone a long time. Is there anything else I need to know?"

"Daisy, I wouldn't have led you to that room if I were worried. He's Luke Braden, so you know about what he used to be like in high school, but I haven't heard anything bad in the last few years. I mean, he's a Braden. They have a great rep here and in Weston. Besides, I know you, and you'll make him tell you the real scoop. Do you need a chaperone on your date?"

She laughed as she unlocked her apartment door, even though she knew he was only half kidding. He'd come along if she asked him to. With the dirty thoughts she'd had all day about Luke, she probably did need a chaperone.

"I'm twenty-nine. I think I can handle him as long as he's not an ax murderer, and I doubt my dad would sell hay to an ax murderer. I just wanted to see if you knew anything else."

She ended the call, red flags waving loud and clear in her mind. She had no idea why she was willing to risk her reputation on a guy she had a wicked crush on. She trusted her gut instincts where Luke was involved, and her instincts were to trust him—but she wasn't sure she could trust herself.

Daisy had been lucky when she'd found an apartment that would rent to her on a month-to-month basis. After living on her own for so long, she didn't want to stay at her parents' house for an extended visit. She liked having her own space, and she was sure that by now they were used to having their own space, too, even if they missed her. She showered and dried her hair, taking an extra minute to look at herself in the mirror. She fingered the ends of her hair again. Seeing her mother's beautiful blond hair made her miss her own lighter hair color. She pushed the thought away and weaved around unopened moving boxes as she changed her outfit for the fifth time. She'd put most of her belongings into storage until she decided where she was going to be living, but she'd brought her medical books and clothes, her *necessities*. Unpacking seemed like a commitment to staying in Trusty, and she wasn't willing to go that far. For now, dodging boxes was just fine.

She heard Luke's motorcycle in the distance, and her stomach fluttered. She ran a comb through her hair one last time. She was lucky. Her hair still felt silky even though it was dyed, and it had just enough natural waves to negate the need for heavy styling. Her black sleeveless sweater would be the perfect weight for the brisk evening. She had no idea where they were going on their date, but she was dressed appropriately for just about anywhere in Trusty. She'd worn her favorite pair of jeans instead of the short skirt she'd wanted to wear, in anticipation of riding his motorcycle—and hoped that the extra material would serve as a reminder to keep her clothes on around Luke.

She answered the door and felt her cheeks flush at the sight of Luke, freshly showered and sporting a lazy smile. Sensuality rolled off six feet of solid muscles wrapped tightly in low-slung jeans and a T-shirt like sugary sweetness wafted from a bakery. And Daisy was starved.

"Hi." Like everything about Luke, his voice was deep and easy.

"Hi." She felt her steely resolve slip away like melted butter.

He handed her a single red rose. "You look beautiful. I almost didn't recognize you without a needle or bandage in your hand."

She took the rose, her eyes never leaving his, and for a second—or thirty—she stood there, rooted to the ground. His smile widened, and she blinked away her stupor.

"Sorry. Come on in." She stepped aside as he passed. His eyes danced over the still-packed boxes that lined the far wall as she went to the kitchen and put the rose in a vase. "This was so nice of you."

"Did you just move in?" He waited for her just inside the door.

"Two weeks ago. I haven't had time to unpack, and I'm only here for a few weeks anyway, so why bother?" She joined him by the door, and it struck her how similarly they were dressed. "We look a little like we called each other to match outfits."

Luke looked down at his clothing, as if he'd forgotten what he had on. "Indeed it does." He pointed to the door. "Want me to go home and change?"

She laughed. "Half of Trusty will be wearing jeans and T-shirts tonight. In fact, probably most of Trusty." He was naturally easy, relaxed. Her nerves tied themselves into a hundred different types of knots, and she envied that about him.

"Shall we?" He opened the door.

"Where are we going?" Out in the hall she waited

as he checked to be sure her door had locked behind them. *Hm*. It had been eleven years since anyone had looked after her in that intimate way—and eleven years ago it was her father checking the locks. She realized how similar checking the locks was to how Luke had kept her safe all those years ago. She liked seeing that protective side of him toward her.

"It's a surprise." He placed his hand on the small of her back as they walked through the dimly lit parking lot toward his motorcycle. A wave of heat pulsed beneath his touch. Daisy had dated a guy in college who drove a motorcycle, and the memory that stuck with her was how she'd thought that straddling the bike, and her date, would stimulate sexual feelings when she rode, and she'd been surprised when they didn't. Her body was already humming with desire at the sight of Luke—and walking close, with the breeze at her back and his masculine, musky scent wrapped around her, sparked fires in all the right places. *Wrong places. Oh God*. Maybe she did need a chaperone.

"I should have asked if you minded riding a motorcycle," he said as he picked up a helmet.

"It's okay. I don't mind."

He helped her on with the helmet. "You look cute as hell."

She doubted that, but he'd just earned bonus points by saying it with such sincerity.

"I won't drive too fast, but you need to hang on tight."

He climbed on in front of her, and she put her hands on his hips. She'd forgotten the awkward feeling of not knowing how close to sit. He took her hands from his hips and drew them all the way around him, until her breasts pressed against the hard planes of his back and her hands were flush against his rock-hard abs—and heat warmed the area between her legs. When he started the engine, it heightened her arousal. As they drove out of town and onto the highway, being that close to Luke and the vibrations of the engine made her body hum. *This is way better than holding you in my dreams.*

They drove into Allure, Colorado, two towns away, and Luke slowed as they rolled down Main Street. Allure was about the same size as Trusty, but while Trusty was a small ranch town and everything about Trusty smelled of horses, leather, or hay, Allure was more suburban, with restaurants and bars, and a quaint, brick-paved village that was lit up year-round with white lights, giving it a perpetual holiday feel. Luke drove past the Village and all of the restaurants along the main drag. When he turned down a dirt road and the lights of a Ferris wheel came into view, Daisy remembered about the county fair. She hadn't been in years, and she felt a smile press her cheeks as they parked in the field of cars and climbed from the bike.

Her body was still vibrating even after she was on solid ground. She put her hand on the bike to steady herself as Luke helped her take off her helmet.

"I hope you haven't already been to the fair." He brushed a lock of hair from in front of her eyes with his index finger.

"I actually haven't been in years." The intimate gesture took her by surprise, as did his choice of where to go on their date. She'd expected him to take her to the local pub for a beer and try to feed her a burger and fries in hopes of getting laid. She was relieved, even if a little disappointed that maybe he didn't want her in that way, and once again, intrigued, by this man whom she realized she'd judged unfairly based on a reputation he'd had when she'd left town eleven years ago. If anyone should know better than to judge someone unfairly, she should. *Well, I'll just have to make up for that.* She grinned at the dirty thoughts that conjured up.

"Was the ride okay?" He locked the helmets to the bike and settled his hand on her lower back again, sending another shiver of warmth through her.

"Yeah. I hope I didn't hold you too tight."

The right side of his lips lifted. "I doubt you could ever hold on too tight."

Why did everything he said sound sexual? If Kevin had said the same thing, she would have wrapped her arms around him and squeezed until he pleaded for her to stop, just to prove she could. There would have been nothing sexual about the words or the touch. If she were to wrap her arms around Luke, she had a feeling they'd have to pry her off with a crowbar.

They crossed the grassy field that served as a parking lot, and headed toward the lights. The air smelled of buttered popcorn, hot dogs, and livestock. Daisy felt herself smiling. She wouldn't have even thought of going to a fair. She looked up at Luke, and at that very second he looked down at her. The air between them sizzled. They meandered through the crowds. Shouts from the rides and laughter filled the air. Arms shot out from the cars on the Ferris wheel as they went around and around. Dozens of people waited in line for the carousel, while parents stood off to the side taking pictures with their phones and waving at their children. The din of laughter grew as they neared the bumper cars. Just being at the fair eased Daisy's nerves, and when Luke slid his hand into hers and pulled her toward a funnel cake vendor with a spark in his eyes, she realized that she was breathing normally for the first time in two weeks. She wasn't thinking about work, or her father's injury, and she wasn't counting the seconds until she could leave Trusty and get started on her *real* career.

LUKE BOUGHT A funnel cake and tore off a piece. "Mm. Open up."

Daisy crinkled her nose. "Do you know how bad that is for you? I haven't had a funnel cake in years, and just the smell of it makes me drool."

"Who cares? You're not eating twelve." He drew his thick, dark brows together and gently coaxed her. "Come on. One night of yumminess never hurt anyone. Besides, you can't go to a fair and *not* have funnel cake."

"How can I turn down logic like that?" She opened her mouth, and he popped it in and then ate a piece himself.

"You can't tell me that isn't delicious."

She closed her eyes for a second, savoring the sinful treat. "Sinfully delicious. The best dinner ever."

"I'm not that cheap. I'll still spring for a hot dog," he teased.

They finished the funnel cake as they strolled

through the fair, and Luke felt the initial tension he'd sensed in Daisy fall away.

"Do you want to eat now, or have some fun first?"

Daisy narrowed her eyes. "I'm trying to reconcile the Harley-driving guy who wrestles with fences and uses duct tape for Band-Aids with the idea of a carnival being *fun* to you." She ran her eyes down his body, and holy hell, did it turn him on. "What other surprises lie beneath your tough exterior?"

Christ, he wanted to take her right there, feel her body pressed against him and kiss her until she couldn't think straight. He'd show her what lies beneath...

Holy hell. I need to get a grip. He shook his head in an effort to bring himself back to reality.

"What can I say? I'm a complicated guy." He'd chosen the fair because he'd be less likely to act on his desires as quickly as if they'd gone out for a drink. He hadn't realized it at the time that he'd made the decision, but now he realized he was leaving the old Luke behind. Sort of. He couldn't help but think about how sexy she was, even if he was trying not to act on it. "So? Food or fun?"

"I'm not very hungry. Let's go on a few rides first."

He narrowed his eyes. "How daring are you?" It was a loaded question, given that she was sexy enough to make him want to drag her behind the bumper cars to make out.

She shrugged. "Kinda sorta daring?"

He took her hand and led her to the line for the haunted house. "Let's put you to a test on ground level first. If you can handle being scared with your feet on the ground, then we can turn it up a notch." *Like, on my bed*. Shit. He had to stop mentally going there. He needed a distraction. She was too cute, and feisty.

"The haunted house? I'm more afraid of things in the dark than heights or speed. When I first moved into my apartment in Philly, I slept with every light on except my bedroom light. For a month."

He closed the gap between them, leaned in close, and rested one hand on her hip, then whispered, "Scared by things that go bump in the night? I'll have to remember that." Everything she said made him picture her lying beneath him in his big, comfortable bed. He'd take away all those fears of the dark and replace them with things she'd never want to forget.

The haunted house was set up inside a double-wide trailer. The line moved quickly, and when they pushed through the dark curtain that served as a door, the interior was pitch-black. The air was stale and humid, and Daisy hooked a finger into his belt loop. He wrapped an arm around her shoulder and held her close. Her breathing was hitched, and when he settled his hand on her upper arm, it was covered with goose bumps. The floorboards creaked beneath their feet as they followed the darkness through what felt like a hallway. The floor began to undulate and Daisy's other hand gripped his abs—sending a wave of heat to his groin. He tightened his grip on her shoulder, trying desperately to rein in his desires. She felt so good pressed against him, touching him...

The floor swelled and swayed beneath them, causing them to stumble from side to side. Flashes of light up ahead briefly illuminated the path toward intermittent screams and a tremulous *wooooo*. A skeleton dropped from the ceiling inches ahead of them and Daisy screamed. Luke pulled her close and pushed the skeleton aside.

"You okay?"

"Yeah." She was shaking.

A black-gloved hand grabbed Daisy's arm. "Luke!"

He held tight and drew her closer. She pressed herself against him. It felt like she would crawl under his skin if she were able. Another flash of light up ahead, and a screech filled the air as a ghostly figure passed before them, causing Daisy to suck in a breath and freeze.

"It's okay. It's not real," he reassured her.

She slid her hand up to his chest. "Your heart isn't racing like mine." She drew away a little, and he knew she was making an effort to be brave.

The darkness filled with eerie, shaky howling. Something flew by their heads, screeching as another flash of light illuminated a bloody image by the wall. Daisy plastered her body against Luke again. She was barely breathing as he guided her through the dark tunnel around a bend. He felt guilty that he was loving the feel of her against him while knowing she was terrified.

"It's okay. It's almost done." Light trickled in through the dark curtains at the exit. She clung to him, and when they came out into the night, he held her trembling body close. They were chest to chest, and he could feel the frantic beating of her heart against his.

He tipped her chin up with his index finger. "You okay?"

Embarrassment heated her cheeks. "I'm sorry." She pulled away, but he held tight, keeping her against him.

"I'm not." Her lips were a breath away, his hands flat against her back. He lowered his mouth to hers, and she closed her eyes in anticipation of their kiss. A couple barreled out of the exit and slammed into them. Luke kept his grip on Daisy and swooped her to the side as the laughing couple stumbled past them, breaking the intimate moment.

Luke looked into her wanting eyes. He wanted—*needed*—to kiss her, and he could tell she was hoping for the same thing.

A man's voice broke their trance. "You stupid bitch," he hollered.

An icy shock ran down Luke's spine. He scanned the people walking past, and his mind rewound to a party years before, when he'd seen Daisy across a grassy field. She was breathtaking in her frilly tank top and jeans shorts, with white-blond hair that swept across her shoulders. He'd wanted to tangle his fingers in her hair and kiss her luscious lips. And in the next breath she was gone. He'd gone looking for her, and when he found her, she was fighting off a drunken guy he didn't recognize. Luke had stepped between the drunken slob and Daisy, and he vaguely remembered pushing the guy away before turning around. But when he did, Daisy was gone. She'd disappeared as quickly as she'd appeared—and he'd gone back to his partying like the bonehead kid he was.

Now he shifted his eyes to Daisy, who was clinging to the waist of his jeans. She was safe. She was right there with him.

"Damn you. I said back off, bitch." The man's voice sent Luke's pulse racing. He scanned the crowd again and locked eyes with the tall, blond man. Darren Treelong. *Goddamn it.* Darren was from their hometown, and he was a drunk. He wore his hair in the same style he had in high school, long and shaggy. He was younger than Luke, and Luke didn't know him personally, but he knew of him because of the rumors that ran through town about his drinking, and that was enough.

He tightened his grip on Daisy's hip, and the muscles in his jaw bunched. Daisy turned toward the voice and gasped.

The woman Darren was yelling at stood with her shoulders rounded forward, her eyes trained on the ground. Luke knew the woman was also from their hometown. She was also younger than him, and he assumed, Darren's wife. While he knew just about everyone that was his age or older because of his older siblings, he hadn't been friends with the younger crowd. By the look in Daisy's eyes, she knew the woman well, and she ached for her. And by the sway in Darren's stance, and the out-of-control, wide-eyed stare he had on the woman, Luke assumed he was drunk.

"Janice," she whispered to herself.

Luke's voice was dead calm, serious. "Is she a friend of yours?"

Daisy looked conflicted. Her eyes darted to the woman and back to Luke. "Not a friend, but we went to school together. Her name is Janice."

Janice reached for Darren's hand. He tore his arm away and raised his hand. In the next breath, Luke stepped between them. Daisy gasped behind him.

"Hey, buddy. Is everything okay?" Luke asked in a deep and serious voice. He stood firm between Darren and Janice and held his hands out to the side, blocking Darren from reaching Janice.

"We're fine," Janice said with a shaky voice.

Darren stepped closer to Luke, swaying a little. "Get the fuck away from my wife."

Luke held his palms up in surrender. "Hey, no worries. I'm just making sure there's no trouble here. You want me to call you a cab?"

Tears streamed down Janice's cheeks. People looked over, hesitated, then moved past quickly.

"I'm fine," Janice pleaded through her tears. "Let's go, Darren. Please, let's just go."

"Shut up, or I'll shut you up," Darren snapped. He pushed Luke's chest. "I don't need no fucking cab."

DAISY WAS ROOTED to the ground as the memory of the night Luke stood up for her came rushing back. She'd been at a party, and a group of high schoolers from another town had shown up. One of them had been trying to kiss Daisy, and no matter how hard she tried to push him away, he was too strong. Luke had grabbed the guy's arm and wrenched him away, throwing him into a group of his buddies. She couldn't remember what Luke had said, probably because at that point she'd run toward her car, but he'd done the same thing he was doing now, putting himself in harm's way for someone he barely knew. He was at least four inches taller than Darren, his broad shoulders and layers of muscle clearly outweighed him, and still Darren pushed forward, chest to chest with Luke. Luke's hands fisted. His jaw clenched and unclenched.

"Take a step back, dude," Luke demanded. "I'm not going to let you threaten her. I don't care if she is your wife."

Daisy's brain kicked in and she reached for Janice. "Come on. Back away. Come on, Janice. We'll get you out of here." *We? How?* Shit, she had no idea, but Luke was right. She couldn't just let her get bullied. No one else was stepping in to help, and it turned her stomach.

Janice wrenched herself free. "We're fine, Daisy. Get him away from Darren or Darren will hit him. Please." Janice grabbed Luke's arm and pulled, yelling through her tears, "Please, just let him go. I'll take him home." She looked up at Darren. "We'll go home, right, Darren? You'll let me drive you home?"

The veins in Darren's neck bulged, matching the adrenaline-infused veins on Luke's arms and snaking up his neck.

"Cab?" Luke offered again.

"No fucking cab. She'll drive me home." Sweat beaded his forehead and upper lip as he staggered away, mumbling beneath his breath, "Asshole."

Luke grabbed him by the arm, and through gritted teeth, he said, "Touch her, and I'll hunt you down and make sure you can never do it again."

Janice dragged Darren away. Daisy stared at Luke's back as it rose and fell with each heavy breath.

His fists slowly unfurled, and she realized she was trembling, as a tornado of fear and admiration stormed inside her.

GODDAMN IT. LUKE closed his eyes and breathed deeply to regain his composure before facing Daisy. The last thing he needed was to get into another fight. The entire town would know about the confrontation by morning. *Damn it to hell.* He'd never been able to just sit back and watch guys like that, but since he'd bought the ranch and had begun to settle down from the restless kid he'd always been, things had changed. The other aspects of his life had calmed and settled, but his tolerance for this type of situation had declined and his reactions to such things had become visceral and immediate. He had no idea what had caused the change in his reactions, but he knew too damn well that he needed to try to figure it the fuck out and fix it.

He felt Daisy's hand on his back.

"Hey, you okay?" Daisy asked in little more than a whisper as she came around to his side.

He looked into her beautiful blue eyes and his gut clenched. "Yeah. Sorry. I…uh…I have a thing about guys like that." He watched her eyes darting to the people who were milling around them, eyeing him cautiously, and he felt guilty as hell for embarrassing her.

"All these years, and I've never seen anyone do that. I mean, I've seen it in movies." Her voice grew serious. "It was terrifying."

Terrifying. Great. He let out a loud breath and looked away.

"And impressive as hell." She stepped in the direction of where he was looking, so he had no choice but to meet her gaze. Her shoulders were tense, pulled up high. Her voice was firm and determined, like anger and compassion all wrapped up in a beautiful, confused package.

"It's not impressive." His pulse raced, and standing there was only making it worse. He needed to walk, to drive, to get the hell out of there.

"Well, I don't know many guys who would do that, especially to him. Darren's been in trouble with the law—"

"Yeah, I know all about trouble with the law." He headed for the parking lot. "Let's just go."

"Go?" She walked fast to keep pace with him.

"Yeah. Sorry. I didn't mean to screw up the night." He ran his hand through his hair, irritated with himself for stepping in again. Hadn't he learned his lesson when he was arrested?

"Go? No." She stopped walking.

He turned, frustration building in his chest. The weight of knowing he'd caused an issue that could come back on Daisy pissed him off. Maybe Wes was right and he was the last person Daisy needed in her life.

"No?"

She shook her head. "Why should we leave? You didn't do anything wrong."

He rolled his eyes. "Yeah, I did. Come on." He headed for the parking lot again.

"Why? Because you stood up for Janice? At first I wasn't sure, you know?" Compassion filled her voice as she walked beside him. "But then I looked around and saw all those people just walking by, doing what everyone does—looking the other way as if some woman's life wasn't being torn to shreds right there in front of them. Everyone in Trusty has ignored the way he drinks and the way he's treated her for years. I mean, *years*. I have never heard about him raising a hand to her, but still. You have to know this, Luke. You *live* there." She crossed her arms.

He'd heard the rumors.

"Then you come along, and you didn't share classrooms with her for twelve years, or watch her bury her father in fifth grade...or get teased by her in high school. And you stepped in and put a stop to it."

"Daisy, I didn't put a stop to it. Guys like that will go home and do God knows what to her when he has her alone—and maybe worse than he would have if I hadn't stepped in."

"No, he won't," she said softly.

She took a step forward, reaching out to him as if her touch could make it all okay. Luke knew better. Nothing would make it all go away. Something was driving him to step in like that and he needed to understand what the hell it was. Later. Right now he needed to get the hell out of there.

"Yeah, he will. Come on." He walked determinedly toward the parking lot.

"Wait." She grabbed his wrist. "I heard what you said to him at the end. Darren might be a mean drunk, but he's never actually hit her that I know of. Has he?"

He shook his head. He didn't know Darren or his wife well; he only knew of them. There had been stories around town for years about his drinking and the way he mouthed off, but never about him hitting his wife. But when he saw him raise his hand, Luke wasn't taking the chance.

"You'd have heard if he did. Trusty doesn't keep secrets very well."

"Exactly. Another reason you don't need to be seen with the likes of me." He took a step forward, and she held on tight. He looked down at her hand gripping his wrist. "Daisy, listen. You're a beautiful, nice person. You've probably got guys lining up to take you out. Let me take you home, and tomorrow, when the shit hits the fan, you can write tonight off as a bad decision."

"A bad decision?" She let go of his wrist, and he wished she'd grab it again. "Wow, really? I've been blown off by guys before, but not after begging them to spend time with me. Fine. Let's go."

Christ. Most women would be glad to leave trouble behind. They walked in silence toward the parking lot, and when they cleared the carnival exit and the crowds fell away, Luke slowed his pace.

"I didn't mean that I made a bad decision by going out with you."

"I know you didn't." She held her chin up high, her shoulders back, and stared straight ahead as she stomped toward the motorcycle.

"Daisy, you don't know anything about me. You've been away for years." He stepped in front of her, blocking her path. "I need to find my way around trouble, not start it."

She pressed her full lips in to a firm line.

He'd hurt her feelings. Luke could sweet-talk a woman into bed in under ten minutes, but he sucked at dealing with real emotions or connecting on a deeper level—and sweet-talking Daisy into bed hadn't ever been on his agenda. He wanted more from life than sleeping with women, maybe even more with Daisy. Changing his personal life wasn't as easy as he'd hoped, but after what Wes had said, the last thing he wanted to do was prove he was exactly who Wes expected him to be.

"I'm trying to save you from getting wrapped up in this shit and having to deal with it back home. Why are you so angry?" He searched her eyes, but she looked away, her arms crossed, brick wall securely erected between them.

"Because." She blew out a breath and dropped her hands with a frustrated groan. "Because I was having fun being with you. Like, the most fun I've had in a very long time. I wasn't thinking about the rumors circulating about you getting arrested, or about how my body gets all hot for you for reasons unknown, or any of that. I thought, maybe, just maybe, we could have fun together. Then you go and get all heroic, and I'm a little rattled, and then I'm insanely impressed. And now you're telling me that I made a mistake. So that means my judgment is all fucked up, and I don't see it, because I'm still looking at you and wanting to get to know you better." She crossed her arms again. "I swear, just being in Trusty messes with my head."

Luke was struck dumb. She wanted to get to know him better? After everything he'd just said? He was too nervous and befuddled to think straight. He fell back on his fail-safe response and flashed a cockeyed grin. "You're getting all hot for me?"

"Oh my God. Is that what you got out of that?" She pushed past him.

He grabbed her and drew her back, bringing them thigh to thigh, her breasts pressed against his stomach. Her eyes filled with worry—and the urge to kiss her was so strong that Luke had to pull back to keep from settling his mouth over hers.

"Daisy, I suck at this stuff." He didn't recognize his own voice, which had suddenly begun spouting honesty like it used to rattle off pickup lines. "I didn't know what to say to you, so I tried to make you laugh. It's what I do. I can flirt my way out of any situation, and I'm not proud of it."

She arched one of her thinly manicured brows, her mouth still set in a firm, angry line.

"Okay, maybe a little proud, but...You just said you wanted to get to know me better." Suddenly the truth became hard again, like pushing rocks from his throat. "You might find that I'm not who you think I am."

"So what?" Her eyes were fierce, her body rigid against him.

"So what?"

"Yeah. So what?" She pulled from his grip. "So I've wasted a night."

He took a step back, unsure of what to say. *So I've wasted a night?*

"I..." One look at the determination in her eyes stole his breath. He scrubbed his hand down his face, completely baffled as to the right thing to do. He wanted to kiss her until the tightness in his chest eased, until he couldn't remember what had caused it in the first place, and at the same time, he liked her—really liked her—and he wanted to release her from ever knowing him so he didn't cause her pain or shame. He drew his shoulders back and gathered his courage to do the right thing.

"I'm done wasting other people's nights."

Chapter Five

THERE WEREN'T MANY things that could take the piss and vinegar out of Luke after a night like last night, but as he stepped onto the dewy grass of his three-hundred-acre ranch and inhaled the pungent scent of horses, hay, and the crisp morning air, he felt the tension that had gripped him like a vice begin to ease. He'd stewed all night over his reaction to Darren, and as much as he wished he hadn't stepped in, he couldn't shake the feeling that he'd done the right thing.

He went through the motions of his morning chores—checking the fencing for damage, ensuring the horses were well and accounted for and the waterers were working. The sun rose over the crest of the Colorado Mountains, illuminating the peaks and valleys of their majestic silhouette, and as the last hope of dawn gave way to the morning light, he breathed a little easier and thought about Daisy.

Beautiful, smart, feisty Daisy.

She'd surprised the hell out of him last night, but

Wes's comment had grated like sandpaper the whole way back to her apartment. The look on her face when he'd left her at her apartment made him tense again. Luke knew how to handle most women, but all of Daisy's reactions were anything but what he was used to. Even after their ruined evening, she'd reached out to him, wearing her desire for him on her sleeve and wanting to understand why he was pushing her away. How could he explain it to her when he didn't understand it himself?

Luke couldn't think about Daisy and all the things he needed to figure out right now. His horses needed him, and at least understanding them came easily.

Luke raised gypsy horses, and he'd quickly become known as one of the finest gypsy breeders in the United States. He had six mares, a mature stallion, one young stallion, and three young stock counting on him. There were stalls to be cleaned and horses to be groomed and checked, and three of his mares were heading toward the fence. They were a needy group, always hungry for affection, and as they crossed the pastures, feathering completely covering their hooves, their abundant, silky manes and tails flowing in the breeze, pride swelled in Luke's chest. He'd used a good chunk of his trust fund and hand-picked quality, thickly feathered horses, and he cared for them as if they were his own kin—which, at the rate he was going, might be about the only kin he ever had.

As they pressed their muzzles against his chest, nudging one another out of the way, vying for his attention, his remaining tension faded away. The horses had a way of doing that. He understood his horses so well he practically knew what they were thinking, but women? If only…

His vibrating cell phone pulled him from his thoughts. The sun had barely risen, and after last night, he knew damn well who it was going to be. He pulled his phone from his pocket and headed for the barn as he answered.

"Go ahead, Wes. Rip me a new one."

"Whoa, bro. Give me a…" Wes grunted, and the telltale sound of wind caused a staticlike sound on the line. "Break."

Luke pulled open the barn doors, inhaling the familiar scent of leather, hay, and his magnificent horses. "Please tell me you're not calling while scaling a mountain." Luke walked to the door that led up to the apartment above the barn that Emily was renovating and opened it.

"I don't do that much scaling anymore." He huffed and groaned. "Okay, that's better. Sorry. We've got a big group coming in today. I was just getting the camping gear and saddles ready." Wes's life was anything but boring. Luke had enjoyed the few pioneering trips he'd gone on with his brother, but while Wes's fulfillment came from roping cattle and teaching people how to ride horses, hunt, fish, run cattle, with a few high adventures thrown in, Luke had found solace in his horses and the success of his ranch, just as their uncle Hal Braden had in Weston. Luke, like his uncle, hated to say goodbye to the young stock he bred for a living, but he felt good knowing they went to good homes. Also like his uncle, he'd never sell the broodmares or stallion, and this year, he'd gotten so close to one of his young horses, that he knew she was there to stay, too.

"If you're calling to give me hell, make it fast. I've got training to do." He took a few steps up the unfinished stairwell and peeked at the framed interior, then descended the stairs and headed back into the barn.

"I'm not calling to give you hell. I'm calling to say I was proud of you. You didn't flip the guy this time."

He heard the smile in his brother's voice. "I'll take my kudos where I can get them." Luke headed back to the supply room.

"I've been trying to understand something." Wes's voice grew serious. "In high school you saw guys do that shit all the time. Why're you all of a sudden acting like you're Chuck Norris, there to save the day?"

He realized that Wes never knew about how he'd stepped in to save Daisy from that asshole so long ago.

"Hell if I know." He stood in the middle of the twelve-stall barn and focused on Wes's questions. Ever since he'd bought the ranch, he'd been thinking about family, specifically his father, Buddy Walsh. At least Buddy'd had the good sense to sign over his parental rights to their six children to their mother, and their mother'd had the good sense to change their names back to her maiden name, Braden. *The fewer daily reminders of him, the better.*

None of Luke's siblings would talk about Buddy. Pierce and Ross, the eldest, were barely five and six when Buddy left, and Jake, Emily, and Wes didn't remember a damn thing about him. For as long as Luke could remember, asking after his father's whereabouts had been taboo.

Luke was a well-educated man. He knew that being abandoned by a parent could have all sorts of ramifications on kids, and even if his siblings didn't claim to think about him, the latest turn in Luke's behavior had him looking in Buddy's direction for answers. He sucked in a deep breath and steeled himself against what he assumed would be *shut the hell up*.

"Wes, do you ever think about Buddy?"

For a beat, the only sound was the wind against the phone. Luke paced, and when Wes finally answered, he sounded disengaged.

"Nope. Never."

"Never?"

"Why would I? I never knew him. In my mind, Mom pretty much had us alone."

Luke nodded as he paced, rubbing the back of his neck. He knew his brother couldn't hear him thinking, but he was processing what he'd said. He understood where Wes was coming from, but he couldn't shake the feeling that he needed some answers. He was thirty years old, and he wasn't sure if he could—or if he should—move forward until he had his past under control.

Wes's voice broke the silence. "Luke, what's going on, man? Why are you asking about Buddy? Hell, why are you thinking about him? He's just some asshole, and he left us all."

"Maybe that's why. How could a guy leave his kids and never look back?" Luke grabbed a shovel and headed for the stalls to work out his frustration. "Don't you want to know why?"

"Nope. Don't care, and whatever you do, don't mention him to Mom. Pierce will tell you that one thing he does remember was that it wasn't easy for her. Moving from Weston to Trusty was probably the best thing she ever did. For all of us."

They'd lived in Weston near their uncle Hal, their mother's brother, until Luke was six, when his mother bought the property in Trusty. Luke hadn't thought much about the move, or Weston, for that matter, and now he was curious about why they'd moved.

"I wouldn't say anything to Mom. I'm not stupid. Hey, why did we move to Trusty?"

"I was eight or nine. I don't know. Hell, I didn't care. Moving here meant we had all that acreage to ride dirt bikes and cause trouble." Wes laughed. "You okay, bro? You want me to swing by after work? We can have a beer and hang out?"

"Nah. I'm good. I've got to get a move on, though."

"Wait. I want the scoop on Daisy. How did she feel about what went down? And by the way, I thought I told you to stay away from her."

"And you thought that would work?" Luke didn't give him time to answer. "She thought I did the right thing. Hell, I thought I did the right thing."

"That's because you did do the right thing, Luke. No one's faulting you for that, except maybe you. You think everyone's looking down on you, and they're not. We're one hundred percent behind you."

"Then why the hell do you care if I go out with Daisy?"

"Listen, I was a dick yesterday. I didn't mean what

I said. I was half-cocked about Ray quitting and I took it out on you. I shouldn't have." Ray Mulligan had worked for Wes for two years, and he quit a few weeks earlier to follow his fiancée to Texas.

"You didn't find a replacement yet?" Luke worried about him. Without Ray, Wes and Chip rarely caught a break.

"Nah. Working on it. Anyway, I've been thinking about the whole Daisy thing since I heard about what went down at the fair." Wes sighed. "Think it through. You do business with her *father*, and from what I've heard, she's only here for a few weeks. You really want to see *that* look in Mr. Honey's eyes?"

Luke tossed the shovel into a pile of hay and headed back out of the barn to get some air. He knew the look his brother was referring to. The *you-slept-with-my-daughter-now-I-want-to-kill-you* look. He'd seen it a handful of times...or more, which is why he'd been more careful about only dating women from outside city limits since he returned to Trusty after college. And since buying the ranch, even his jaunts out of town to satisfy those urges had lessened.

"You're probably right. She's probably better off without me hanging around, anyway." His chest constricted at the thought.

"Yeah, I'm usually right."

Luke heard the smile return to Wes's voice.

"But that doesn't mean shit, and we both know it. How does Daisy feel about you hanging around?"

Luke watched two foals playing in the pasture. "How should I know?"

"Maybe you should let her decide what's best.

We're guys. From what Emily and every woman I've ever dated tells me, we don't know shit."

Luke used to believe that was true, but the more he thought about his father, the more he thought that maybe he was onto something. Maybe he *did* know shit after all. His thoughts turned to Daisy, and he knew damn well that he wasn't going to be able to walk away.

"IF I HEAR about the fair from one more patient, I'm going to smack someone." Daisy slapped a file down on the counter. Her father couldn't get well fast enough. She must have been crazy coming back here to the big-eared, big-mouthed town. The clinic had been busy all day, and three patients had told her that they'd heard about what happened between Luke and Darren—and warned her about Luke having been arrested. She still had no idea what he was actually arrested for, and neither did they, but that didn't stop them from perpetuating gossip ranging from theft to driving drunk. Luke had been a perfect gentleman with her last night, and after walking her to her apartment door, he declined coming in for a drink and left after thanking her. *Not* kissing her. She was still fuming a little over that, too, despite everything that was going on.

"Want me to follow you around and smack them for you?" Kevin stood beside her at Kari's desk.

She sighed, drawing comfort from his support. "No. It's just...You should have seen him, Kevin. He didn't do anything wrong."

"I know." Kevin shuffled papers and shifted his

eyes to the receptionist, Kari Long, who also shifted her eyes away.

"What?" Kevin's eyes were doing that nervous jumpy thing they did when he was hiding something.

Kari tucked her dark hair behind her ear and bit her lower lip, her eyes darting between the two of them. "Leo and I took the girls to the fair last night. I wanted to catch you this morning, but we were so slammed I haven't had two seconds to breathe." Kari patted Daisy's hand. "I saw the whole thing, and you're right. He didn't do anything wrong. I thought he was totally cool for stepping in, and so did Leo. Very manly."

Daisy banged her forehead on the counter. "So did I."

"Then why the head bang?" Kari asked.

"Because..." Daisy glanced at Kevin, having already shared her dating woes with him.

"Because Luke wants to keep Daisy's reputation intact." Kevin wrapped an arm around Daisy. His button-down shirt was neatly tucked into his khaki slacks, and between that and the empathetic look in his eyes, he could have been a therapist for the day instead of a nurse.

"I'm not even sure if I'll see him again."

Kari rolled her eyes. "Good Lord. He's worried about your reputation? From what I've heard, you spent forever trying to repair your rep."

"God, I hate this town." Daisy pressed her lips together, disgusted that the rumors and having to defend herself still got under her skin so many years later—and angry with Luke for thinking he knew what was best for her.

"Hon, put that stuff out of your mind. I have bigger problems to worry about than who other women are sleeping with." Kari shuffled papers on the desk and let out a frustrated sigh. "Our family doctor's practice has three physicians who see patients on a rotating basis, and they're so booked that they can't get the girls in for their physicals until September thirtieth, which doesn't help since the preschool won't take them without it."

"I can do a physical," Daisy offered. "All you had to do was ask."

"You're always so busy. I hate to bother you, and physicals aren't exactly urgent care. Besides, from what I hear, there are at least thirty other kids in the same situation. I hate to abuse my position here, but that would be such a big help."

"Pfft." Daisy waved a hand. "Are you serious about the other kids? There are that many who can't get appointments?" Annual physicals were an important part of health maintenance, especially in children. "Let me think about this for a day. Maybe I can set up a clinic for the physicals and fit the others in, too. That wouldn't take too long, if I can get approval from the clinic." *And as long as the clinic could be done before I leave town.* It dawned on her that holding a clinic on her own would look good on her résumé, too. *Hm.* Not a bad idea at all, if she could fit it in.

"Oh my God. Really?" Kari's eyes widened with hope. She grinned so widely, Daisy thought she might jump up and hug her.

"Yeah, but don't spread the word yet. I need to get

authorization." Daisy glanced through the glass that divided the reception area from the patients, and her stomach sank. "Janice is here?" *Please don't let her be hurt.*

"Yeah, she asked to see you. Want me to bring her back?" Kevin asked.

"I don't really have a choice, but sure. Let's get this over with." Daisy headed back to find an open exam room with her stomach tied in knots. She slipped into the only open room just before Janice walked in. She did a quick visual inspection—*no bruises, not limping, an angry scowl on her face. Great.*

"Hey." Janice crossed her arms and jutted her right hip out, looking like the same hateful teenager Daisy remembered.

She forced herself to be professional. "Hi, Janice. How's Michael?" Daisy tried to push aside the nervous vibrations rattling through her.

"Fine. He's with my mother. I'm not here because of Michael."

Daisy drew her shoulders back and reminded herself that she wasn't in high school anymore. She was a professional, a grown-up, and whatever Janice had to say, she could deal with. She hoped.

"You shouldn't have let Luke step in like that. I would have gotten Darren out of there." Gone was the matronly, compassionate woman of yesterday.

Daisy met her icy stare. "Janice, I know it's none of my business, but how can y—"

"You're right. It's none of your business. How about remembering that next time?" She ran her eyes over Daisy's lab coat. "You think that just because you went to med school that you know best? Or that you and your hotshot boyfriend are better than me and Darren? Well, I've got news for you…"

"That's not it at all, Janice, and you know that. Everyone in this town ignores how Darren treats you, and Luke—who isn't my boyfriend, by the way—was the only one who would stand up for you. How can you not see that?"

"Pfft. Not your boyfriend? You're the same slut you were in high school." Janice spun on her heel and opened the door.

Daisy reached behind her with a trembling hand and pushed the door closed. "Oh, no, you don't, Janice. You're not going to come into my place of employment and spread your nasty lies about me." She closed the gap between them. "I was never a slut, and you know it. You and your friends were the ones whoring about, not me. And you know what? Maybe Luke should have let Darren push you around. Maybe then you'd stop doing it to others." She whipped the door open and stormed down the hall and directly into the bathroom.

"Whoa!" Kevin zipped his pants and headed for the sink. "Now you're following me into the men's room? Babe, if you really want me that badly..."

Mortified that she'd walked into the wrong bathroom and shaking like a leaf from the confrontation with Janice, Daisy burst into tears. Kevin wrapped his arms around her.

"Hey, I was kidding. What's wrong?"

Daisy buried her face in his chest and let the tears flow, and as he'd always been, he was her willing, soothing sponge.

"Janice?"

She nodded.

"That bitch."

Daisy laughed through her tears.

"Some things never change. But some things do." He pried himself from her arms and looked down at her with compassion that only a true friend could have so readily available after so many years of listening to the same old stuff.

"You're not that same girl anymore, Daisy. You're a doctor. You're above the crap. You've made it, and unfortunately, you're now even more worthy of being jealous over. And the fact that you waltz into town and catch the eye of Luke Braden only adds to that. Take it as a compliment."

"Right. A compliment." She wiped her eyes. "I'm so sick of it all. I gave her hell for what she said, but I can't help it. Every time I hear her say things about me, it throws me right back to the halls of tenth grade."

"I know. But until you move away from Trusty, you need to toughen up."

Daisy leaned against the sink, her nerves finally calming. "God, I hate this town. You know what the worst part is? I just blamed her for everything and said that Luke should have let Darren push her around. How could I say that? That's wrong on so many levels."

"Oh, I don't know." Kevin washed his hands, then leaned against the counter beside her. His shirt was a little rumpled as he leaned back on his palms, looking at her like only he could—seeing the years of pain and knowing that maybe she was right.

"No. It definitely is. I mean, she's not a bitch because she was born that way. Think about it. Her father drank himself to death, her mother was never home when she was growing up, and I know now what I didn't know back then. All those guys she slept with? And Darren? She was trying to fill her daddy's shoes. Psych 101." Guilt tightened in her chest for having said such horrible things to Janice. She just wished she knew why Janice turned all that anger toward her.

"True. There is that."

Daisy's cell phone rang, and she dug it out of the pocket of her lab coat. "Sorry, Kev. It's Mom. She's going to give me crap about Luke. I just know it."

"Just answer it."

She sighed, then feigned a smile. "Hi, Mom. I'm flying around. What's up?"

Kevin mouthed, *Liar*.

"Sorry, Daisy. I thought you'd be off work by now. I heard about the fair. And Luke."

"I can't talk about all that right now, Mom." She mouthed *Luke* to Kevin.

"Okay. I...Sweetie..."

"Go ahead, Mom. Just make it fast." She pictured her mother pacing the kitchen floor, nibbling on her lower lip, trying to figure out what to say. She should have told her mother about the date. She'd probably hurt her feelings.

"It's just...Daisy, I just think it's funny, you know? Luke breeds those beautiful gypsy horses, and I was talking with Margie on the phone today about how funny it is that you can judge a horse by its papers, but you sure can't judge a kid by his parents. Luke's father never stepped up to the plate for his own children—thank God they had Catherine—and Luke stepped up for a girl he barely knew." Her mother sighed again. "I'll let you go, but with all the talk going around, I thought I should, I don't know, remind you not to lose sight of how remarkable that is."

After her mother hung up, Daisy stared at the phone.

"What?" Kevin asked.

"She thought he did a good thing, which is good, I guess." *Except that it doesn't matter, because he never even called.* She shoved her phone in her pocket. "Ugh. Kevin, this has been the strangest twenty-four hours. I need to focus." She took a deep breath. "About Janice. Should I apologize? I need to apologize. I do."

He shrugged. The universal sign for *who the hell knows* and apparently the underlying theme of her life lately.

Chapter Six

AFTER A CRAPPY day, Daisy wanted to have a glass of wine—and stare at her offer letters until she came to a decision about where she was going to work. She needed to do something to keep from thinking about Luke, and planning her future was the perfect outlet.

The sun hung low in the sky, and as Daisy crossed the parking lot, she took a minute to enjoy the peacefulness of the evening and to admire the mountains in the distance. Philly seemed a million miles away. She'd spent the last eleven years there, and she'd been so glad to get out of Trusty that she'd never looked back. Before the incident with Darren, she was having such a good time with Luke that she was actually starting to think that not looking back had caused her to miss out on the parts worth remembering. Maybe coming back to Trusty wasn't the worst thing she'd done this decade.

She exhaled loudly and headed to her car.

"Hey."

Luke's voice sent a shudder through her. She turned, and just the sight of him brought the feelings of the evening before rushing back. He smiled a slightly embarrassed, slightly flirtatious smile that sucked the air from her lungs.

Holy. Smokes.

He held his hands up. "I know you might not want to talk to me, but I couldn't stay away. I thought about you all day, Daisy." He held her gaze, but the flirtatious spark she'd seen changed to something else altogether. Genuine sincerity.

"I thought about you, too." She was surprised at the steadiness of her voice, given the nervous flips her stomach was doing.

He took a step closer to her, and Daisy swallowed hard. "Can we go someplace and talk?"

"I'd like that." Why did he make her heart go crazy? She had a plan. Go home. Drink. Decide on a future. And with a handful of words, he'd swept those plans away without a trace.

Luke moved closer again, so close the air between them shifted, heated, and she swore, *sparked*. He placed his hand gently on her hip. "I'm sorry for yesterday."

"Mm-hm." She couldn't form a sentence to save her life. The muscles in his chest twitched as he spoke, and the heat of his hand on her hip sucked her brain cells from her head.

"No confrontations. I promise." His eyes darkened, sending a shiver through her.

"I'm not worried," she managed. Daisy held her breath, anticipating the kiss she'd dreamed about all night as he lowered his face to hers. His whiskers scraped against her cheek. She closed her eyes, drinking in the feel of him as his warm breath whispered across her skin.

"Thank you."

She wanted to reach out and stroke his cheek, to feel the line of his jaw and that muscle that bunched on the side when he was tense. The anticipation of the night, of the kiss she'd been dreaming about for years, was tangling her thoughts into knots. Heat coiled low in her belly, and in the next breath, before he could pull his lips from beside her cheek, Daisy threw caution to the wind. She pressed her hands to his cheeks, drawing his full, soft lips to hers. The first second was one of shock—for both of them—a tentative, cautionary grazing of their lips. The second was one of gratitude, and the next sixty? Gloriously intimate stroking, tasting, sharing of each other's mouths. *Delicious.* One of Luke's hands settled on the small of her back, his other buried beneath her hair as he deepened the kiss. Daisy felt her body become lighter, and as he made an utterly male and sensual sound of appreciation deep in his throat, the heat that had coiled in her belly spread like wildfire throughout her limbs. She breathed in through her nose, and his masculine, earthy scent seeped into her pores. His thumb stroked the sensitive skin on the back of her neck, and as their lips drew apart, he kept her close, lips grazing, thighs touching.

"Sorry," she mumbled against his lips. "I was afraid if I waited any longer, I would be too nervous to talk."

The right side of his lips cocked into a smile. "Daisy Honey, what kind of guy do you think I am?" He pressed another soft kiss to her lips, then shook his head, as if he were trying to clear his thoughts. "Wow. I was *not* expecting that."

She felt her cheeks flush, and he pulled her close again, initiating another greedy, hot kiss. If heaven had a taste, she was sure it would taste like Luke, lusciously sweet and strong, but somehow gloriously soft, too. Her knees weakened, and when he drew back, she was a little dizzy with lust.

"Wow." It came out as one long whisper. She felt his heart slamming against his chest as fast and as hard as hers, and was glad that she wasn't alone in feeling the world spin.

"Are we going to kiss all night? Or should we go talk?"

She bit her lower lip as embarrassment settled in, and she had a fleeting thought about how she'd just kissed Luke—taken the kiss from him—in a way akin to what she'd been accused of so long ago. The thought swirled and burned for a hot second before she quelled it and tossed it aside. She wasn't that girl, never had been, and she'd be damned if she'd feel bad about kissing the man she'd spent years pining over.

She thought getting that kiss out of the way would enable her to think more clearly, kick her nerves to the curb, but—*wow*—was she ever wrong.

He arched a brow. "Don't get any ideas. You're not making me a notch on your belt." He reached for her hand.

She froze. "What?"

"What? I was kidding." His smile faded as understanding bloomed in his widening eyes.

She was rooted to the ground, reliving high school all over again.

His brows knitted together. "Hey, Daisy?" He settled his hands on her hips again. "I was honestly kidding."

She took a deep breath. *Of course you were. I'm an idiot.* "Okay. Sorry." *Jesus, Trusty is so not the place for me.* Daisy was aware of how quickly she could spiral from a place of confidence back to the girl fighting a bad rep. She loathed the power those girls—and the stupid rumors—had on her. She swallowed against the pain of the past and drew her shoulders back, regaining her confidence. It felt good to move past those rumors.

"I struck a nerve, huh? Well, if it's any consolation, I'm obviously fighting a rep, too."

"I'm not fighting a rep." She didn't mean to snap, but even though she said the words, she knew she was still fighting that rep—even if only in her head. She took another deep breath and closed her eyes to calm her nerves. "I'm sorry. Yes, you struck a nerve, but I'm fine. Jesus, this place makes me a little crazy."

"Hey, look at me."

She drew her eyes to his.

"I have a great idea. Let's start over."

She rolled her eyes. "I'm fine, really."

"Damn, and I was looking forward to reliving that kiss."

Five minutes later, Daisy was wrapped around him on the motorcycle, pressed against his back with her skirt tucked beneath her, and feeling warm all over despite the cool air whipping through her thin cotton skirt.

LUKE CLIMBED FROM the bike, already missing the closeness of her body pressed against him. Usually, when he kissed a woman, it was with one outcome in mind. Getting laid. For the first time ever, he wanted to continue kissing her, to hold her, to soothe the worry he'd seen in her eyes when he joked about being a notch on her belt. He wanted to memorize the feel of her against him, the taste of her lips, and the press of her fingers on his biceps. But he hadn't kissed her. She'd kissed him, and she'd shocked the hell out of him by doing so, stirring new and different desires in him, which had helped him resist taking the temptation further.

The patio of Twilight Restaurant was lit up with colorful tiki lights. The restaurant had recently opened, and tonight there was a band playing outside. They offered picnic-style seating on the lawn, and Luke thought it would be the perfect place to relax and get to know each other, but after that amazing kiss, relaxing was not coming quite so easily.

He reached for Daisy's hand as they made their way across the crowded lawn to a free picnic blanket. She took his hand easily, comfortably, and he was relieved. He was out of practice as far as real dates went, and his stomach felt funny. It had been a long time since he'd been nervous around a woman, but he was realizing that everything about Daisy was evoking different emotions. People swayed in their seats to the beat of the music, and as they settled onto the plaid picnic blanket, he noticed that Daisy's shoulders swayed seductively to the tune, too.

"I hope this is okay. I thought we could listen to music, have a little dinner, and maybe get to know each other better." Luke's typical dates had consisted of a quick beer at the local watering hole and an hour of pleasure before escaping to the safety of his house. Planning tonight's date with the hopes of Daisy's acceptance had supercharged his anticipation, and now the smile on her face told him he'd made the right choice.

"They opened a few months ago, right? I've been wanting to come here, but I haven't had a chance yet. This is perfect."

They watched the band for a few minutes, and Luke spotted the waitress, Lynn Haverty, heading their way. He knew her from around town, and as Daisy caught sight of Lynn and her body went rigid, he realized that they'd been in the same graduating class. Lynn wore black slacks, a white button-down shirt, and a name tag that said, HI, I'M LYNN. She flashed a smile at Luke, and it faded when she looked at Daisy.

Lynn tucked her wavy dark hair behind her ear and ran her eyes between them. "Hey, Luke, Daisy. Heard about the fair last night. Darren's such a jerk."

Daisy tried to smile, and Luke could tell by the shadow of worry in her eyes that it was forced.

Luke nodded. "Hey, Lynn."

She leaned in closer to Luke and lowered her voice. "Dude, that guy deserved so much more. Tell you what. I'll bring you a bottle of wine on the house.

My treat."

"You don't have to do that." Luke was glad to see he wasn't being criticized, but he didn't want to be singled out for what happened with Darren, especially while he was with Daisy.

Lynn swatted the air. "Oh, please. How often does someone stand up to Darren?" She took their orders and disappeared into the restaurant.

Luke noticed that when Lynn left, Daisy breathed a little easier. Someone else might see Daisy and think she was a beautiful girl enjoying a musical evening. Luke saw something more. In addition to the worry pooling in her baby blues, tension rode her fingers as she gripped the blanket. He realized that with Daisy, he was noticing many things, like how her shoulders tensed when he'd joked about her reputation, and on the opposite end of the spectrum, the way she'd melted against his back on the motorcycle—which was the best sensation of all.

She was leaning on her right hand with her legs tucked to her other side, watching the band. Luke covered her fingers with his, and she lifted her gaze to him.

"Hey, you okay?"

She smiled a little, and he felt her fingers unfurl beneath his. "Yeah."

Lynn brought them the bottle of wine, and Luke felt her fingers grip the blanket again. "You guys enjoy. If you need anything, just flag me down."

"Thanks, Lynn." He picked up Daisy's rigid hand and uncurled each finger; then he laced his between them and brought them to his lips. Once Lynn was out of earshot, he moved closer to Daisy. "Want to spill the beans on why she makes you tense?"

She looked at their intertwined hands with a furrowed brow. Luke withdrew his hand.

"Hey. That was sweet. Give me your hand back." She reached for his hand.

"Either you're really hard to read, or I'm worse at this than I thought."

She laughed a soft, feminine laugh that was music to his ears. "It's totally me."

"Wanna clue me in?"

"Not really, but I will." She glanced in the direction Lynn had gone.

"Hey, no pressure."

"No. It's okay. You know how you said something about my reputation?"

"Yeah, and you wanted to clobber me for it?"

"Yeah, right. When I was in high school, the girls around here were pretty cruel. They started rumors about me sleeping around and doing all sorts of things I never did, and the guys who were in their clique that they said I had done those things with sort of ignored it, but they never stood up to say it wasn't true." She shrugged.

Luke read right through the shrug to the hurt in her eyes, and it pissed him off that she'd been treated that way and that he hadn't done something more to stop it at the time. He'd been a teenager himself and wrapped up in what was going on in his life. The town ran rampant with rumors, and half the time they were white noise to him. He'd probably known about her rep back then, only she was younger, too, like Janice and Lynn. And he'd been a typical teenage kid. Like most teens, unless something was in his face—like it had been the night of the party when he'd stepped in on Daisy's behalf—he was too wrapped up in his own shit to notice anyone else's.

"I know, Daisy. I know about the rumors, and I know they weren't true. I'm sorry you went through that, and I'm sorry I wasn't more aware back then. I was a stupid kid, like everyone else. I was focused on my own stuff, or the next party, and leaving for college." He shook his head, feeling like a heel.

She lowered her eyes. "You were the only one who ever publicly stood up for me, and that meant the world to me. Besides, it was a long time ago, and I should be over it."

Thinking of his father abandoning him, he said, "Some things cut deeper than others. I wish I had done more. I'm curious about something, though. You don't have brothers or sisters, right?"

"Nope. Just me."

"I was in my own world in high school, you know? Lost in that indestructible, selfish phase. But if anyone had said those things about my sister, Emily, I still would have pummeled them. Since you didn't have a brother to step in, did your dad do anything?"

"I have to tell you something funny first. When I heard you say Emily's name in the diner, I had forgotten she was your sister, and…I was a little jealous."

"Really?" He arched a brow. He liked that. He liked that a lot.

"Yeah, but we're not going to talk about it." She

held his stare for a second before continuing, leaving no room to discuss the way she'd just blown his mind.

"My father?" She looked away for a beat, and when she looked back, she shrugged. "Not much. I guess I never would have expected him to. He was so busy with the farm and the business, and he never paid much attention to gossip. My mom, now, she was right there in the thick of it with me. She'd come into my room at night and reassure me." She looked away, as if watching a memory unfold before her eyes. "You're going to laugh, but I remember asking my mom to change my name long before high school. When I was little. I was eight, ten, maybe. I came up with all sorts of names I thought were stronger, and I can still see her shaking her head and looking at me like she completely understood. But she didn't agree to change it. She said I should be proud to carry my grandmother's name." Her eyes widened and her tone grew more determined. "And I am. I'm proud to be Daisy and I'm even proud to be Daisy Honey, because I'm proud of my family, but it sure wasn't an easy name to grow up with."

"And now?" He remembered when he'd first seen her in the diner, the way she'd threatened him when she told him her name and how cute he'd thought it was. Now he knew better. She'd been fiercely defending herself from judgment.

She sat up a little straighter. "Now..." She sighed. "Now I am who I am, and it still stings when I see the girls who were so cruel, like when they come see me at the clinic with their kids, and I have to take care of them without judgment. They don't even necessarily look at me with the same snotty looks now, but I still feel that zing of pain, you know? My body flashes ice-cold and my defenses go up. But mostly, I think it just made me stronger."

"Pain has a way of doing that. It must have been hard to come back to Trusty."

"Harder than I thought it would be, actually. I have two job offers on the table, but when my dad got hurt, coming here seemed like the right thing to do while I decided which one to accept." She took a sip of wine.

"Well, I'm sure glad you're here. What's your specialty?"

"I just finished a residency in family practice, and I can't wait to get started in a practice. The clinic is great, but there's so much more that I want to be exposed to, and that's not going to happen here." She met his gaze and held it. "What about you? Your family has such a strong reputation. How did it feel to come back into town with an arrest on your back after your trip with Wes?"

"Wow, you really don't sugarcoat, do you?" She was a delicate combination of strength, vulnerability, and cutthroat honesty, and he liked it. He liked her. Very much.

"It's not a strength of mine." She ran her tongue along her lower lip, leaving it slick.

He lifted his glass in a toast to keep from leaning forward and kissing her. "To being direct."

She clinked his glass. "And to avoidance."

Her smile was so cute that after they took a drink, he couldn't resist. He pulled her into a sweet, wine-laced kiss. "Sorry. It was killing me. I thought if I didn't kiss you soon, I'd be too nervous to talk."

She covered her eyes. "Great. I'll never live that down. If anyone saw us, it'll just confirm what they already think of me."

He pulled his cell phone from his pocket and pretended to text. "I'll just send a note to the papers in case they missed it."

She swatted his arm. "I answered your question. Your turn."

Luke contemplated his response. *It sucks. I did the right thing, and I don't understand why, or why it makes me feel like a pariah.* Nothing sounded right in his head, so he fell back on the comfortable shrug.

"Come on," Daisy pleaded. "Let me in a little. I told you my dirty secret."

He narrowed his eyes. "That was your dirty secret? How the hell did you get a rep if that's your best secret?"

"I never said it was my *best* secret." She wiggled her shoulders in a *take-that* tease.

"Ah, now we're getting somewhere. Note to self: Use more accurate semantics." Lynn brought their dinners, and they listened to music while they ate and talked about music and books and life in general. Anything to keep Luke's mind off of her original question, which nagged at him like a paper cut.

An hour later, they'd finished dinner, and they were both much more relaxed.

He pulled her close and wrapped her in his arms as the band played a slow country tune. He loved the way she fit against his body, and he loved the smell of her hair, which carried the fresh scent of a meadow after a predawn rain. He paid for dinner and reached for her hand.

"Want to go for a walk?"

"Um. Sure." Her forehead wrinkled again.

"You do take walks, don't you?"

She shrugged. "I guess. I work all week, and I help my parents, so I don't have much time for taking walks."

"Let's make time." He pulled her to her feet, and she grabbed his waist to stabilize herself on the bumpy grass. They were thigh to thigh again, their hearts beating fast. He ran his finger down her cheek. "I like this."

"This," she said in a breathy voice.

"This position we keep finding ourselves in. Pressed up against each other, like it's where we belong." He felt her fingers press in to his sides, saw the desirous look in her eyes. Oh, yeah, she felt it, too, but now that he understood that she was still recovering from the rumors in her past, he held back. He wasn't interested in a one-night stand with Daisy, and Wes's reminder that she was there for only a few weeks nagged at him. He forced himself to take her hand and walk toward the parking lot.

"Come on." He helped her put her helmet on. Damn it. Even that didn't squelch the urge to kiss her. She'd surprised him in front of the clinic, and he'd been so lost in the tantalizing warmth of their kiss that he hadn't been thinking clearly. Maybe Wes was right, and she didn't need to be the talk of the town when she was here—but he wasn't sure he was strong enough to ignore the passion that was brewing between them.

"Where are we going, and why are you in a hurry?"

"Because I want to kiss you, and if I don't walk away now, I'll kiss you right here, and I'm not sure I'll be able to stop." Her eyes widened, and in one swift move, he put his large hands around her rib cage and set her on the bike. "And, Daisy Honey, maybe I used to be that guy, but I'm not now. Not with you." He climbed on the bike, and she wrapped her arms around his middle and pressed her warmth against him. He was sure his heart would burst right through his chest.

ADRENALINE PUMPED THROUGH Daisy's veins as the bike roared to life and Luke drove away from the restaurant and through town. Luke was easy to be with. He was considerate and kind, and so damn handsome that he took her breath away, but there was also something mysterious about him, and it had nothing to do with his arrest—which he'd successfully avoided talking about. When she'd asked him about it, he had a serious look in his eyes, like he was trying to keep something trapped inside him. She hoped he'd feel comfortable enough to share it with her, maybe even on their walk. Luke was revealing sides of himself that she'd never guess he possessed, like the tender, romantic side of wanting to take a walk. She wanted to take a walk with him—after they filled the ache of need that swelled between them and at the moment was creating so much heat that even with the cold air against her skin, her body felt white-hot.

Luke drove to the edge of town to his ranch. The driveway was long and cut straight through acres of beautiful pastures. Daisy had seen the property a million times from the road. She knew he'd bought it from the Framinghams, who had lived their whole lives in Trusty. When they passed, their only son, who had moved to New York twenty years before, hadn't wanted to hang on to it. When Daisy spotted the house, she was surprised to see that it no longer looked or felt anything like the Framinghams' property. The house had been remodeled using cedar and stone. There was a wide front porch with nice wicker furniture and flowers and low shrubbery planted along the walkway. He turned down a dirt path toward the large wooden barn, which had also been renovated, and as he cut the engine, Daisy heard horses whinnying.

He took off his helmet as he stepped from the bike and looked like one of those cool guys in a magazine again, all sexy and hot, his hair alluringly mussed. He then carefully removed her helmet and brushed her hair from her face.

Her body was still humming from the engine as she slung her leg over the bike so she was facing Luke. Daisy knew she was doing nothing good for her reputation, and she pushed the thought away. She was too old to be worried about such nonsense. Those thoughts had even crept into her mind when she dated in Philly. As she looked at Luke, whose soft, hungry gaze held hers, she hoped that one day those thoughts wouldn't haunt her every move around men. *Around him.*

She loved Luke's face. The way his eyes were at one moment tender and empathetic and in the next breath, filled with lust, the sharp edge of his jaw, so rugged with a few days' stubble and so soft when he was clean-shaven. She pushed the thoughts of the past away, allowing herself to feel the emotions as they washed through her. She'd never wanted to kiss every part of a man's face before. It was usually lips she was after, but with Luke she wanted to taste that rough exterior and make her way to the sweetest spots that lay beneath. She took his face in her hands and allowed her instincts to guide her as she pressed soft kisses to the edge of his mouth, feeling him exhale against her lips. He shifted between her legs, and she tightened her thighs around his muscular hips. Luke didn't try to kiss her back as she caressed his cheek and slid her mouth to the sharp line of his jaw, pressing kisses to his rough stubble, then up along his chin in a trail to his lips. His eyes were closed, and Daisy felt the bunched muscle of his jaw relax beneath her fingertips.

Luke's forehead met hers, his eyes still closed. "Daisy." A breathy whisper.

"I know."

His hand slid beneath her hair, his thumb stroking the back of her neck as he gently gathered her hair in his hands and tilted her head to the side, then finally, blissfully, took her in a slow, evocative kiss. She rocked her hips into him and his other hand pressed firmly on her lower back, pulling her against him. Instinct took over again as she wrapped her legs around his and he deepened the kiss. He sucked her lower lip as he drew away, causing an erotic rush of heat through her center.

The moon was nearly full, casting a misty glow over the pastures. Crickets chirped in the tall grass, and the sounds of the horses trickled in.

"No one has kissed me like that before," he admitted.

The past scratched at her mind. She'd never been this aggressive before, had never felt the desire to—until Luke. The tether to the hurtful rumors drew her back. Was she proving them right? His eyes were nearly black, and a breath later, when he rested his head on her shoulder, she felt the weight of him press against her. It wasn't the impassioned weight of an impatient lover. All those ripples of hard muscles and tension molded to her body with the familiarity of a favorite spot, as if he'd been there before and never wanted to leave. *Screw the past.* She wasn't that girl and had never been. She wanted Luke in ways she'd never wanted anyone else. She'd spent years thinking of him, hoping for this very second, and she'd be damned if she'd let anything ruin it for them. She shut off that part of her mind with a sigh, and focused on Luke, whose lips were soft as he kissed her neck, then laved her skin with his hot, wet tongue, working his way up. Daisy closed her eyes, savoring every second of his touch.

She ran her fingers through his hair. "God, Luke. What you do to me is..."

"Crazy." He kissed her again, stealing the breath from her lungs and replacing it with his own. "Daisy."

"Yeah?" She hoped she'd actually said the words.

She couldn't even open her eyes. Her body was floating in a dangerous sensuous zone she didn't want to leave.

"Do you feel it?" His forehead rested against hers again.

"The connection?" One hot, long breath.

"I don't connect. I never have."

Oh God, she was leaving in a few weeks and couldn't think about what that meant. She could only feel for his face in the dark and kiss him again.

"Luke," she whispered.

"Mm."

"You're..." She kissed him again. "Connecting."

Chapter Seven

NIRVANA. THAT WAS the state Daisy instilled in Luke. Her touch was like velvet, and her kisses were magic, whisking away his worries. He didn't understand why and he didn't care to. All Luke knew was that for the first time in his life, he felt different. Better. Right. *Connecting*. Nothing stuck with Luke. Not women, and before the ranch, not jobs, either. He'd always been restless, and the ranch and his horses had changed that significantly. But he'd never felt what consumed his body and mind when he kissed Daisy. The feelings weren't even definable. He wanted to kiss her, hold her, protect her, not rush to have sex with her. He wanted to know what made her sad and what caused that flinch of reservation he'd felt right after she'd kissed his face with so much love. He searched his mind for the meaning of it all and couldn't remember ever feeling like that before. Not with a single person. He wanted something more, and as much as he'd planned on keeping his distance, and as much as it scared him and made his heart go all sorts of crazy, he wanted it bad.

"Walk with me, Daisy." He reluctantly took a step back and lifted her from the motorcycle. As difficult as it was to pry himself away from her, he didn't want to just fall into bed with Daisy. He wanted to get to know her, to date her, even if she was in town for only a few weeks. She was the only girl he'd ever felt that way toward, and he wasn't about to ignore it.

She took his hand and it felt natural, a perfect fit, as they walked toward the pasture where two of his broodmares were anxiously awaiting his attention. Daisy gasped a breath, and Luke knew it was at the beauty of the horses. Gypsy horses were heavily feathered around their hooves, much more luxuriously than a Clydesdale or a draft horse, and their abundant manes and tails gave them almost humanlike characteristics.

He stroked the black-and-white horse's cheek. "This is Chelsea. She's a tobiano, see?" He stroked the back of the horse's neck. "Her base coat is black, and see how the white patches cross over her spine? That's what sets her apart from other pinto patterns. Look at her legs. See how they're solid? They're not always, but usually they are in tobianos." Chelsea pushed her muzzle into his chest and he kissed the bridge of her nose.

"You can pet her." He took Daisy's hand in his and stroked Chelsea's cheek.

"She's so soft, and...loving. Look at how she's practically trying to bury her nose in your chest."

"Yeah, my girls love affection. This is awful to say,

but with her powerful frame and thick feathering, she reminds me of Anna Nicole Smith. Remember her?"

That earned him another sweet laugh.

"I'm serious. Look at how luxurious her mane is. When she's out in the pasture running and her mane is flowing behind her, it's a match." Chelsea's mane was thick and full, and when just groomed, it hung to her knees.

"She's gorgeous. Your *girls*?" She arched a brow. "I love that."

"Yeah? They are my girls. I love them." A chestnut-colored horse with white feathering over her hooves nudged Chelsea aside and Luke laughed. "This is Rose. She's a little pushy." He kissed the soft space between her nostrils.

Daisy petted the horse, and Luke felt her eyes on him. "Was it hard for you to come back to Trusty after being away at college?"

He took her hand again and walked along the fence line. "Not really. I mean, my whole family is here, and I knew I wanted either a horse ranch or a farm, so for me, it really wasn't much of a question of if I'd come back."

She nodded. "I can see that."

"It's not like that for you." He knew it wasn't, and when she shook her head in confirmation, he expected it. "I guess not, given what you went through when you were younger."

"Do you remember standing up for me?" She stopped walking and looked up at him.

She was so beautiful with the moonlight glistening in her eyes and the hopeful look in her eyes. It was hard for him to concentrate on talking rather than taking her in his arms again.

"Yeah." He nodded. "I had forgotten about it until after seeing you again at the diner, but yeah, I remember. We were at a field party. I can't remember whose party it was, but I was pretty drunk." Like most teens in the rural town, weekend nights were spent drinking too much and hanging with friends until the sun came up. "Some guy had his hand on you. I remember that, and I remember the look in your eyes." It had nearly slayed him that night, the mixture of venom and fear he'd seen in her eyes as she fought off the guy, all the while scanning the people around her to see who was watching.

He slid his hand to the back of her neck and settled his other on her hip, then stepped forward, hoping to protect her from the memory. "I remember, Daisy." She was breathing hard, her breasts brushing against his stomach with every inhalation. "I remember how you looked scared and angry, and I remember tearing the guy away from you, and when I looked back, you were gone." He brushed his thumb along her neck and she lowered her eyes.

"Hey," he whispered.

She met his gaze.

"There was one problem with that night. You forgot to leave a glass slipper." It was a good thing she hadn't. He'd been nowhere near ready for a girlfriend back then, and even back then Daisy had been girlfriend material despite her reputation: smart, strong, and based on how she'd reacted the other night, loyal. He wanted to protect her and love her like he'd never loved a woman before. *For her*, not for him.

She blushed, and more frightening sensations trampled through him. Every breath heightened the anticipation of kissing her again. She pressed her hands to his chest and Luke pulled her against him, aware of everything around them. The horses whinnying in the distance, tree frogs and crickets singing in the night. The smell of the thick grass and the pungent scent of horses and hay. And then there was Daisy, her skin slippery from the heat. The floral scent of her perfume sent his best intentions off balance. He lowered his lips to hers in another deep kiss, and she rocked her hips against his hard length. Her moan of pleasure filled his mouth, stealing what little resolve he'd been clinging to. His hand slid down the curve of her ass, and he pressed her body against his, holding her there, feeling the beating of her heart against him. He tangled his hand beneath her hair and tilted her neck back, giving him better access to her silken skin. He kissed and sucked her salty skin until all that was left was desire seeping from her pores.

He forced himself to pull away and rested his forehead to hers again. "Daisy, we should stop."

Her hands were still pressed to his chest, and she gathered his shirt in her fists and held on tight, as if her life depended on being there. With him. She didn't need to say a word, because he felt it too. A connection of more than wanting sex. Of wanting something deeper. Needing something deeper. He let out a shaky breath.

He searched her eyes as her fingers trailed the wave of muscles across his chest. She closed her eyes and kissed the center of his chest, pulling a moan from his lungs.

"Daisy," he whispered again.

She looked at him again with the same wanton look he felt. "I want this, Luke. I'm not a kid. You don't have to protect me."

Like hell he didn't. She'd cracked through some silent barrier to his heart that only his family had been privy to, and yeah, he had to protect her. He wanted to. But hell if he was strong enough to protect her from his desires.

"We don't have to go any further. I really like you, Daisy." He paused to swallow and to try to slow the pace of his words and maybe his racing pulse. "You're only here for a few weeks. We can just..." *Be friends? Nope. Somehow they'd skipped that altogether, left it in the dust back at the diner.* He couldn't even try to convince her it was worth fighting. Instead, he wrapped his arm around her shoulder and walked with her up to his house. Luke had lived there two years, and since he'd been staying away from women in Trusty, he realized, as he opened the door and watched Daisy walk inside, he'd never brought any of them home.

He closed the door behind them and took her in his arms again, then kissed her softly. Her fingers slipped under the edge of his shirt to his bare skin, sending heat searing through him and spurring him to deepen their kiss as he swept her into his arms and carried her across the hardwood floor and down the hall to his bedroom. When he lowered her feet to the floor, they were both fighting to breathe between hot, deep kisses. Luke reached behind him and tore his shirt over his head. Daisy's soft, wet mouth found his nipple, and she sucked and licked until he thought he'd lose his mind. He brought her mouth back to his, taking her in another greedy, needful kiss as he drew her shirt over her head—their lips parting just long enough for her top to slip through; then he kissed his way down to the center of her glorious breasts, freeing her bra in one easy move and tossing it aside. Her fingers tangled in his hair and drew his mouth to her taut nipple. She arched against him, sighing loudly. He had to have more. Taste more. He filled his hands with her full breasts, brushing her nipples with his thumbs as his mouth moved south. Daisy sucked in a breath as he gently lay her down on his king-sized bed, then traveled south again, rolling the waist of her skirt down low on her hips and kissing her freshly exposed skin as he divested her of the skirt and her white, lacy thong. Then he kissed his way back up her body, gyrating his hips against her naked sex. Jesus, he was never going to last. She was so soft, so beautiful. He gazed deeply into her eyes.

"You okay?"

She nodded, her eyes closed.

"Look at me, Daisy."

Her eyes blinked halfway open.

"We can stop. I'm not one of those guys who will get pissed if we don't go any further."

"Luke." She swallowed hard. "I want this. I want you."

Hearing those words sent a shudder through him. He kissed her again, feeling her need in every stroke of her tongue and in the press of her hands on his shoulders, urging him lower as she lay there, completely open to him.

"Christ, you're beautiful."

Eyes still closed, she bit her lower lip and pushed his shoulders again. Jesus, they were on the same page. *Connecting.* He moved down her delicious curves to the slight protrusion of her hips, taking each one into his mouth and loving it as she writhed for more. Her knees fell open, and he splayed his hands on her lower belly as it rose and fell with every needy breath while his lips rode the soft plane of her hip down to her sex. One soft lick and he was a goner. She was so wet, tasted so sweet, and when she spread her legs further, he took her inner thighs in his hands and helped her efforts, then brought his mouth to her, licking, stroking, circling her most sensitive spot as she sucked in tiny breaths, driving him out of his frigging mind. He slid his fingers inside of her, drawing another seductive sound from her lips. He licked her harder, up one side of her folds and down the other, lingering when she arched against him, stroking her with his fingers as she grasped at the comforter.

"Oh God..."

He knew. He felt it, too. Could barely breathe as he licked harder, faster, feeling her inner muscles tightening around his fingers. He slowed his pace, holding her on the brink.

"Luke. Oh God, Luke."

He thrust his tongue deeper, tasting her desire, feeling the pulses of pleasure that made her body twitch and tremble as she came apart beneath him.

She came down slowly, panting, reaching for him. He laid his cheek on her thigh for a beat, his body awash with desire.

"I want you, Luke."

A shiver pulsed through him as he slipped from his jeans and briefs and took a condom from his wallet. He slid on the latex sheath and settled his hips above her. He wanted to tell her how his heart was filling his chest and how she wasn't just another stress release, but he looked into her eyes and no words came, only the need for intimacy. *For Daisy*. He pushed into her slowly, savoring the feel of her, knowing he wouldn't last long, which really sucked, because he was a damn good lover. Their eyes locked, their hot, slick stomachs slid against each other until he was buried deep and they both gasped a breath. He had to *move*. Had to feel her moving with him. As if she read his mind, she wrapped her legs around his hips, and they moved in perfect sync, kissing, loving, pawing every bit of flesh they could reach.

"Luke," she said in another long breath.

"I know. I'm right there with you."

Their lips met again as he thrust hard and deep. Her hips bucked, her head fell back, her lips parted, and her breath came in short, fast bursts. Her thighs tightened around him as she cried out his name, and he followed her right over the edge with his own fervent release.

HOLY. MOLY. DAISY'S body tingled from shoulder to toes. She didn't want to open her eyes and break the divine spell of being close to Luke. He nuzzled against her neck, and he felt oh so good. She felt his weight lift from her chest, felt the heat of his stare. Then he pressed a tender kiss to her lips, and her eyes fluttered open. Jesus, he was gorgeous. He had that sex-hazed look, the one that looked like a sigh felt, and a smile crept across his lips.

"Wow, Daisy. That was nowhere near what I had planned for us tonight," he said with a serious tone.

"Me either." Was it? Lord knew she'd wanted him from the moment she set eyes on him in the diner. While it wasn't an actual plan, she definitely didn't regret it.

He rolled onto his side, pressed his chest against her, and wrapped his strong arm around her. She would be perfectly content staying in the safety of his arms forever.

"You've got goose bumps."

"I'm okay." It had been so long since she'd been intimate with a man that she wondered if she'd just forgotten how incredible it could be. She couldn't remember ever wanting to crawl under a man's skin and seed herself into his core like she did with Luke.

Holy crap.

She didn't know if it was a good thing or another symptom of how crazy being back in the town made her.

He ran his finger down the center of her stomach, drawing her attention to his dark-as-night eyes. She felt the quiet awkwardness of after-sex-with-a-new-partner but saw none of the same in his eyes.

"Your mind is going in a million directions. I see it in your eyes, and I feel it in your body." He cupped her cheek. "Talk to me."

Was she that transparent? She had so many things swirling through her mind—her feelings for him, the details about his arrest and whether those details might make things worse for her, given the reputation she was trying to move past. She should have found out the facts before she ever locked lips with him, but she had followed her instincts, and now that she'd been with him, she needed to know, because she *wanted* to be with him. Badly.

With a sigh, he rested his head beside hers. "Is it weird that I want to go take down all those girls who made up rumors about you?"

No. It makes me like you even more. He'd protected her all those years ago, and there was no denying the feelings that were blooming wider with every breath. This was it. Lying naked beside him, vulnerable to his getting upset and sending her away. Risking it all. She turned onto her side and looked into his eyes.

"Is that why you were arrested on that trip? Because someone said something about a girlfriend?"

His eyes narrowed, seemed a little colder, but they never shifted away. "No."

She held his gaze, feeling the tension of her question thickening the space between them. She could follow her heart, and she could follow her lust, but she couldn't—wouldn't—*open* her heart without knowing exactly what she was dealing with.

He brushed her hair from her cheek. "It wasn't for a woman, and I haven't had a girlfriend in forever. When I said I don't connect, or never had connected, I meant it." The muscle in his jaw bunched again. She really liked him. Probably too much for a guy she'd have to leave in a few short weeks, but still, she forced herself to push a little harder, no matter what the risk.

"Luke, I sort of need to know."

He fell back on the pillow again with another sigh.

"Please?"

When he faced her again, it was with a guarded look in his eyes. "Why is it that I don't need to know the details of your past and you need to know mine?"

That shook her a little. "My past?" She swallowed against the insinuation. "I don't have a past."

"I know, Daisy, but even if you did, I wouldn't care. If you told me that you slept with every guy in your graduating class, it wouldn't change what I feel when I'm with you." His voice was sincere, and the hurt in his eyes was real, almost tangible.

She wanted to stop, didn't want to push any harder. But Daisy was too smart to be ignorant. "Is it that bad, Luke? Because now I'm getting a little scared that it's something I *should* be worried about." She lay back and stared up at the cathedral ceiling. She should have thought about this before she was lying naked in his bed. She crossed her arms to keep from trembling.

"No. It's not bad. Daisy, what happened, I feel like it's tied to my past in some way. Long ago, stuff I don't even have the answers to. I just thought...You know what? It would be really great to be trusted for the man you know me to be, not..." He paused. "Never mind."

She turned to face him again. "Then trust me. Connect with me."

He was silent for a beat, and her pulse kicked up a

notch.

"I thought I just did."

She touched his stomach and felt his muscles tense. She splayed her fingers and pressed a little harder. She pushed herself up so she could look into his slightly confused eyes. God, she loved his eyes. "We did connect, physically. Share all of yourself with me. Emotionally, mentally, and physically."

He opened his mouth, as if to talk, and then pressed it tightly closed.

"Luke, look who you're talking to." She smiled down at him, knowing he knew just what she meant. "If I can deal with the crap I dealt with, I can deal with whatever this is, and if not, I'm gone in a few weeks anyway." She shrugged like it didn't matter, but the words sliced unexpectedly through her.

He reached up and touched her cheek. His brows knitted together, and when he spoke, his voice was soft, his tone tender.

"I'm not good at this, Daisy. Look, I like you, and I felt something I've never felt back with you, but I'm not good at…sharing those parts of myself. It doesn't come easily like it does for you." He came up on his elbow, and for a long moment they stared into each other's eyes, sharing a silent message of *what the hell do we do? Where do we go from here?*

She saw fear in his eyes at the idea of really letting her in. Daisy knew all about calming patients and gaining trust, but in the man department she was a little flustered. All she could do was lead with honesty and hope that he felt enough for her to do the same.

"Okay. I get that, I guess, but how can you expect

me to get close to you when I have no idea what I'm up against?"

He brought her hand to his lips and kissed it, melting her resolve a little.

"Trust?"

"Two-way street. You have to trust me enough to tell me."

"Fair enough." He held tightly to her hand. "You didn't deserve the rep you had. I don't deserve the gossip about what I did. Is that good enough for now? The charges were dropped. That should tell you something about me."

She wanted it to be enough, but it wasn't. The words tumbled from her lips. "Luke, being with you tells me something about you."

His eyes softened, pleaded. "Then trust it, Daisy." He searched her eyes, and she couldn't think of a thing to say. "Or don't."

Her stomach took a nosedive. "Or don't?"

"I can't change my past. Yes, I was arrested. I didn't do anything wrong, and I hate having to explain it away. I hate feeling like a cretin when I shouldn't. But most of all, I hate knowing that if I don't explain it, you'll probably never see me again."

Her body craved him, but her mind—her sharp, trustworthy mind—told her not to play with fire. She tried to figure out how to explain what she couldn't put into words in her own mind.

"I spent years fighting lies and misconceptions. I know how hard it is to live under the veil of gossip, and while I believe in you, I don't want to fight something I don't understand." Daisy sat up and tried to steel herself against the feelings that whirled around inside of her so she could get up, get dressed, and leave.

God. I don't want to leave.

His arm slid around her waist from behind. "Oh, sweet Daisy, you're right."

She closed her eyes, feeling the weight of guilt for pressuring him and sighing as relief washed it away.

She turned to face him and pulled the blanket up over her chest. His hooded eyes held a mix of emotions that tangled together and tugged at her heart. She didn't say anything, and she knew by the way his shoulders dropped a little and the way his gaze softened, that she didn't have to.

"Daisy, I know nothing about being a boyfriend and everything about avoiding deeper relationships, so you'll have to be patient with me." He reached for her hand.

"You know how to connect. You just have to follow that guarded heart of yours." She was drawn to Luke's honesty, his warmth, and even the strength of his silent struggle. She was supposed to leave in a few weeks. She needed to guard her own heart, not teach him how to open his.

He continued with a serious tone. "I was working for Wes at the time. Dais, what happened at the fair isn't that uncommon for me."

Dais. She loved that.

"I wish it was, but I have trouble keeping my mouth shut with guys like that." He paused, she assumed to let his words sink in, which they did.

That she knew from the high school party in the

field when he'd stepped in to rescue her, but she wondered if it ran deeper.

"What do you mean, they aren't uncommon? Do you get in a lot of fights?" Her stomach clenched at the thought. She was all for chivalry, but fighting was a whole different situation.

"No." He shook his head. "You saw me at the fair. I tried to talk him down, not push him around. Even when he pushed me, I didn't strike back." He ran his hand through his hair with a loud sigh. "You know, I want to tell you all this, but sitting here naked, it's a little disconcerting. I need to pace. Can we get cleaned up and maybe sit outside and talk?"

Oh, thank God. "Yes, please."

After rinsing off and dressing, Daisy felt much less anxious, and she could tell by the way Luke wrapped his arms around her and pressed a soft kiss to her lips that he did, too. She followed him through the large, open great room. A stone fireplace ran straight up the wall to the exposed beams on the cathedral ceiling. The mantel was covered with framed photographs of horses, which she assumed were his, and his siblings. Two chocolate-brown sofas formed an L before the fireplace with a heavy wooden coffee table in between the sofas and the hearth. Daisy noticed several horse magazines and green living magazines on the coffee table. An overstuffed armchair and ottoman were tucked into a cozy reading nook lined with bookshelves. A reading light arced over the armchair, giving the area a warm, inviting feel, like the rest of the room.

"Do you want some wine or something?" Luke

pointed past the bar that separated the living room from the kitchen.

"No, thanks."

He opened the door, and a chilly breeze swept past them.

"Hold on one sec." Luke went back into the living room and grabbed a throw blanket. "Here." He wrapped it around Daisy's shoulders, then draped his arm around her. "Let me know if it's too cool outside. We can talk in here if you'd rather."

She loved that he'd thought of the blanket. "I'd rather be outside."

It was a beautiful, starry night, and being with Luke, knowing he was opening up to her, and seeing how difficult it had been for him to do so, deepened her feelings for him.

Luke paced the slate patio. "Before I tell you, I just want you to know that I wasn't trying to keep it from you." He took both her hands in his. "I wanted you to like me free and clear of that incident. Regardless of it, really, and I know that wasn't fair. I'm sorry if I seemed evasive."

"It's okay. I do understand what you mean. Even now, if someone mentions the rumors from high school, I want to either run the other way, tell them to go to hell, or beg them to believe that it wasn't true." She hated how it felt to say that aloud, to admit she even felt that vulnerable.

He drew her close and leaned his forehead against hers again—another thing she loved. "I hate that you went through that at all. You know what, though? We have common ground. And considering I've never connected with anyone on the same level that I feel a connection with you, I'm not surprised."

Even if they hadn't come together physically, she felt closer to Luke right now than she'd ever felt to any other man. Common ground. She'd never felt like she had common ground with anyone. Daisy always felt like she had to work harder to prove herself than anyone else.

Luke kissed her forehead before taking a deep breath and pacing again. "Okay, so here goes. One of my brother's clients came to his dude ranch for an overnight trail ride with his wife and another couple, and I went with Wes to help him out. The guy kept yelling at his wife. I'm not talking about just telling her she was doing something wrong. Every move this woman made was wrong in his eyes. He was a big guy, probably my height and a good thirty pounds heavier than me, and she was this petite woman. Sweet as the day was long. And every time he yelled at her or told her she'd never get it right, out of respect for my brother, I bit my tongue."

"What did your brother do?"

"Nothing. We exchanged a few looks, you know, like *what an asshole*. But then we were packing to go down the mountain, and my brother had gone ahead with the other family and the guy grabbed his wife's arm. I saw her flinch. It wasn't the flinch of a woman who was surprised. It was the practiced flinch of a woman who knew what was coming next, so I stepped in. Like I did at the fair, only this guy wasn't drunk, and when he pushed me and I tried to talk instead of fighting, he threw a punch." He was breathing harder now, still pacing a path in front of Daisy. "I caught his hand before he hit me and tried to talk him down, but he pulled his arm free and threw another punch. I blocked it, and…"

"And?" Her voice was thin and quiet.

"I didn't hit him, if that's what you're thinking. I flipped him. He wasn't hurt, but his ego was damaged. Wes came back looking for us, and I didn't know until afterward, but he saw the guy swing at me the second time, and he saw me flip him." His eyes darted nervously around the patio.

"Flipped?" *Flipped!*

Luke shrugged. "I studied a little martial arts when I was at college. Trust me. Flipping him was about the nicest thing I could have done besides walking away. And I couldn't walk away."

"And you were arrested for it." She could imagine the scene unfolding in her mind, much like it had at the fair, and she felt herself open a little more toward him. Not just for what he went through, but for his honesty and for that vulnerable and defensive look in his eyes that she understood so well, because she'd lived the feelings he was experiencing. The annoyance at having to explain himself, the swallowing of his pride, and…the relief once it was all out on the table.

Luke nodded, and when he spoke again, his tone was softer, easier, as if the weight of his actions had been lightened. "Assault. It was our word against his, and from what I understand, his wife refused to back his story." He shrugged, only it wasn't his typical *whatever* shrug. This shrug was slow and heavy. An it's-okay-if-you-still-don't-want-to-see-me shrug. "He dropped the charges."

She took a step closer to him and touched his hand, stopping his pacing and drawing his attention to her.

"Thank you for telling me."

"I wish I never flipped the guy, but to be honest, I can't say I wish I never stepped in."

"Unless you're not giving me the whole story, it doesn't sound like you did anything wrong."

Luke looked away, and the muscle in his jaw bunched again. He dug his phone from his pocket and handed it to her. "Wes's number is in there. Call him. He'll tell you exactly what went down."

She put the phone back in his hand and covered it with hers. "Trust is a two-way street, remember? I don't need to call Wes. What I meant was—and let me be sure to say it clearly." She stepped closer to him and wrapped her arms around his neck. "Based on what you described, which I fully, one hundred percent believe, you should be *proud* that you did the right thing."

He folded her into his arms. "I can't tell you how many people have told me that I did the right thing, and I've been battling believing it until just now. Jesus, Daisy. You dropped a cake. How did I get lucky enough to catch something so much sweeter?"

Her world cracked open and he slithered right in.

Chapter Eight

DAISY'S STOMACH HAD been tied in knots all day over talking to the administrator about holding a clinic for the kids' physicals before the school year started and in anticipation of seeing Luke again. She sighed as she left the administrator's office and was glad for the distraction when her cell phone vibrated. She smiled when she saw the text was from Luke. Just seeing his name on the screen of her phone sent a little thrill through her. She opened the text and a picture popped up of Luke's face pressed to the cheek of the most adorable little horse she'd ever seen. The caption read, *Come by after work and meet Shaley.* Her shift at the clinic was over in ten minutes, and she could think of nothing she'd rather do than see him and meet that cute little horse. He'd called her while she was on her way to work to say good morning, and he'd said that he'd thought about her all night. She'd had to repress a squeal of delight like a fourteen-year-old crushing on the coolest boy in school, because she'd spent the night reliving their time together.

"Romeo?" Kevin glanced at her phone.

She sighed. "Am I that transparent?"

"Let's put it this way. You either had great sex last night with your new man, or you're wearing vibrating underwear like Katherine Heigl wore in *The Ugly Truth*," he whispered.

She swatted him. "Shh. Oh my God. I can't believe you remember that scene." The movie had been on pay-per-view one night when they were on the phone commiserating about something or other, and they'd watched it while they talked.

"That's awful." She bit the inside of her cheeks to keep from smiling.

"That's worse. Now you look like...Oh never mind. What did the wicked witch say?" Kevin had deemed the administrator of the clinic, Ashley Brunt, *the wicked witch* the first week he'd worked there. She looked down her nose when she spoke to the employees. She was a stickler for rules, short-tempered, and hardly ever left the chair behind her enormous wooden desk—or as Kevin called it, *her throne*.

"What do you think she said?" Daisy stalked down the hall. "She said we're an urgent-care center, not a well-care facility, and that if the parents need to have physicals done in a timely fashion, they should find more equipped GPs. Can you believe that? I mean, talk about coldhearted. She lives here. How can she go to sleep at night knowing there are kids who aren't getting their well-care checkups?"

"You're surprised? She is the wicked witch, you

know, not the fairy godmother. So what now?" Kevin was giving her his I-know-you're-not-giving-up squinty-eyed look.

"I'm thinking."

"Want to grab a beer while you think?"

"I can't." She felt the tell-all smile return.

"You're seeing Luke? Good for you. You deserve a little fun."

"Thanks, Kev. John didn't show up, so I need to cut my dad's hay today, too, and tomorrow I need to bale it. After I see Luke for a few minutes, my budding romance and my free weekend will both be pushed aside with one fell swoop while I play farm girl." She banged her head on Kevin's chest.

"Now, now, drama girl."

She glared at him. Drama girl was their term for the girls who played out annoying theatrics in high school. "Didn't I ever teach you not to taunt a frustrated female?"

"I thought Luke relieved all of your frustration. Now you're just being greedy."

She lifted her hand as if to swat him, and he held up his hands in surrender.

"I'm kidding. Sorry." His bangs flopped into his eyes, and he tossed his head to the side to clear them. They flopped right back into place. "I'll help you tomorrow. What time?" Kevin's family owned a farm at the other end of town, and while they were primarily sheep farmers, they had a small hay field as well.

"Really? God, I love you. Nine? Does that work?" Thank goodness. She was surprised that John hadn't shown up to cut the hay, but her father's farm wasn't his responsibility. *It's not mine, either.* She didn't mind helping him, but she had hoped for more time with Luke.

"Yup. I'll meet you at your dad's. Come on. I'll walk out with you."

Daisy gathered her things and hung up her lab coat. "Do you think I'm making a huge mistake? I mean, I really like Luke, and I'm leaving in a few weeks." She needed to make time to review the offers again and to think about what she wanted from them. This weekend. She'd definitely do it this weekend.

"Part of me wants to convince you to marry the guy, just to keep you in Trusty instead of New York or Chicago. You know you won't find any friends there who are as great as I am."

She rested her head on his arm. "You can come with me. Nurses can work anywhere."

Kevin sighed. "I'm afraid I'm a true Trusty boy, and someday I'll find a non-Trusty girl to sweep off her feet." Kevin loved Trusty as much as Daisy hated it, despite the gossip. He'd kid about wanting to leave, but Daisy knew better. He never missed the Christmas tree lighting at the center of town. He got excited before the town parade in May each year, and he stayed until the last of the confetti had been thrown. He never seemed to crave the fast pace and same level of experience that Daisy did, and despite it all, their friendship was solid and he supported Daisy's desire to flee Trusty—even when she knew he'd rather she was right there beside him, singing Christmas carols and throwing confetti.

"We'll find you someone. I just know it. So? Mistake?"

"No pressure in that question," he said sarcastically. "The way I see it, you're here now, and you enjoy spending time with him." He shrugged. "What's the harm?"

"That I'll really fall for him and then leaving will be ten times as hard."

"When you're taking someone to bed, follow your heart and not your head. You're the one who taught me that, remember?"

"I was drunk and hundreds of miles away. When was that? Our freshman year of college? I was drinking when I said it, and I meant for you not to overanalyze like you were. Remember that phase you went through?" She deepened her voice to sound more like Kevin. "What message will I send her if I text too often? What did that look mean? She slept over. Does that mean I *have* to ask her out again?" She rolled her eyes.

Kevin opened the door to the clinic and they walked out to the parking lot together. "I thought it was very sage advice."

"It was, for an eighteen-year-old. I think I have to use my head and my heart."

Daisy had her nose in her purse, searching for her keys while she and Kevin walked to the parking lot.

"Daisy?"

"Hm? Where did I put those darn keys?" She finally felt them and whipped them out with a victorious smile, jingling them in front of Kevin.

Kevin held her gaze. "For once in your damn life,

listen to your heart and let your head take a little nap." He headed for his car. "See you tomorrow. Nine o'clock."

It wasn't a nap she was worried about where Luke Braden was concerned. Ever since last night, her heart had been doing the hundred-yard dash while her head was playing hooky altogether.

LUKE STOOD BESIDE Rose in the center of the barn. Rose was a six-year-old chestnut broodmare and the mother of Shaley. Luke took great care when grooming his horses, and as he brushed the tender skin of Rose's face with the soft brush, he swore he saw a contented, grateful look in her dark eyes. She bent her neck and leaned her forehead against Luke's chest. He pressed a kiss to her hard head, then rested his cheek against her for a breath, enjoying the connection. Before moving to Trusty when he was six, Luke and his siblings had spent a lot of time at their uncle Hal's horse ranch, and while Luke had a difficult time bonding with people, horses stuck to him like glue.

Luke used that same soft brush on Rose's underbelly before moving to the thick, blond feather around her hooves. He was careful around the bones in her lower legs, as they were closer to the surface and could be sensitive if knocked with a comb or brush. Like most gypsy horses, Rose was good-natured and patient. She seemed to enjoy the grooming process as much as Luke did. Luke's stock of gypsy horses were affectionate creatures, fast learners, and he raised them well. The offspring usually started out as pocket ponies, following on his heels whenever they could.

A breeze swept through the open barn doors, drawing Luke's eyes to the front of the barn for the tenth time that hour in anticipation of Daisy's arrival. As crazy as it was for a man like Luke, he missed her. He'd seen his cousins fall in love over the past few years, and just like in the movies, they fell fast and hard. Luke had never imagined himself being swept up in love, or even wanting to be, but Daisy stirred all sorts of emotions in him that he'd never felt before. He couldn't help but wonder if that is what his cousins had felt. All those warm and unfamiliar feelings also had him thinking about his parents, and more specifically, his father. His mother wouldn't talk about his father, but he wondered if someplace deep inside she still missed him, or if she loathed the very thought of him.

He wondered if his father ever thought of them after all these years. Did he miss his children when he left? Did he ever try to reconcile? Those were things he hadn't given much thought to until recently, and now he couldn't let those wonders go. He tried to push the thoughts away and focus on Rose.

Luke set the grooming brushes and combs aside and spread his hands on Rose's chest, then closed his eyes, concentrating on matching the cadence of her breathing. Once they were in sync, he ran his palm across her back, pressing firmly as he moved down her chest, along her belly and hips, drawing tension away from her spine. He became aware of each of Rose's muscles, the way her coat felt thinner around her knees, and the curve of her belly as he followed the point of her hip south. Luke had found that massage helped him to relax as much as the horse. He felt a change in Rose's breathing as he moved along her chest, and his thoughts turned to Daisy. There was nothing erotic or sexual about touching Rose, and he wasn't thinking about a sexual touch with Daisy. He was thinking about bonding on a deeper level. He wanted to learn where she was the most sensitive, what calmed her—and what revved her up. He wanted to know more about her—what had driven her into medicine, what she dreamed of, and what she feared.

And he knew he was jumping the gun.

When he finished the massage, he came around to Rose's head again and pressed another kiss to her face. "You're a good girl, Rosie."

"Is it crazy that I'm jealous of that horse?" Daisy stood in the doorway, watching him with the dreamy look girls got in their eyes when they saw kittens or puppies.

Her smile shot right to Luke's core as he crossed the barn and took her in his arms. "God, I've missed you." When he lowered his mouth to hers, she kissed him hungrily, anxiously, clinging to his chest like she had last night. They came apart breathless, and he held her against him in a warm embrace. "I'm happy to give you a rubdown. How long were you standing there?"

"Long enough that I was practically panting for your affection. That was amazing. You both looked so…peaceful. Can I pet her?"

"Of course." He watched Daisy with Rose. "My cousin Rex's fiancée, Jade, taught me about horse massage. It's a great way to bond with the horses."

Daisy ran her hands through Rose's thick mane. "Women would kill for this type of hair. You are a lucky girl." She petted the soft spot between the horse's nostrils and gazed into her eyes. "She's really beautiful. Don't you wonder what she's thinking about? What are you thinking, Rose?"

Luke had seen too many people treat horses like they didn't have feelings. They'd pet them with the emotion of touching the cold steel of a car, or led them to the pastures with about as much care as if they were pulling a wagon of hay. It was disconcerting for Luke, and as he listened to Daisy talking to Rose, it warmed him all over.

"She's Shaley's mom, the four-month-old filly in the picture I sent."

"Oh my God. She was so cute, I could barely stand it."

"Now I'm jealous of my foal." He untied Rose and they walked her back out to the pasture. The other horses ran to the gate to greet them. Shaley was among the group.

Daisy stuck her hand through the fence and petted Shaley. "She's so cute. How do you stand it?"

"I spend a lot of time training, grooming, giving them rubdowns. I get more time with my girls than anyone else." He leaned against the fence and watched her eyes widen as Shaley went to Rose and began to nurse.

Daisy sighed. "Look at that. The maternal connection always blows me away, with people and animals. I mean, childbirth is not easy, and instead of taking all that pain out on the baby, mothers forget the pain and they nurture and love the very thing that caused it." She shook her head. "It's incredible."

"It's kind of crazy that paternal instincts aren't as strong." He couldn't believe he'd said it aloud.

Daisy hooked her finger in the waist of his jeans. "Thinking about your father?"

Yes. He shrugged.

"Father's don't carry babies for months and get attached to them before they're born like mother's do."

"True, but sometimes they stick around for years and then disappear." He had no idea why he was revealing his most intimate feelings to Daisy, when he barely admitted them to himself. The compassion in her eyes was so vivid and clear that he fought against it out of embarrassment, and he looked away. "Stallions are the same way. They kick and bite. Maybe it's a male thing."

She pressed her palm to his cheek and drew his eyes back to hers. "You don't kick and bite. And these horses aren't your offspring, but you nurture them as if they are. It's not a male thing. I think it's a chemical thing. Think about it. Some mothers do horrible things to their children, or abandon them, and some fathers do the same. So it can't be related to the sex of the parent. It has to run deeper. Otherwise all fathers wouldn't feel connected to their children. Right?"

"Dr. Daisy has arrived." He brought her hand to his lips and kissed it.

"Your dad left before you guys moved here, right?"

His chest tightened. "Yeah. He stuck around until a

few months before I was born."

"Does caring for the young horses and seeing the way the broodmares nurture them make you think about him?"

Luke slowed his pace. How could he have missed the connection? As much as buying the ranch had helped him become less restless, it also made him want to settle down in his personal life. Of course it was that desire to settle down that had him thinking more and more about his childhood and about Buddy. He was nowhere near ready to talk about this.

"I didn't ask you to come over to talk about something so heavy. Do you have time to grab dinner?"

"Actually, I have to cut my dad's hay. John didn't show up, and since there's no rain in the forecast, this is the perfect weekend to get it done."

"He didn't show up?" Luke knew John Waller had been helping Daisy's father since he injured his back. He was a responsible man and a loyal friend. Luke was surprised to hear he'd leave her father hanging.

Daisy shrugged. "I learned a long time ago never to expect too much from people. He has his own farm to take care of. I'm just happy I'm here to help."

"I'm not sure what it was like in Philly, but here, it's okay to rely on people."

She rolled her eyes. "That's not the Trusty I know."

"Sounds to me like you still see Trusty through the eyes of a scorned teenager." *No wonder you're in a hurry to leave.*

"Probably." She fiddled with the seam of her shirt.

"That's a shame, but it makes sense." *Looks like we*

both have something to learn about connecting. "Come on. I'll help you cut your dad's hay." He draped an arm over her shoulder.

"You don't have to help. I know how to do it, and I'm sure you have stuff to do here."

"Chores are never done on a ranch, so sure, I could work until midnight, but none of them would be as much fun as being with you or as meaningful as helping your father." He pulled her close and kissed her cheek.

DAISY'S PARENTS WERE inside when they arrived, and since it was already late, Daisy went inside to see her parents while Luke went to work. He drove Daisy's father's tractor, cutting the hay under the evening haze, and he thought about Daisy. He hadn't planned on talking to her about his father, but once the words came out, he was glad they had, even if he'd had to cut the conversation short for fear of becoming too emotional. She hadn't pushed him or talked so much that he couldn't think, and she'd watched him so intently that he couldn't help but feel as though she was doing so for more than just curiosity.

She might even care.

He hoped she did.

Chapter Nine

DAISY AWOKE SATURDAY morning to the distinct smell of coffee and horses. She pulled Luke's navy comforter up to her chin, stared up at the cathedral ceiling, and tried to piece together the sounds sifting in through the open window. Gravel crunching beneath heavy tires. A horse whinnying. A female voice. *A female voice?* Daisy bolted up in bed. She and Luke had come back to his place after cutting the hay at her father's farm, and they were going to bale and store it with Kevin's help this morning. They'd stayed up half the night talking and the other half making love. Maybe she had heard wrong. She closed her eyes and listened. She couldn't make out what was being said, but the voices were definitely Luke's and a woman's, and they weren't outside. They were inside and dangerously near his bedroom door.

She shot a look at the clock. Seven o'clock. Holy cow. That was later than she'd slept in forever. She darted into the bathroom wearing nothing but one of

Luke's T-shirts and took a quick shower. Everything in Luke's house had a masculine touch. Earthy hues mixed with a splash of navy and a touch of maroon. His shower was oversized and had two sprays, one up high and the other about waist height—very decadent. *How great would that feel if we were...Oh my God. Stop it.*

She'd never get out of his shower smelling feminine. He had men's American Crew body wash and shampoo. She was surrounded by the smell of him, and if she wasn't going to see her father in a few hours, she would relish in it. She needed to go home and wash off Luke's smell so her father didn't wonder if she'd bathed in *him*, and while she was at it, she needed to stare at those offer letters that she'd been ignoring. She'd worked hard and she wanted a meaningful career, but even though she hadn't accepted that first date with Luke in hopes of finding a relationship, and despite telling herself she wasn't going to get involved, she had feelings for him. *Big feelings*. Feelings she was having a hard time pushing aside.

I just have to commit to a job; then it will be easier to leave.

I can't stay in Trusty.

She rolled her eyes at the thought. No, she definitely couldn't. She finished showering, dressed—in last night's clothes—and when she opened the bathroom door, she found Luke sitting on the bed with a fresh cup of coffee and that sexy smile that stole her breath and sent her best intentions down the drain. He rose to his feet.

"Hey, babe." He placed his hand on her hip and kissed her cheek. "You smell like me."

"I know. It was either that or not get clean."

He set the coffee cup down on the dresser and wrapped his arms around her waist.

"I'll buy you whatever you need to be comfortable and smell delicious."

Oh boy. It would be so easy to fall into Luke's life. She loved curling up against him and falling asleep in his arms and waking to the sounds of the farm—

"Luke?"

And some strange woman's voice.

"In here," he called.

A pretty face popped into the bedroom. "Daisy! Luke didn't tell me you were here."

"Daisy, I'm not sure if you remember Emily, my sister?"

Emily came into the bedroom with open arms, and as Luke let go of Daisy, Emily pulled her into a hug. She was a few inches taller than Daisy, and though she was older than Luke, with her youthful, slender body and vivacious personality, she could pass for twenty-five. "Oh my gosh. How are you? You dyed your hair."

Daisy had been a few years behind Emily in school, and she'd known of her but would never have recognized her, much less have been on a hello-hug basis. She didn't have time to think or respond before Emily continued with a welcoming, friendly smile.

"I like it darker. You're working over at the clinic, right?"

"Yeah." Daisy reached up and touched her wet hair, wondering if Emily was used to finding women in

Luke's bedroom.

"Luke, give her a hair dryer. Sheesh." Emily walked into his bathroom and opened the cabinets under the sink. "I know you have one. I left my hair dryer here when I stayed over that night we had mimosas. Remember? You never gave it back." She came out of the bathroom and made a beeline into the hall. "Where'd you put it?"

"Sorry," Luke said to Daisy. "Emily's a little pushy."

"It's okay."

Emily came back armed with a hair dryer. "Told you. Found it in the linen closet. Here." She handed it to Daisy. "Take this as a good sign. He never has women stay over, so he has no clue as to what you need. You'll have to give him a list. Or even better, we'll go shopping for extras and stock up on your stuff. Lord knows I could use a girl's day out."

"Emily," Luke said.

"I just want to get to know your girlfriend."

The *G* word sent a little thrill through Daisy. She couldn't help but like Emily—and wonder where she'd been all her life. She could have used a female friend all those years ago. "My stuff?" She looked at Luke.

"Hey, I'm all for it." He smiled.

"I'm...only here for a few weeks." *I think.*

Emily put her hand on her hip. "Huh. Really?" Now they were both looking at Daisy.

"Daisy, why don't you dry your hair and we'll give you some privacy." He shuffled Emily out the door while Daisy wondered what the hell just happened.

Daisy heard Emily say, "Wishful thinking much?" before Luke closed the bedroom door. *Wishful thinking much?*

After Daisy dried her hair, she went in search of Luke and found him in the riding ring with a young stallion. She admired the silhouette of the mountains. Rounded peaks and valleys played across the horizon. She inhaled deeply, filling her lungs with the crisp morning air, so different from the air in Philly, which was heavy and polluted. Even the scent of manure didn't dampen the freshness of the morning. In the years she'd been gone, she'd forgotten how much she loved mornings—and the scent of hay. From the second she'd set foot in medical school until her residency ended, Daisy had been on a dead run—to study, complete labs, make the grades, handle rounds, study, study, and study some more—and she knew that once she accepted a full-time job, whether in Chicago or New York, she'd continue on that hamster wheel.

She inhaled again. If she had forgotten something as wonderful and simple as the crisp sting of fresh air in her lungs, what else had she forgotten? She sank down to the grass to watch Luke while he was unaware of her presence. He seemed so content and happy here, that the more time she spent with him, the more she questioned why she wasn't. She mulled over his comment about her seeing Trusty through scorned teenage eyes and she knew he was right, but seeing Trusty through anything else was not an easy task.

The young stallion had a saddle on its back, and Luke led him to the edge of a tarp that was spread out on the ground. The horse's neck was bowed, his ears sharply forward. Daisy had been around horses all her life, and she was familiar with what horse handlers called bombproofing, teaching the horse how to properly react to stimuli that might spook him. The horse leaned forward and blew out through his nose. Luke didn't flinch. He held loosely to the lead, speaking calmly and confidently, stroking the horse's back as if the tarp were no big deal. The horse blew out through his nose, sniffing the tarp again. Luke was standing beside the horse, talking, looking around, and when the horse finally relaxed its bowed neck, Luke took another confident step forward. She couldn't make out what he was saying, but he stood close to the horse, and she noticed that he was using the same slow strokes that he'd used the evening before when he was massaging Rose. He led the horse forward again, and he continued the same pattern of talking to the horse as they crossed the tarp. Luke was patient, and each time the horse hesitated, he calmed him, gaining his trust.

Daisy was mesmerized by his confident demeanor and the way his body showed no outward signs of frustration. She remembered the way he'd reacted to Darren, the way his entire body had tensed and how he'd protected Janice without hesitation, and she realized that he was a protector. It's who he was, and watching him with the horses confirmed something else that she was coming to understand about him. Luke was a lover. He loved with his entire being.

When he completed the exercise, Luke walked to the side of the ring. He spotted Daisy in the grass and waved her over. As he opened the gate, the horse nudged him from behind. Luke turned to face him, and the horse pressed his forehead to Luke's chest. The horse trusted him.

He knows you're a lover, too.

LUKE REACHED FOR Daisy's hand as she joined them. He took the saddle off Skyler, then led him toward the pasture. "Hey, babe. Sorry I didn't wait inside, but I wanted to fit in a little training before we left for your dad's."

"That's okay. I need to go home and change before we go anyway, so take your time and you can meet me there."

"Dais, I'm really sorry about Emily. She stops by a lot. I shouldn't have called her into the bedroom. That was inconsiderate."

"She gave you crap for that, didn't she?"

He opened the gate, and Skyler joined the other horses. "You might say that. I just wasn't thinking about if you'd be embarrassed and I should have been. I was excited for her to meet you. I mean, I know she knows of you, but for her to meet you as my girlfriend." He stopped by the barn and drew her close, gauging her reaction to his use of the word *girlfriend*. That was a term Luke hadn't associated with since high school, and even then it was mostly the girls who had labeled themselves as his girlfriend. That is, until they saw him with another girl and realized just how wrong they were. *Girlfriend*. He liked that term in relation to Daisy. It fit. It felt comfortable, rolled off his tongue as easily as *Dais* and *babe*.

"Luke, you know I'm supposed to leave in a few weeks." She held his gaze, even if the conviction in her voice wasn't reflected as confidently in her eyes.

She'd said it clear as day. She was planning a future far away from Trusty, and he had no business hoping to keep her there.

"Yeah, I know." He ran his hand through his hair. He shouldn't care, not after just a few days. But he did, and it hurt like hell. "Do you really dislike it here that much?"

She sighed. "Yes. No. I thought I did."

They walked up to the cars in silence.

"Daisy, I won't try to talk you out of leaving Trusty, but…just know that I really like being with you."

"I like being with you, too. More than I probably should, Luke. I knew when you asked me out that I was leaving. I worked so hard to prove myself and to secure job offers in places where I could learn and grow in my field."

Her eyes filled with determination, but when she spoke again, her voice quivered a little.

"I didn't expect…" She stepped closer and hooked her finger in his jeans.

He looked down at her hand, focusing on it. He loved when she did that, linked the two of them together. When he met her gaze again, there were no words left to say. He lowered his mouth to hers and kissed her. When he tried to draw his lips away, she leaned in to him, prolonging their connection until the need for oxygen drew them apart and she looked up at him with sorrow in her eyes.

"I know, babe. I didn't expect it either."

Chapter Ten

DAISY AND KEVIN had just finished getting the tractors and the baler set up when she heard Luke's motorcycle rumbling down the long dirt driveway. Her stomach fluttered, and Kevin, dressed in jeans and a tank top, crossed his arms and watched Luke drive in.

"I'm glad he ended up telling you why he was arrested. I would have hated to have to tie you down to keep you two apart." Kevin's brown hair was rumpled and his shirt was streaked with grease from checking the equipment.

"This is why I never felt bad about not having brothers. You've always got my back." Daisy's pulse sped up when Luke stepped from his bike. She'd just seen him earlier, in the same snug Levi's and black T-shirt, and he still took her breath away. He locked his helmet to the bike, and she noticed that his sleeve was hung up above his muscle, exposing his barbed-wire tattoo. She'd seen it up close and personal last night when she'd run her tongue along each sharp line of the design, and for some reason, the sight of it upped his heat quotient and sent a sinful reminder of pleasure humming through her.

"Sorry I'm late." Luke's hand found her hip, and he kissed her softly. He nodded at Kevin. "Kevin, right? You went to school with Daisy, and I met you at the clinic when I came in for my tetanus shot. Good to see you."

"You too. Glad you could come out today. How's your arm?"

"I've got the best doc around. It's nearly healed." He smiled at Daisy.

"Then let's bale some hay," Kevin said.

Luke nodded toward the porch. "How's your father feeling?"

Daisy's stomach tightened. Her father stood with his arms crossed at the edge of the porch, watching them. Last night, he'd asked all sorts of questions about Luke cutting the hay, but it hadn't been enough to get him off the couch and outside. As glad as she was to finally see him outside, she worried about what her father might say to them. She moved closer to Luke. "Come say hi to my dad. He's a little bit of a control freak when it comes to his machinery and the farm, so try to overlook it."

"Little bit?" A smile spread across Kevin's lips. "That's the understatement of the year." When they were younger and Kevin would come over to study or hang out with Daisy, if they went outside, her father's voice usually followed them out the door. *Stay off the equipment.*

"Shh," Daisy said as they neared the house.

"I know your dad, Dais."

"Oh yeah. I forgot." She went up on the porch to greet her father. "Hi, Dad. It's good to see you outside. Are you and Mom going to take a walk today?"

His eyes were trained on Luke. "Not today, darlin'. Luke, Kevin. How are you boys?" Her father's jeans hung loosely around his middle, and his broad shoulders no longer stretched the material of his button-down shirt.

"Doing just fine, sir," Kevin answered.

Seeing her father on the porch without the camouflage of his favorite recliner, Daisy noticed he'd lost more weight than she'd thought, and as much as she hated to admit it, he looked older, weaker. She was used to seeing him in the fields or working on one of his machines, or even working at his desk, and she realized that she was still having trouble putting the pieces of his new lifestyle together in her mind.

Luke stepped onto the porch, right hand extended. "Nice to see you, sir."

Her father's eyes ran up and down Luke, lingering over his tattoo.

Daisy held her breath and caught a knowing glance from Kevin. She knew he was holding his breath, too.

He shook Luke's hand. "Haven't talked to you in a while."

"No, sir. I've been training my young stallion and tending to my young stock. You know how that is."

Her father pressed his lips together and nodded. "Yes, sir. Sure do." He narrowed his gaze. "Is it true you got arrested for hitting a man?"

Holy shit. "Dad, it's not what—"

Luke inhaled deeply. "No, sir. I was arrested for stopping a man from hitting his wife." His eyes never left her father's.

Daisy couldn't breathe. Kevin took a step closer to her. She felt his elbow against her back and knew he'd done it for support.

Her father's lips pressed into a firm line again.

Daisy felt like she was balancing on a seesaw, with her father on one side and Luke on the other. She loved her father, and she felt herself falling for Luke with every breath she took. Luke stood proud, strong, and confident while Daisy felt her knees weaken. She was afraid to breathe.

Her father drew in a deep breath, and Daisy was sure he'd tell Luke thank you but no thank you and send him on his way. He nodded, a single, curt nod.

"Daisy said you cut the hay last night. The windrows are pretty close to the same width as the baler pickup." Her father's eyes ran up and down Luke. Windrows were the lines of cut and raked hay, and her father had always been meticulous about them.

"Yes, sir. I made sure of it. The quality of the bale starts with the windrow, as you know. The baler should be able to pick these up evenly, without creating a thickening in the middle, and the hay should be dry enough now not to be above eighteen percent moisture."

If Luke was nervous, he showed no outward signs of it. Kevin tapped Daisy's back with his elbow, and she remembered to breathe. She glanced at Kevin and he lifted his chin, as if to say, *Look at him go.* She returned her attention to her father and Luke, trying to ignore the bundle of knots in her stomach.

Her father lifted his chin and looked down his nose at Luke. "That's right."

Holy cow. They were speaking the same language. Her father's scrutinizing gaze softened. Luke held his hand out once again and her father shook it.

"We've got you covered, sir, but I think we'd better get started. Even with three of us, it's going to take us all day to get this done."

They headed back to the barn. Luke walked between Daisy and Kevin, acting like nothing out of the ordinary had just taken place, when in fact, Daisy's world had just spun on its axis, and somehow she hadn't fallen off.

"Sorry about that."

Luke slipped his arm around her. "What?"

"Her father," Kevin answered.

"Pfft. He's a hay farmer. This is your family's livelihood." He shrugged. "He wants to know things are done right."

"You must have worked on a hay farm," Kevin said.

"Only every summer since I was yay high." Luke held a hand at his waist. "And I studied ag in college."

"You did?" Daisy realized there was a lot she didn't know about Luke; then again, they'd known each other for only a few days.

Luke's voice filled with confidence. "My uncle Hal owns a horse ranch in Weston, and before we moved to Trusty, I spent a lot of time there. I've known what I wanted to do since I was a kid. The art of cultivating land, raising crops, feeding, breeding, and raising livestock? What could be more fulfilling than that?"

"So you never even debated studying anything else? That's how I was with medicine. I knew from the time I was a teenager it's what I wanted to do."

"Never. Ag was a part of me, and when something touches me that deeply, nothing can pry me away." Luke's eyes blazed a path to Daisy, and she was sure Kevin would be scorched by the heat. She was relieved when Kevin spoke, cooling the fire.

"So you totally understood her father. You weren't bothered by his attitude?"

The knots in Daisy's stomach twisted a little tighter.

Luke tucked her hair behind her ear. "Not at all. You call that an attitude? That's a man protecting his family's income."

Daisy was still thinking about *nothing can pry me away.*

DAISY DROVE THE tractor across the driveway, pulling the baler behind. The engine roared and rumbled beneath her as she drove toward the hay field, remembering when she was young and her father had let her ride on his lap while he cut the hay. He was a serious man, and when he was working the fields, he was even more focused than usual, and although as a child Daisy might have thought she was out having fun on Dad's lap, her father had used those times to teach her. He'd narrate every move he made with the tractor, why he avoided some areas or sped up at others. She thought about the way he used to bring her out at night to close up the sheds and the barn and realized that even then he was teaching her. *Look for critters before closing the door. Always hang your keys on this hook. There's nothing worse than wasting time because you can't find your tractor keys.* She ached with the realization that the tractor she was driving was the one her father fell from.

Kevin and Luke were working the baler. Daisy stopped the tractor at the sight of three trucks coming down the driveway, kicking up plumes of dirt in their wake. She climbed off the tractor and headed toward the barn, where they were pulling in and parking.

John Waller stepped from the first truck. Daisy recognized his black cowboy hat and tall, lanky figure. He waved, and she lifted her arm and waved back as she crossed the field.

"John, I didn't think you were coming." Daisy steeled herself against the anger and hurt that rattled off like gunfire in her mind as she surveyed the others who had come to help. Mack Boiler and his brother, Chad, whom she'd gone to school with—and who had jumped right on the *make fun of Daisy* train, and the person who surprised Daisy the most, Darren Treelong.

"I had to run out of town this week to deliver livestock and I got hung up, but I'd never leave your pop hanging, Daisy. You should know that."

Yes, maybe she should know that about John, but she'd learned during study groups and shadowing sessions in her residency that people didn't always keep their commitments, and her memories of Trusty didn't include many people reaching out to her. She'd never in her wildest dreams—or nightmares—think that the other men would come out to help.

"Thanks for coming." Her muscles tightened and burned as she met Darren's gaze. He squinted against the sharp glare of the sun and shoved his hands in his pockets as he dropped his eyes to the ground. Gone was the bravado he'd boasted at the fair. *You're sober.* Daisy sensed Luke behind her, felt the heat of his body, the protection of his strength.

"Darren, thanks for coming out to help." Her nerves prickled. She didn't know what to expect, if he and Luke would go head-to-head, or if he'd verbally lash out like Janice had. She forced herself to continue. "We really appreciate it."

Darren gave one curt nod. "Thanks for taking care of my boy."

Michael. Of course. "You guys know Kevin, and this is Luke Braden."

Luke shook John's hand. "John, how's it going?"

She'd forgotten that they knew each other. She watched the exchange and understood what Luke had meant about being able to rely on the help of others. He'd trusted that John would be there. She hadn't realized how cynical she'd become about the people in Trusty, and now she bristled against the cynicism.

"Good, man. I probably should have called David, but I was slammed."

"No worries. I'm glad we can all work together." Luke shook the other men's hands. When he faced Darren, he didn't run his eyes down his body in judgment or pull his shoulders back with a show of strength. He offered his hand, as he had to each of the other men.

"Good to see you, Darren."

Darren eyed his hand. A lifetime seemed to pass in what was probably only ten seconds before Darren slid his hand from his pocket and shook Luke's hand with another curt nod.

"Let's get this show on the road." John was quick to give directions and move things along. Farm people knew that idle times could lead to heated moments when there was a past between two men, and by now, Luke and Darren's run-in had become breakfast conversation.

Daisy hung back for a minute, struck by the generosity of these men coming together for her family. Seeing Darren show up to help her father despite having become the talk of the town because of Luke stepping in, and watching him and Luke work side by side, she saw a hint of what Luke had been so sure of. She felt a thickening in her throat, but the hurt high school girl was still wearing a cloak of armor that was impossible to shed.

Daisy went to join the men and work her father's farm.

She still had something to prove.

Chapter Eleven

THEY WORKED THROUGH the hot, dry afternoon and long after sunset. Luke was glad that the others had turned out to help. He'd known they would. He'd rarely been let down by his friends in Trusty. Gossip ran swiftly, but so did loyalties, as he'd seen firsthand with the way the others had treated him around Darren. They'd treated Luke as if he were just another guy—not the guy who stepped between Darren and his wife. Darren wasn't warm with Luke, but he hadn't been confrontational, either, and that was enough for him. It was a start.

He, Kevin, and Daisy stood in the barn. They'd just finished putting the equipment away, and everyone else had left. Daisy's eyelids were heavy. She stood with one hand on her hip, her back against the barn wall, looking adorably sexy and exhausted in a pair of cutoffs and a dirt-streaked tan tank top that clung to her breasts.

"Were you surprised they showed up? Your dad's

a great guy. No one's going to leave him hanging." Luke whipped his shirt off and used it to wipe sweat from his face; then he shoved it in his back pocket.

"You know, I never thought of him as a *great guy*. A hard worker, a strict father, a loving parent, even if not outwardly so." She licked her lips. "But the words *great guy* never really came to mind. They...um..." She cleared her throat, and the way her eyes lingered on his chest told him that it wasn't a tickle of hay that caused her need to pause.

Luke repressed a smile. He loved knowing his body had an effect on her, especially since he felt a jolt of desire every time he caught a glimpse of her sexy curves. There was something incredibly sexy about a petite, beautiful woman driving massive farm equipment.

"I'm glad they came to help, but I didn't expect it."

"Well, this has been fun, but I've got to rock and roll. I'm working my way through *Game of Thrones*, season two." Kevin shook Luke's hand. "Great to see you, man." Kevin smiled at Daisy. "Do you want me to come by tomorrow to help clean up anything left on the field?"

"You're never going to find a woman if you spend your weekend nights with a DVD." She teased him. "Don't worry about tomorrow. You're the greatest for offering to help, but I can take care of it. I really appreciate your help today, though. Hey, Kev, I've been thinking about what Kari said about all those kids needing physicals. If I do it, are you still game to help? I mean if I can work something out or get Ashley to change her mind."

"You know I will. But don't count on Ashley. She's not likely to budge."

Daisy pulled Kevin into a hug despite the sweat and grime covering his entire chest. It was clear to Luke how much they cared for each other. They were as comfortable as he and his siblings were, and he was damn glad that there was a striking difference between that comfort and the passion he saw in Daisy's eyes when she looked at him.

Daisy fiddled with the ends of her hair. Her body glistened from the heat, and when she met Luke's gaze, he was drawn to the tired, seductive, shy look in her eyes.

"I love that you're still thinking about helping those kids."

"Thanks. I'm still undecided. Just mulling it over."

"You know I'm coming to help tomorrow, right?" He closed the gap between them and slid his hands beneath the edge of her shirt, settling them on the heated flesh of her waist.

"You don't have to."

He'd waited all afternoon to kiss her—really kiss her, not a quick and appropriate peck, but a hot, wet, passionate kiss. He lowered his mouth to hers and—oh yeah—she wanted it, too. She wrapped her hands around his neck and deepened the kiss, sending them both stumbling until her back met the hard barn wall.

"Jesus." He kissed her again, tasting the need on her tongue as she eagerly swept and stroked his mouth. "I swear you're an aphrodisiac. How can it be that after spending all these hours together, I still miss you?"

He kissed her cheek, then settled his mouth on her neck and sucked the salty, sweet taste of her. She pressed her hips to his, breathing hard as he kissed his way across her shoulder, then back up, taking her in another greedy kiss.

"Luke." His name came out like a warm brush of wind as his hands slid beneath her shirt and cupped her breasts.

She felt so good—too good to pull away. He lifted her shirt and pulled the cup of her bra down, then lowered his mouth to her breast, unable to suppress a moan of pleasure as she buried her hands in his hair and held him to her.

He reluctantly pulled back and met her lust-filled gaze.

"Daisy." He swallowed hard.

She took his lower lip into her mouth and sucked, stealing his ability to think.

"Yeah?" she whispered as she dropped her hand to his crotch and stroked him through his jeans.

Fuuuuck. He grabbed her wrist. "I can't. Not in your parents' barn."

She stuck her lower lip out, and he had to take her in another deep kiss.

"You're killing me."

"Follow me home."

Ten minutes later, they were kissing their way into her apartment. Luke kicked the door closed behind them as she lifted off her shirt and tossed it, and her bra, to the floor.

"Holy Christ, Daisy. You're like a wicked fantasy standing there in Daisy Dukes and cowgirl boots." He drew her close, and a guttural moan stole from his lungs at the skin-to-skin contact.

She lowered her lips to his chest, pressing wet kisses along his pecs. She hooked her fingers in the waist of his jeans and flicked her tongue over his nipple, pulling another hungry groan from deep within him. He wrapped one strong arm around her, and in two steps she was against the wall. He tore open her shorts and yanked them down to her boots. *Damn boots.* Her lips parted. Her tongue took a slow ride across her lower lip as she reached for the button of his jeans. He snagged his wallet and she grabbed his hand.

"Do you always use a condom?" she asked.

"Without fail. I've never trusted anyone enough not to."

"Do you trust me?"

"More than anyone in the world." Luke could hardly breathe. He'd always been careful when it came to sex, and with Daisy, he ached to feel her, really feel her. *All of her.*

"I'm on the pill, and I'm clean."

"Jesus, Daisy. I'm so damn clean you could eat dinner off of me."

She bit her lower lip, then, breathing hard, asked, "I...believe you that you always used a condom, but...how clean?"

"Tested and confirmed at my last checkup."

The darkening of her eyes sent a shot of lust through him. He shoved his jeans down to his knees, then pressed his body against hers and kissed her again. His hard, naked length pressed against her quivering body. She pushed him away with a narrow, hot stare. In the next breath, she took him in her mouth and cupped his balls as she stroked, fondled, and sucked him into a frenzy of delirious need.

"Holy...Daisy." He closed his eyes, clenched his teeth.

She ran her hands up his thighs, pressing hard as she licked his hard length, lingering on the tip, teasing him until every nerve sizzled and burned. Her mouth was hot and wet. Knowing he'd never last, he pulled her to her feet, then pressed her to the wall with one hand, using the other to tug off her boots. He lifted her easily as she wrapped her legs around his waist and lowered her sweet center onto his hard shaft until he was buried deep, and they both stilled at the closeness.

"Daisy," he whispered. Holy hell, he'd never felt anything so tantalizing in his life.

She covered his mouth with hers, and he pressed her back to the wall again, using it to support each powerful thrust. She gripped his biceps, emitting a streak of erotic, sexy, needful noises between heavy breaths.

"Oh...Luke..." she whispered. "Ah...uh..."

He couldn't speak. Heat burned deep in his belly and exploded like ice through his limbs. Daisy arched into him as she cried out his name, and he buried his face in her neck and grunted through his own powerful release.

Chapter Twelve

LUKE WAS UP long before the sun rose Sunday morning. Daisy was sprawled over him, one thigh covering his, her arm draped across his chest. He didn't want to move, and he knew that if he was going to have time to help her at her father's farm today, he had to get over to the ranch and get his morning chores done. But she was so warm against him, and when he was with her, every part of him felt full. It didn't matter where they were or what they were doing. He just loved being with her, and it made him wonder about the emotion everyone knew as *love*. What did that word really mean? He loved his family in a way that was deep and true, but deep and true only scratched the surface of what he felt for Daisy.

How could four letters hold so much meaning? When he thought of the term *I love you*, it conjured up feelings of closeness and trust, but the words that filled his mind to define what he felt for Daisy went much further. *Depth, truth, mindfulness, passion, stability, friendship, understanding,* those were the things he associated with Daisy. Closeness and trust were the base, but feeling all those other connections—*depth, truth, mindfulness, passion, stability, friendship, understanding*—the ones that sewed them together like an intricate quilt, those had to be rare, because he'd never felt them all bundled up in one person before.

His mind circled back to his father. How could he leave them so easily? Daisy sighed, and he reflexively kissed the top of her head. Not only could he not imagine her leaving in a few short weeks. He knew he could never be the one to leave her. He also knew that if he was ever going to be able to look at her and not have it clouded by unanswered questions about his past, he had to deal with the skeleton in his closet, and Daisy had decisions of her own to make.

He glanced at the envelopes he'd noticed last night on her dresser. *They're my offer letters.* He hadn't asked after her decision last night, didn't want to think about it, and it turned out it was all he could think about once she'd fallen asleep.

A few weeks will never be enough.

A lifetime might never be enough.

It killed him that he might never have the chance to find out.

AFTER GROOMING THE horses, Luke stood by the pasture watching Rose nurse Shaley. The sun had brought a warm, dry morning, and a sense of urgency consumed Luke. He needed to put his past to rest. It was the only way he'd ever have a future. He debated calling his brother Pierce. He knew how Pierce felt about Buddy, and he wasn't sure roping him into what Luke needed to ask for was a good idea. Pierce hadn't ever allowed a single conversation about his father in the past, and as Luke's chest constricted, he knew not to expect anything different today. With a deep breath, he set his feet in motion and paced as he pressed Pierce's speed-dial number.

"Hey, Luke." Pierce yawned. "How's it going?" Pierce owned casinos all over the world, and Luke had no idea what part of the country he was in today, but his brother's voice was gravelly and tired.

"Good. How about you? Did I wake you?" Through real estate investments and good business sense, Pierce was a self-made millionaire. As the eldest, he was focused, determined, and fiercely protective of Luke and their siblings. He'd been away at college by the time Luke was eleven, but he'd called, visited, and watched over him with the diligence of a parent.

"Nah, just jet-lagged. I'm over in Weston visiting Treat before heading home to see Mom and everyone. Jesus, his daughter, Adriana, is so freaking cute. She's almost a year old now, and Treat's like a pile of mush around her. He said having a daughter has been life changing."

Life changing. That's exactly what Daisy was. "Yeah, a six-six pile of mush." Luke laughed at the thought of his imposingly large cousin softening around his daughter. He'd seen Treat and his wife, Max, with their daughter, Adriana, a few months ago, and even he had melted at Adriana's incredible cuteness.

"How are you doing, Luke? I hear you're seeing Daisy Honey."

"Who told you, Em or Wes?" The Braden grapevine was as bad as Trusty's.

"Emmie. She said she found her in your bedroom." Pierce laughed, a deep, hearty laugh. "Dude, you called Emily in to meet her? Emily can't keep a secret."

"Daisy's not a secret, and yeah, Em gave me hell for it. It's not like Daisy was in bed. She was fully dressed. We were talking."

"Talking? You must really like this girl." Pierce went through women like some people went through chewing gum. He would probably never settle down.

"I know you'll razz me for it, but, man, Pierce, Daisy...She's everything. She understands me. She's smart, and caring, and it's like we're made from the same cloth, you know? I can't get enough of her."

"Luke, you're talking like you love her." Pierce's tone was serious.

"Yeah. I know. I'm falling pretty hard." *So damn hard it hurts.*

"Better you than me. So what's up?"

"I need a favor."

"Anything."

You might not think that once you hear what it is. "I want to track down Buddy." Luke rubbed the prickling nerves on the back of his neck.

"Buddy?" Pierce sounded fully awake now. "You sure you want to go there?"

Luke ran his hand through his hair and paced. "I know that."

"Listen, first and foremost, whatever you decide to

do, I don't want you talking to Mom about him. She had a hard time after he left. I don't remember everything, but there are a lot of arguments that I wish I could forget. There's nothing good about him, Luke."

Luke knew his brother's efforts to dissuade stemmed from his protective nature.

"I didn't imagine that there was."

Pierce's voice softened. "Luke, are you sure you want to go there? I'm happy to do it if you really want me to, but you may find out some things that you wish you'd never known." Luke pictured Pierce's dark brows drawn together, his eyes contemplative as he rubbed his clean-shaven chin.

Luke ran his hand through his hair and paced. "I need to understand why he left and never came back, Pierce. He's never even fucking met me."

Pierce's voice softened. "I know it hurts, bro, but really, this guy's not worth your time or energy."

"I get that. I don't know if I'll do anything with the information, if I'll actually go see him or not, but I feel like I need to get closure on this whole thing." He was sure of it now, as sure as he knew he'd already fallen in love with Daisy.

"I know you need closure, and I'll help you get the information you want, but you've got to know that these things don't come without consequences."

Luke shook his head. "I know. No one else seems to give a rat's ass about his leaving. Pierce, look at who I am. I've never been able to connect with a woman—not until Daisy. That's strange as shit, isn't it?"

"Dude, does it look like any of us are *connecting*?"

"Whatever. So maybe he fucked us all up. I don't

know. I only know that I've finally found someone I love." There, he'd said it. Out in the open. "And every time I look into her eyes and think about moving forward, Buddy's hand lands on my shoulder." He shrugged. "Look, if you'd rather not help me find him, it's okay."

Pierce sighed loudly. "You love her?"

"Yeah, man. I do."

"Luke, we all carry crap around from our past. I'm actually a little impressed. You must love her to want to dig up this shit." The compassion in Pierce's tone was tangible.

"I never knew I was hiding behind anything until Daisy wanted to know what happened when I was arrested, and I knew if I didn't tell her, I'd lose her. That's kind of when it all clicked. I didn't do anything wrong. There was no reason not to tell her, but something in my fucked-up head made me afraid to say anything. I'm sure that's because of Buddy leaving. All that psych 101 shit, you know. Father abandonment issues. Will everyone leave me? All that kind of shit. The more I thought about it, the more I realized I was a classic example. I never get close to anyone. I don't even let women try." Luke paced and looked up at the house, feeling a sense of pride in all he'd accomplished, despite his father leaving. "Don't you see, Pierce? I couldn't walk away from Daisy. It's time for me to put this guy behind me, and the only way to do that is to face it head-on."

"Women can make even the strongest men realize their weaknesses. You sure you want to go down this road? I'll help you, but you need to be sure."

Luke headed back up toward the barn. "Yeah. It scares the shit out of me, but I want to be with Daisy, and I can't move forward without clearing up the past."

"Has anything in your life that was worth a shit not scared you?"

"Here I thought you'd give me hell for falling in love. It's not exactly the Braden way." The fact that all of Luke's siblings were still single—and he was the youngest of them all—didn't evade him.

"Sure it is. All of our Weston cousins have fallen in love and gotten married. We're just slower to the plate."

He heard Pierce's smile, and he was glad for his support.

"I'll talk to Treat and see if we can use some of his sources to track down Buddy, but from what I've heard, your girlfriend is only in Trusty temporarily. You know that, right? Word around town is that she's only there until her dad gets better; then she's off to bigger and better things."

"Yeah, I got the memo." *And I hope she changes her mind.*

"Okay. I'll see what we can dig up and I'll call you when I've got something to tell you. Just promise me that you'll think long and hard before you take the next step. I'd hate to see you do this only to find that Daisy's moved on and you're stuck knowing a bunch of shit you would rather not have in your head."

Luke knew damn well he'd be thinking of it far more than he wanted to. If he had any hopes of a future with Daisy, he had to reconcile his past.

Chapter Thirteen

SUNDAY AFTERNOON DAISY and Luke worked for three hours in the hot sun at her father's farm. They'd cleared the fields of the remaining hay bales that had fallen apart or jammed on the stacker. While they were in the fields, Daisy had seen Mrs. Caden's car drive down the driveway and she wondered why Janice's mother was there. She imagined Janice's mother giving her mother hell for what Luke had done, and the thought sickened her. She was relieved when they'd come back to put away the equipment and Mrs. Caden's car was gone. She pushed the thought away as Luke came out of the equipment shed. She loved watching him work, all testosterone-laden brawn. Tanned and ripped. *Manly, sexy, delicious*. She shuddered, thinking about the evening before. Her stomach fluttered as Luke reached for her hand. He pulled her close with a devilish grin, and in that second, his tough exterior fell away. She loved those first moments when they came together. The instant their thighs touched, when his entire body melted against hers before he took a breath and the strength returned and he gathered her in against him. She loved the complexities of him, and she wasn't sure he even knew how complex he really was. His mind was always churning. She saw it in his eyes, thinking, planning, wondering. The lazy smiles and easy nature ran deep, but he was anything but simple. He held her close, and she felt the heat of his body envelop her as desire replaced the tenderness she'd seen in his eyes.

"Stop looking at me like that." Daisy felt her cheeks flush, though the last thing she wanted him to do was stop.

"Like what?" He nuzzled against her neck. "Like I have an insatiable appetite for you?" He lowered his mouth to hers.

When they drew apart, she was breathless. "God, you're good at that."

Luke smiled, and a soft laugh escaped his lips. "It takes two to kiss, Dais." His cell phone vibrated and he pulled it out. "It's Emily. She has the drawings for the apartment above the barn, but I've got another change for her."

"You're going to drive her crazy and she won't ever get to finish." Daisy ran her finger down his chest.

"It's a simple change this time. I just want to move a wall and create a small alcove." He texted Emily back, then shoved his phone in his pocket.

"Do you make those changes to drive her crazy?"

He shrugged. "It's like the last bit of restlessness I have or something. It never feels done. Hey, while we're on the subject of workspace and changes, I know you're bummed about your boss saying you can't hold that clinic, but what about doing it someplace other than *at* the clinic? Couldn't you do it anywhere else?"

"You've been thinking about this, too? I can't stop thinking about it. Yeah, I can. I mean, I have insurance, and I'm licensed, so it wouldn't be a big deal, and it's only physicals, so we don't need a lot of space. I just need to figure it all out. Maybe I'm biting off more than I should."

Luke narrowed his eyes. "Why? Is it too much? Are you too tired after work?"

"No, but it's not like the people here really like me that much. I mean, most of the parents of the school-aged kids are the people I went to school with, and you know...They may not even *want* me to do their kids' physicals." It was a painful thought she'd been nursing for the past two days. What if she offered to do the physicals and no one but Kari showed up?

He folded her into his arms. "You do realize that you've been gone from this town for so long that those people have probably matured by now. I'm sure they don't still harbor the jealousy that made them say all those things."

"I think you have Trusty confused with Mayberry." She wrapped her arms around his neck and rested her head on his shoulder.

"Whether a few people love you or hate you isn't what this decision should be about, Dais. You studied medicine for a reason, which I assume was to help people."

"Of course," she murmured against his neck,

soaking in his strength and support, not to mention his delicious, masculine scent.

"Here's the bottom line. Would you be doing the physicals for the parents or for the kids?"

"Kids, of course." She pushed out of his arms. "Kids need annual checkups. You wouldn't let your horses go unchecked, would you?"

He grinned, and she knew he had purposely egged her on.

"Then nothing else should matter. Open the clinic, and those who come, you help, and those who don't?" He shrugged. "Their loss, but at least you've done all you can to help the people who matter. The kids."

While in medical school and during her three years of residency, Daisy had come up against jealousy and competition. She'd gone face-to-face with some of the most stubborn professors, and arrogant doctors had challenged her. She was used to adversity. Support, however, came less often. She could count those she could *always* rely on on one hand: her parents and Kevin. And now, she realized, she could add a fourth person to that list. Luke.

"Thank you for reminding me of what really matters." She was unable to take her eyes off of him. He had an entire ranch to deal with, and she knew he was wrestling with thoughts of his father, and he was still carrying the burden of his arrest, and here he was, focusing on her issues, and he was right. For a guy who claimed not to know how to connect, he was connecting on so many levels that she couldn't imagine ever disengaging from him.

Or ever wanting to.

"You're welcome, and I know it's not my place to be proud of you, but I am. I love how you saw a need and offered to help instead of doing what most people who worked as hard as you might do—help Kari and let the others fend for themselves." He buried his hands in her hair and cupped the back of her head. "You're really special to me, Dais. I can't wait for you to get to know my family better."

Her heart did a little dance. Things were moving fast, but everything about being with Luke felt right. She'd dated enough guys to know that what she felt for Luke was completely different, and it wasn't the toe-curling, mind-blowing sex, or the way her body caught fire every time she saw him. She felt safe with him, respected, happy, and comfortable. She loved the care he took with his animals and the way he respected her father's ways. Most of all, she really liked who he was. He stood up for what he believed in, and he stepped outside of himself to help others. He trusted. He believed in others, and those were attributes she could learn from. She knew things with Luke were different, because when she wasn't with him, she never stopped missing him.

She also knew she had entered dangerous territory. Territory that had her pushing away her decisions about employment and reconsidering all she'd ever believed about her hometown. She should probably put some space between them, focus on the clinic and her offers of employment.

One look into his dark eyes and she nearly melted on the spot.

If his family was anything like Emily, she knew

she'd love them. A streak of worry skittered through her. Luke must have seen it in her eyes.

"What is it?"

She swallowed hard. She was way too old to be worried about this crap. *Goddamn Trusty.* "I always worry about people who know of me but don't really know me. All those years of rumors..."

"Dais, that was years ago. Kick it to the curb." He pressed his cheek to hers and whispered, "Don't worry. I won't tell anyone that you can be a very naughty, sexy temptress."

After a hot streak raced through her and she caught her breath, she swatted his arm.

"Look at me." He waited until she met his gaze. "Seriously, even if those rumors had been true and you'd slept with the whole town, my family wouldn't care. I adore you, and they will, too." She opened her mouth to say she hadn't, and he cut her off.

"I know you didn't, but it wouldn't matter if you had."

She couldn't think of a darn thing to say and couldn't have pushed words past the lump that had lodged in her throat if she'd wanted to. Instead, she kissed him, and the worry drifted away.

"Come say hi to my mom?"

He smiled. "Absolutely."

She took his hand, and on their way out of the pole barn, she saw him eyeing the older, smaller barn that they used for storage.

"We don't use that barn for much anymore. Once the loft elevator broke, Dad was too busy to worry about fixing it; then he got hurt and, well..."

"What's wrong with it?" He squinted, and she felt him pulling in that direction.

"I'm not sure. The chain or something."

"Let me take a quick look. Does he keep his tools in there?"

"Luke, you don't have to do that. We can hire someone." She took a step toward the house, but Luke was already heading in that direction.

"Why hire someone when I'm here? If it's really just the chain, I can have that fixed in no time."

"You've done so much already."

"Dais, I don't mind. Besides, your dad's hurt. The last thing he needs to do is worry about finding someone to take care of this. It's probably killing him that he isn't taking care of everything else. Don't you think?"

She didn't think. She knew. But she was surprised that Luke could understand that. Knowing there was no convincing him otherwise and loving that he'd take his time to help her father, Daisy showed him where her father kept his tools, and while Luke went to work fixing the elevator, Daisy headed to the house to get them cold drinks.

She found her mother on the porch, drinking a glass of lemonade, and remembered Janice's mom had been there. She took a deep breath, steeling herself against whatever had gone down.

"Hi, Mom. Was that Janice's mom's car?" *Please tell me that she didn't bitch you out for what Luke did.*

"Yes. She brought a dish of lasagna. Wasn't that sweet? I swear, you never realize how great a community is until you need them."

"Really? I was worried that she came to give you a hard time about Luke and what happened at the fair."

"I think she was thankful that he stepped in. What's all this I hear about you setting up a clinic for school physicals?"

Daisy's breath caught in her throat. The Trusty grapevine was fast, but how could the news have traveled that quickly? She hadn't mentioned the idea to anyone other than Kari, Luke, Kevin, and Ashley. "How do you know about that?"

"Janice told her mother that you were setting up a clinic."

"Janice? How on earth did she hear that?"

"Well, are you?" Her mother's face was a mix of seriousness and hope.

"I don't know. Gosh. How does word spread so fast around here and change into *plans* when I've barely had the thought in my own head? Kari must have said something to someone, and by the sound of it, the whole thing is taking on a life of its own. I have no idea what I'm thinking about doing. Ashley won't let me do it at the urgent-care office, so I'd have to figure out a place to do it, and it's a big job. I'll have to order vaccines and schedule times to see them in the evenings and weekends." Despite her earlier misgivings, she felt the hum of excitement building inside her, similar to the thrill she'd experienced delivering babies during her residency. *The birth of something new.*

"If anyone can do it, you can."

"Thanks for the vote of confidence, Mom. I'm considering it."

Her mother had never thrust her opinions on Daisy. She had a quiet way about her, like when Daisy had first mentioned that she was applying to medical school, her mother had simply raised those thin blond brows of hers with a hopeful smile on her lips. Much like she was doing right now.

"How did it go in the field?" Her mother offered Daisy a drink of her lemonade.

"Great. We're done."

Her mother patted the chair beside hers. "Sit with me a minute." She looked more rested today. Her eyes were brighter and the worry lines across her forehead weren't nearly as pronounced as they'd been the other day.

It felt good to sit down and relax. "I was going to bring Luke in to say hi, but when I told him Dad's loft elevator was having trouble, he wanted to take a look at it." She looked in the direction of the old barn and saw Luke kneeling by the loft elevator engine.

"Did he, now?"

"Yeah. I told him that we could hire someone to do it, but he didn't want Dad to worry. How's Dad? He goes to rehab tomorrow, right?"

"Yes. You know your father. He's not going to tell me if his back gets any worse, so I have to gauge his progress by silent signals. I think he's doing fairly well. He's not groaning much these days." Her mother smiled and then reached for Daisy's hand. "How are you, sweetie? You're working long hours at the clinic and then helping here. Are you doing okay?"

"I'm fine. I don't mind helping Dad, and with everyone who showed up, it was actually kind of fun."

Her mother patted her hand. "Your father appreciates all that you do. He does seem to be doing better, and you saw he was outside today. I have hopes that he'll be up and around in a few weeks." Her mother squinted in Luke's direction. "Your father said Luke's a smart, nice young man."

Daisy shot a look at her mother. "Dad said that?" *This* took her by surprise.

Her mother smiled. "I know. I was surprised, too, given his history."

"His...you mean Luke's arrest?" Of course she did.

"Well, yes, but it sounds as if he was arrested for doing something quite chivalrous." Her mother knitted her brows together. "At least that's what I heard."

What she'd *heard*. The Trusty grapevine was hard at work again. Daisy had enjoyed spending the last few years away from prying eyes and gossipmongers while she was at school and during her residency. Coming back to Trusty had been a bit of a culture shock, but like riding a bike, it took only a few minutes before it all came rushing back to her. *And makes me want to turn and hightail it out of here*.

She had enjoyed living in Philly, where *hearing* things meant reading about real newsworthy items—world news, medical breakthroughs and political issues, in the newspapers—not receiving a phone call every time a neighbor farted. Even though she was in Trusty by choice and she could pack up her stuff and move away at any time, she'd never abandon her family, and now she had Luke to consider. He'd snuck into her every thought and was clouding her once-urgent need to flee her hometown.

"Mom, does it ever bother you that there's so much gossip in this town?"

"Oh, sweetie, that's like asking if it bothers me that the sun goes down each evening. Trusty is my home. It will always be my home, and no matter where you live, there will be people who talk about you. Not you specifically, but you know what I mean." Her mother set her glass down on the table beside her. "I know how difficult high school was for you, and I hate that you went through that hard of a time. Girls can be so vicious at that age, but you know no one believed those rumors, don't you? I tried to tell you then, but you were too hurt to see it. You must know that now."

"I'm not so sure."

"Oh, Daisy. Be sure. I know you think Trusty is the very opposite of where you envision yourself. It's the epitome of small-town living. We gossip. We don't wear fancy clothes or drive fancy cars, but, sweetie, Trusty is also known for other things. More important things, like forgiveness and community. When your father first injured his back, the community came out in droves, bringing casseroles and helping on the farm. Trusty is home to good people, Daisy."

She couldn't even imagine people coming out in *droves*.

"You're the first person from Trusty to go to medical school—not veterinary school, but medical school—in a very long time. Everyone here is so proud of you, and honestly, I'm tickled pink that you came back, because Lord knows that even with our weekly calls, I went batty with you being so far away. I worry about you. Sometimes a mother needs to put her arms around her daughter and *know* she's okay."

Daisy sighed. "You're guilting me. Don't get too used to it. I'm still considering all of my options."

Her mother shook her head. "Daisy, what about when you have a family of your own? Don't you want family nearby?"

"Don't you think you're jumping the gun? I don't even have my career in line yet."

"I guess. Things are so different for you than they were for me. I can't even imagine what it would have been like for you not to have been close to your grandmother."

An ache of longing washed through Daisy. She'd always been close to her grandparents, especially her maternal grandmother. She'd taught Daisy to bake, and she would read to her for hours. Daisy had spent many weekend nights watching movies and eating ice cream with her grandmother. *We'll keep this treat as our little secret.* She'd missed her so much when she'd gone away to college that they'd called each other at least a few times each month, which was all Daisy could manage with her workload, and when her grandmother died, Daisy couldn't shake the feeling that she was still watching over her. The pain of missing her had eventually eased, except for moments like now, when the sadness in her mother's eyes brought it back.

"I haven't made my decision yet, Mom. I'll keep that in mind." Her voice was thin and weak. She cleared her throat. "Dad's accident was kind of good timing, though, don't you think? If there is such a thing, and I know that sounds bad. Dad got hurt right before my residency ended, and I needed time to decide on where I wanted to live and which job to accept." Thinking of Luke, she said, "It's almost as if I was meant to be here."

"Good timing is one way to think of it. Maybe fate is another." Her mother gazed in Luke's direction. "Have you thought about which job you want to accept?"

"I haven't decided. They're both great opportunities. I'll tell you one thing, though. Working at the clinic has shown me how desperately Trusty needs a doctor. I never realized how many people put off their health care because of a forty-five-minute drive. It's crazy."

"You could fix that, Daisy Lee."

Her mother used her middle name so infrequently that it caught her attention, which she was sure was the whole point. Daisy rolled her eyes.

"We've been over this a million times. I really want to do more than well-care visits, Mom."

"Yes, I know you do, but a mom can hope, can't she? And what about Luke?" Her mother's tone was serious.

"What about him?" She tried to play Luke off as if he were no big deal. The pit of her stomach sank. He was so much more than *a big deal*, and she knew her mother would see right through her facade.

"You've been seeing him a lot, and I see the way you look at him, Daisy. How does he feel about you leaving?"

"I don't know. We haven't talked about it much." Daisy fidgeted with the arm of the chair. She didn't want to think about leaving. "He's probably dying of thirst. I'm going to grab some lemonade. Want me to fill yours?"

Her mother touched her hand. "No, thanks. Sweetie?"

"Yeah?"

"These things have a way of working themselves out."

"Thanks, Mom." She watched Luke put the ladder away. "I have no idea how I can be so attached to him after just a few days."

"Oh, goodness, Daisy." Her mother laughed. "I knew I wanted to marry your father after our first date. No, wait. I knew it after I first noticed him in second grade."

Daisy had never believed in anything remotely close to love at first sight, but she was dangerously close to that big *L* word, and she feared it had the ability to turn the life she'd planned for herself upside down.

Luke crossed the lawn with a purposeful, confident gait. His broad shoulders were squared, and as he neared, his rounded biceps and ripped abs came into clear view. Daisy's pulse sped up.

"Lordy, Daisy. Now, that's one handsome man," her mother said just above a whisper.

"I know, right?" The comment didn't surprise her. Her mother loved her father, but she was still a woman, and a person would have to be blind not to be taken with Luke Braden. "I'm going to grab that lemonade. I'll be right out."

Daisy went inside and filled two glasses with ice

and lemonade. Noticing her father sitting in his recliner with a stack of papers in his lap, she said, "Hi, Dad. Want some lemonade?"

"No, thanks. How did it go out there?" He sounded tired, or maybe bored.

Daisy came around to the front of his chair so she could see his face. Dressed in his typical jeans and plaid shirt, he kept his eyes trained on his papers, his brows drawn together. She'd misread his voice. He was three fingers deep in inventory spreadsheets. Daisy took that as a good sign. Even if he wasn't out and about, at least his mind was ready to get back to work. "Fine. We're done, and Luke worked on the loft elevator on the old barn. I'm not sure if he fixed it or not."

At that, her father drew his eyes up to her. "Did he, now?"

"Mm-hm. I hope that's okay."

Her father pushed to his feet with a low groan.

"Are you okay, Dad?"

"Fine, fine."

She grabbed the lemonade and followed him out to the porch.

"You should be good to go now," Luke said as he climbed the steps. He pulled his shirt from his back pocket and wiped his hands, then nodded at Daisy's mother. "Good to see you, ma'am."

Her mother shook his hand. "Nice to see you, too, Luke."

He nodded at Daisy's father. "How's your back doing, sir?"

"Getting better every day," her father answered.

Daisy and her mother exchanged a *that's-news-to-me* glance. She was surprised that her father would share that with Luke when he hadn't so much as given Daisy or her mother any indication that he was feeling better.

"The chain on the loft elevator was loose, but I tightened it up and it's working fine now." Luke shoved his shirt back in his pocket.

"Thank you, Luke," her father said. He lifted his chin and looked down at Luke. "How's that ranch of yours coming along?"

Luke's smile reached his eyes, and pride filled his tone. "Couldn't be better. My young stock's coming right along. You know how farm life is. Every day the sun comes up is another day to enjoy it." Luke looked down at his bare chest. "I'm sorry for not being dressed, sir, but my shirt is pretty drenched."

Her father nodded, but didn't respond.

"That's okay, Luke. I think David was bare chested for the first twenty years we lived here. Right, hon?" She patted his leg.

Daisy's father smiled down at her mother, then drew serious eyes back to Luke. "At some point we should talk about crops."

"Oh, David, Daisy's only here for another few weeks, and he'll probably want to spend as much time with her as he can before she leaves." Her mother slid a smile her way.

Before she leaves. The thought of leaving scratched like sandpaper. Daisy handed Luke a glass of lemonade.

"Thanks, Dais." He finished the lemonade in one

long drink. He looked down at his sweaty body. "I should probably get back and check on my girls."

It shouldn't bother her that they were going in separate directions. He needed to take care of his horses, and she needed to go home, get cleaned up, and spend some time thinking about her job offers. But as he pressed a kiss to the back of her hand, and she melted again, she knew she'd go home, shower and change, and then get into her Prius and drive straight to his place—with a bag of clean clothes for tomorrow morning, or maybe for the week.

Luke shifted his eyes to her parents. "Sir, ma'am, it was nice to see you."

Daisy had to bite her tongue to keep from sighing dreamily like a fan girl as he walked away, Levi's hugging him in all the right places, bare, broad shoulders swaggering, and all those tanned and glorious muscles bunching and flexing as he reached into his pocket and dug out his keys.

"Nice young man." Daisy's father patted her shoulder, knocking her world a little more off-kilter.

Chapter Fourteen

DAISY WAS WHIPPED by the time the clinic closed Wednesday evening. She'd spent the last few days taking care of stuffy noses, flus, bronchitis, cuts and bruises, and handled a host of other patients that should have been seen by their primary care physicians. At least the construction worker's stitches qualified as urgent care. Caring for the patients at the clinic made her aware of the plethora of needs right there in Trusty. She'd seen firsthand that when medical care wasn't convenient, families were forgoing it altogether, which was not only stupid, but dangerous. Whether she was caring for emergencies or handling well care, she was glad for the distractions because she couldn't stop thinking about the looming deadline for her job offers. She had been staying with Luke since Sunday night, and every time he brought up her job prospects, she brushed it off.

It felt so right to spend time with Luke. She loved going for walks with him and spending their nights wrapped in each other's arms. She helped him take care of the horses in the evenings, and just watching him care for them and love them endeared him to her even more. She knew he'd make a great father one day. He had a big heart. Every time she started to give consideration to the job offers, the thought of leaving Luke was too painful, and she pushed the decision to the back burner.

Too tired to even think about cooking dinner, she stopped by the diner on her way home. *Home?* Luke's house felt a lot like home to Daisy lately, and she knew it had nothing to do with the physical house and everything to do with him.

"Hey there, sugar. You look pooped." Margie set a glass of iced tea in front of Daisy. "It's fresh and supersweet. It'll brighten your day."

"Thanks, Margie. Can I get a salad and a chicken casserole for two to go?" She took a long drink and closed her eyes, relishing in the delectable taste that she'd never been able to match. While she was in medical school, she'd lived on Ramen noodles, ice water, and instant coffee. The few times she'd come home during school breaks, she and her mother would stop in at the diner her first day back, and Margie always had a fresh pitcher of tea waiting for them. It was one of the hallmarks of home, Daisy realized, just like the crisp mountain air that she'd so easily forgotten.

"Coming right up." She slipped the order through to the kitchen and then returned to Daisy. "There's been talk around town about you and Luke." Margie wiped the counter with a damp rag. "All good."

"Yeah?" Talk around town never surprised her, but *all good* sure did. Hearing Margie's comment didn't hit her with the force it would have when she'd first come back to Trusty. Daisy realized that she was softening toward the thing she'd rued the most about Trusty. *Talk around town*.

"Mm-hm." She leaned in close and lowered her voice. "And I hear Janice's mother is finally trying to get Janice to do something about Darren's drinking."

"I'll believe it when I see it." Daisy wouldn't pin her hopes on that change happening anytime soon.

"Yeah, that's the way I feel, too. I wish she would, though. Children learn from their parents, and she has sweet little Michael to think of. He's such a doll."

If Janice had only taken Michael to his doctor sooner, she could have saved him a lot of pain. "Yeah, he is."

Margie leaned over the counter. "So is it true that you and Luke are an item?"

An item. A couple. Now *they* were the talk of the town. Of course they were. What did she think would happen if she spent every night with him? "Yeah, you might say that."

The door to the diner opened and Alice Shalmer walked in.

"Hey there, Alice." Margie waved from across the diner. "Have a seat. I'll bring you some iced tea in a sec."

"Thanks, Margie." Alice had worked at the Trusty library since Daisy was in middle school, and she looked just as Daisy remembered: tall and thin with an angular nose, pointy chin, and black-framed glasses.

She sat beside Daisy at the counter. "Hi, Daisy. How's your dad feeling?"

"A little better every day. Thanks for asking."

"That's good to hear." She set her purse in her lap. "I've been bringing your mom books each week, so she has something to keep her mind occupied. I was even able to find a few on physical therapy that I think she really found helpful."

It seemed that every time Daisy turned around, she learned about someone who had reached out to her family. "Thank you. I'm sure she really appreciates that. She doesn't get out too much these days."

"No, she doesn't. But then again, your father has always been the center of her world. He's a good man. It's a shame what's happened to him."

The center of her world. That was the truth. "Yes, we feel that way, too, but we're hoping he'll be well soon."

Margie brought a glass of iced tea for Alice. "Did you get any new hot romances in?"

Alice shook her head. "I'm behind on shelving, but I've got a new assistant librarian starting soon, Callie Barnes. She's from Denver and smart as a tack. We'll get all caught up." She set her eyes on Margie. "Margie, we need to find you a living, breathing man to live your own romance."

Margie threw her head back and laughed. "No, thank you. Men in books don't talk back, they never get a beer belly, and they stay young forever. And the best part?" She leaned across the counter and whispered, "I'm not the talk of the town."

"Like you'd even care about that," Daisy teased.

Margie was one of the most confident women she knew. She'd seen her stand up to drunken customers, haggle with tourists, and talk frantic friends back to sanity. She couldn't begin to imagine Margie being shaken up by rumors.

Margie placed her hand over her heart and feigned a frown. "I've got a sensitive heart, Daisy. All this..." She waved her hand up and down in front of her body. "Facade. That's all it is. A big fat facade." She set her hands on her ample hips. "And if you believe that, you'll believe that I grew the tea leaves for that drink of yours, too." Margie walked away laughing.

Daisy smiled. "I never realized how much I missed her when I was away."

"Speaking of being away, everyone has missed you, Daisy," Alice began. "But we're so proud of how much you've accomplished. You've done Trusty proud."

Everyone. It was all she could do not to laugh. "Thanks, Alice. I doubt *everyone* missed me, but thank you."

"Oh, you'd be surprised. It's a shame Dr. Waxman isn't here to congratulate you himself. He was always such a card." Alice took a sip of her drink.

"I miss him." She wished Dr. Waxman were there. He'd most certainly congratulate her and dole out a handful of advice about what kind of flack to accept from patients and what to nip in the bud, and she'd memorize every word as it fell from his lips—then he'd probably hand her a lollipop. The thought brought a smile to her lips.

"Speaking of Dr. Waxman." Alice shifted her eyes

to Daisy. "Did you hear about the breast specialist who came into town last year and held a conference at the library? He wanted to hold a clinic for breast exams, and the library hosted the clinic."

"Yeah, I did hear about that. Dr. Ornstein from Denver went to several small towns, right?" She'd known it was a marketing ploy for the breast center he'd recently opened—a clever one.

"Yes, and did you know he caught Millicent Crouch's cancer early enough that she's cancer free now?" Alice shook her head. "If she'd had regular exams here in Trusty, she might have even caught it sooner." She slid a look to Daisy that was very similar to her mother's look when she'd told Daisy that she could change Trusty's medical issues.

"I did hear about Millicent, and I'm glad they caught it early."

Alice gripped the top of her purse, as if she were steeling herself for something. "I was at Sheetz this morning and ran into Cleo, who said that you were setting up a clinic for the kids' school physicals."

No wonder she was steeling herself. "Cleo?" Cleo Topps worked at Sheetz. She was in her late fifties and Daisy hadn't seen her since she'd returned to town.

"Yes, and she also said that some of the girls were helping you. Let's see if I can remember." Alice looked up toward the ceiling. "I think she said that Lynn Haverty and Kari Long were helping you, and Kevin, of course. Betty Laird is already going through the PTA list and taking signups." Betty had been the middle school secretary forever.

"Wait. What?" How could this have happened so

fast? "I haven't committed to the clinic."

"No?" Alice furrowed her brow. "Oh dear. Well, why on earth not?"

Because I have no clinic. Because I haven't had time to breathe. Because...Oh the hell with it. "I couldn't get authorization from my manager at the urgent-care clinic, and I'm living in an apartment right now, so I don't really have space to see patients."

"That's why I was telling you about the breast clinic. The library had to be inspected by the county in order to hold the clinic there, and we kept up that certification. Use it, Daisy. Please."

"The library?" She could just see a sign out front. *Drop off your kid and pick up a book!* "I don't know. I'd have to see patients in the evenings or on the weekends, and the library closes at six."

Alice patted her hand. "This is Trusty, dear, and you're talking to the librarian. One phone call and it's a done deal."

The bells over the front door chimed as Janice burst through the doors with Michael screaming, his little fists clinging to her shirt. Tears streamed down her cheeks, and she was panting hard.

Daisy jumped from her chair and went to her. Her shirt was covered with blood. "Janice, what happened?"

"Oh, thank goodness I found you. The clinic is closed and Darren cut his hand. I was going to ask Margie to call your mom and track you down."

Daisy quickly assessed Janice's face, arms, looking for signs of a struggle. "Where is he? Are you hurt? Did he hurt Michael?"

"No." She drew in a deep breath. "He's home, and Daisy, he's drunk. He won't go to the hospital, but look." She held out the bottom of her shirt. "I'm so scared. Please."

Damn him. Drunk again? Daisy grabbed her purse and called over her shoulder to Margie, "I'll pay later." She followed Janice and drove like a bat out of hell, glad she kept a full medical bag in her trunk.

She parked on the side of the road in front of Janice's small brick rambler and grabbed the old-fashioned leather medical bag from the trunk. It had been a gift from Dr. Waxman when she'd been accepted into medical school. *Do Trusty proud,* he'd said; then he'd corrected himself. *Do yourself proud.* She was trying to do herself proud, but would leaving this messed-up town—and Luke—behind really make her proud?

The front door opened into the living room. The house smelled of stale cigarettes. There must have been a dozen or more beer cans littered throughout the small, cluttered living room. A trail of blood ran between the kitchen and living room like a vein. She followed it down a narrow hallway.

"He's in the bathroom," Janice explained. They found Darren passed out in the bathtub, mouth slack, eyes closed. His hand was wrapped in a bloody towel, hanging over the edge of the tub. The bathroom smelled of urine and the metallic stench of fresh blood. "I told him to stay there. I was afraid the blood would ruin our carpet."

Daisy took his pulse as she gave Janice instructions in a calm, firm voice. "Janice, take Michael to your mother's. I can take care of Darren." At least she hoped she could. She needed help. If Darren woke up, he could go ballistic. "Go, Janice. Now."

"No. I can't. He gets rough when he's drunk."

Damn it. She thought he'd never touched her. Daisy grabbed Janice's arms. "Listen to me. Michael does not need to see this. You're his mother. Take him to your mother's house and keep your child safe. I'll be fine."

Janice nodded but remained still. She was probably in shock. Daisy applied pressure to Darren's hand, hoping he wouldn't wake up until after Janice and Michael were gone. She pulled out her phone and called Kevin.

"Kevin, I need you to get ahold of Janice's mother and tell her to come get Janice and Michael at Janice's house; then come to Janice's. Darren's in bad shape." Her next call was to Luke. "Luke, Darren's drunk and he's cut his hand. He won't go to the hospital. I need to stitch him up, and I need you to hold him for me." She gave him Janice's address, and by the time she hung up, Janice's mother had arrived. *Thanks God it's a small town.* Daisy kept pressure on Darren's hand until Janice and Michael were safely out of the house. Kevin burst through the front door with Luke on his heels. Both men carried first-aid kits.

"Holy shit, Daisy," Kevin said, eyeing the amount of blood oozing over the side of the tub, where Darren's hand had been resting.

"I'm hoping it's not as bad as it looks. I need to clean him up, numb him, then stitch him up, but I want to get a good look to be sure he didn't cut the tendons first. If he wakes up, he could lash out. Can you guys hold him for me?"

They were already moving into place when they heard Janice's neighbor, Mr. Low, calling into the house. "Darren? I saw Janice leave with her mother." He appeared in the bathroom doorway, and Kevin was quick to shuffle him out of the house and lock the door.

"The whole town will know in six minutes," Kevin said as he ran back into the bathroom.

"I've got his back. Kevin, get the front." Luke lifted Darren forward and sat behind him in the tub. He wrapped his powerful arms around Darren's, pinning them to his chest, and wrapped his legs around his waist.

Daisy eyed his expertly placed limbs. "You've done this before."

"You can learn a lot at the right college parties." Luke's tone was dead serious.

Kevin climbed into the tub, pinning Darren's legs beneath him and holding his forearm against the side of the tub while Daisy cleaned and inspected his wound.

"He missed the tendons. It's long and deep, but I can stitch it. Are you guys ready?"

Luke nodded, jaw clenched, muscles flexed around Darren.

"We're good, Daisy," Kevin said.

Daisy's pulse ran wild as she focused on numbing the area around the wound, expecting Darren to wake up and go crazy. Darren didn't flinch. She breathed a sigh of relief. Daisy set to work stitching up his hand, thinking about Janice and Michael. What would she have done if she hadn't found Daisy? Would she have gone against Darren's wishes and called 911? Would he have let her? Would she have just let him bleed? She knew damn well why he didn't want to go to the hospital in the next town over, and it had nothing to do with the forty-five-minute drive. Drunks thought that if they kept their injuries to themselves, no one would ever know they had a problem. That might be true in a larger city, where people were too busy hustling through their high-paying jobs to worry about neighbors, but it wasn't true of Trusty. She thought of her father and of what her mother had said. *Trusty is also known for other things. More important things, like forgiveness and community.*

Darren remained asleep through the whole ordeal. The three of them carried him into the bedroom, removed his bloody shirt, and laid him on the bed. Daisy bandaged his hand so he couldn't rip the stitches out, and as he lay there, passed out, looking pathetic as hell, Daisy felt sorry for him. She had never met his father, who was an alcoholic and had died in a car accident when Darren was young, but she knew his mother, and she seemed to have her life in order. She worked at the town hardware store, lived alone, and she'd done all the right things when Darren was growing up. She'd thrown him birthday parties when he was in grade school and supported him at high school sporting events. But once Darren began drinking, when he was in eleventh grade, she no longer had any control over him. If only she'd been able to get Darren into rehab.

Fat chance. At this rate, he was sure to follow his father's footsteps to an early grave. She felt the weight of Luke's arm across her shoulder.

"You okay?"

"Yeah, of course." She realized she'd pulled Luke from his horses and Kevin from whatever he was doing, which was probably reading, watching a movie, or thinking about meeting a woman. "Thanks for coming, you guys. I'm sorry to have called you, but you're my go-to guys."

"I'll wear that badge proudly." Luke squeezed her shoulder.

"No worries, Daisy. Jesus, how does she live like this?" Kevin disappeared down the hall.

Daisy and Luke followed him into the kitchen. Michael's toys were gathered in bins in the corner of the kitchen and living room. The counters were clean, the table was covered in crayons and coloring books, and amid it all were several empty beer cans. Daisy ached for them—all of them. Darren included. She'd seen guilt weighing him down the other day at her father's farm.

Daisy grabbed a trash bag and gathered the empty cans. Kevin and Luke helped, and in no time, they had the small house clear of them, but there was still broken glass and trails of blood.

"I'm going to stick around and clean up the blood so Janice and Michael don't have to come back and see it. You guys can go. I can take care of this."

Luke shook his head. "And take the chance that Darren wakes up? No way. I'm staying."

"Me too. We can have this done in no time." Kevin

headed into the bathroom.

"You must have other things to do." As relieved as she was, Daisy didn't want to keep Luke from his work.

"I'm not leaving, Daisy." He grabbed a mop from the kitchen closet and headed toward the bathroom while Daisy answered a knock at the door. Lynn Haverty and two other girls Daisy had gone to high school with—and been teased by—Jerri and Tracie—stood on the porch with worry in their eyes.

"Janice called," Lynn explained. "She asked me to pick up clothes for her and Michael. She said she's not coming back." Lynn peered around Daisy. "She said there was blood everywhere. Holy crap."

"I know. We're cleaning it up so she and Michael won't have to see it." Daisy stepped aside and let them in. "He's in their bedroom. Please don't wake him."

"Hi, Daisy," Jerri said as she came inside. "I haven't seen you in so long. Wow, you look great." She hugged Daisy as if they'd been good friends, when they'd been anything but.

Daisy was dumbfounded for a moment, wondering how they could brush off the past and move forward so easily when she was busy tamping down her fight-or-flight defenses. "Thanks." Daisy went to the kitchen to look for rug cleaner and try to get the blood out of the carpet. She heard Tracie on her heels and braced herself.

"I heard you were doing the physicals. Thank you for that. I wondered how I'd get Maddy hers before school started." Tracie had a seven-year-old daughter, who, like Tracie, had freckles across the bridge of her nose and bright green eyes. Tracie's auburn hair hung in a thickly braided rope to the middle of her back. She opened a closet door and pulled out rug cleaner and rags. "She keeps all the cleaning supplies in here."

"Thanks." Daisy went to the living room while the other girls packed Janice's and Michael's clothes; then they joined her and helped clean the house.

"I hate that she's going through this," Lynn said.

"I know. I wish she would have moved out ages ago." Tracie stuffed Michael's rain slicker into a bag.

Daisy was scrubbing the living room carpet when Jerri sank to her knees and began helping her. Her blond hair was pulled back in a ponytail. Daisy held her breath.

"I like your hair darker, Daisy."

"Thank you." Daisy hadn't given much thought to her hair since she'd dyed it. It had made things easier when she was in her residency. Looking like a Barbie doll coupled with a name like Daisy Honey put her a step behind, regardless of her 3.9 GPA. Just as books were judged by their covers, Daisy was living proof that people were, too. Now a wave of defensiveness washed through her, as if she were weak for changing her hair color.

"I'm glad you were here to help, Daisy. I know none of us were very nice to you in high school." Jerri kept her eyes trained on the carpet.

With that little nugget, defensiveness went out the door. Daisy swallowed against the thickening of her throat.

Jerri sat back on her heels. "The truth is, we were awful to you, and we're real sorry. We talk about it, all of us. How bad we feel about what we put you through."

Tracie set aside the bag and looked at Daisy. "I'm really sorry, Daisy. Jerri's right. We're all sorry." She looked down, then glanced back up at Daisy with empathetic eyes. "When I think of Maddy and how upset she'd be, and I'd be, if anyone ever treated her the way we treated you, I…I'm just so ashamed of what I did. What we all did."

Daisy had waited years to hear those words, and they hit her like a sledgehammer to the heart.

Lynn joined them and spoke with a soft and caring tone. "You didn't deserve it, and I have no idea why we thought it was okay to do what we did. I'm sorry, Daisy." Lynn looked at the others and took a deep breath. "The truth is, we were jealous of you."

"You were pretty and smart, and you had this great family who treated you like you weren't just a dumb girl." Jerri shrugged.

The universal shrug that had filled so many gaps recently.

"It's okay," Daisy said just above a whisper.

"No, it's not." Jerri leaned forward and wrapped her arms around Daisy's neck. "I'm sorry."

Daisy's hands were wet and messy from cleaning the floor. She lifted her forearms to Jerri's sides in an awkward hug. "I'm no better. I said some really horrible things to Janice the other day."

"No, you didn't. You said the truth, and she knows it."

Daisy shook her head and blinked away the dampness in her eyes. "No, it's not right. I need to apologize when I see her."

When they were done, Daisy was struck by the way the community pulled together in pockets of friendship and support. Her mother had been right about forgiveness and community. These girls who had been vicious to Daisy for so many years had just spent an hour cleaning Janice's house and gathering her belongings, and now they were hugging and thanking her. *Including* her.

Luke reached for her hand.

"I think we owe Dr. Honey a lot more than a thank-you," Lynn said.

Dr. Honey. Lynn had just given Daisy the one thing she'd strived for her whole life. Respect.

Luke must have known that a lump had lodged in Daisy's throat and stolen her ability to speak, because he pulled her close and asked, "What did you have in mind?"

My protector. Daisy had spent her life proving she didn't need to be protected. Maybe she didn't have it all wrong. She didn't *need* protecting, but it sure as hell felt good coming from Luke.

"The least we can do is help when she does the clinic. Would that be okay, Daisy?"

Kevin cleared his throat, and when she looked up at him, she knew he felt the earth shift with the long awaited change from their youth, just as she had. Luke kissed her temple, and the earth shifted again—to the place it was meant to be.

Chapter Fifteen

IT WAS ALMOST nine o'clock by the time Luke headed down to the pasture for his nightly check on the animals. Daisy had gone back to her apartment to take care of a few things, and they'd decided to stay there tonight. He missed her already. He was proud of the strong and confident way she'd taken control of the situation with Darren. For her to go above and beyond anyone's expectations and clean the house for Janice only proved how kindhearted she was. He'd noticed the way Daisy's features softened when the other women had hugged and thanked her, but when they'd called her Dr. Honey, he'd felt a physical change. He'd had his arm around her, and he'd felt her body deflate, as if someone had opened a valve and released years of tension. He'd had to fight the urge to turn her to him and hold her against him.

The horses were making their way across the field toward him. His mind drifted back to the glance he'd caught between Daisy and Kevin. It told of years of friendship and support, and it had sparked a moment of jealousy. An emotion Luke was not very familiar with, but he knew he'd only recently come into Daisy's life, and he respected their friendship. Kevin had been there for her during her most difficult years, and as much as he wished he had been the one she'd turned to all that time—or even better, that he could have made it stop back then—he took comfort in knowing she'd had Kevin to lean on. He'd tucked away the sliver of jealousy that had pierced his soul and followed the other desires it spurred in him. He wanted to be with Daisy. With her and there for her, which is why he planned on telling her exactly how he felt tonight.

Chelsea was the first to greet him, pressing her muzzle into his chest.

"Hey, Chels." He stroked her cheek while doing a visual inspection to make sure she didn't have any cuts or troublesome burrs. His cell phone rang, and he slipped on his Bluetooth and answered the call from Wes while he inspected the horses.

"Heard your gal did a good thing today."

He heard the sound of rushing water in the background. "Hey, Wes. White-water trip?"

"Nah. Just riverside pioneering this time. Two-nighter."

"How'd you hear about Daisy all the way out there?"

"I have a sweet little brunette who keeps me abreast of things while I'm away."

He heard the smile in Wes's voice. "Right. Clarissa. Well, yeah, Daisy was amazing today, and hopefully Darren will get some fricking help. The guy's a mess."

Luke had been thinking about Darren, and he wondered what would happen when he realized his wife and child were gone. He wondered if it would be a different feeling than what his father felt when he'd left them, and he wondered if that feeling was one of relief or grief.

"Hopefully, it'll be a wake-up call."

"You know, I worked with him over at Daisy's father's farm, and when he's not drinking, he's a nice guy. Quiet, which was probably because he was embarrassed about what went down at the fair, I'd expect, but he was nice enough. I can't imagine what gets into people's heads that they end up that drunk. I mean, you and I, we had our drunken nights when we were younger, but we know when we've had too much to drink, and I sure as hell know that if I didn't, I'd have no business having a wife and child."

"Yeah, I learned a long time ago that we never know what's going on in someone else's mind."

Luke noticed a gash on Shaley's leg. "Aw, crap. Shaley's bleeding."

"Oh, man. Sorry. You need to go?"

"No. I've got my Bluetooth in. I'm walking her down to the barn. Hey, as long as I've got you on the phone, can I bend your ear a few minutes?"

"Sure. What's up? You've decided you're not serious about Daisy and need to know how to bow out gracefully?"

Luke shook his head. He used to be just like Wes when it came to working his way through as many women as he could. Now that Daisy was in his life, that felt like a lifetime ago, like it hadn't even been him, but rather some guy he knew. “Wes, I’ve never been more serious about anything or anyone in my life.”

“So I’ve heard.”

“I guess I have Pierce to thank for that?”

“Emmie.”

“I’m thinking of asking Daisy to stay in Trusty.”

“You asking for my advice?” Wes sounded dead serious.

Luke led Shaley into the barn. “No. I was just airing out my lungs.”

“What do I know about this shit? You really like her that much? That fast?”

More than I ever thought possible. “Yeah, I do.” He inspected Shaley’s wound.

“Well, you know what Mom would say, right?”

Luke smiled. “Christ, how could I have forgotten that? *Love will find you when it’s damn good and ready and not a second before or a minute too late—and when it does, you don’t have a chance in hell in getting away.*”

DAISY WAS STILL reeling from what happened with Darren and from the things Jerri and the others had said to her when she sat down at her kitchen table with her two job offer letters. She’d driven by Dr. Waxman’s house on the way home from Janice’s, and it stirred up all sorts of childhood memories. She remembered the way he’d always asked after her and seemed to know what was going on in her life even when she hadn’t seen him in months. It had made those doctor visits easier. The grapevine snuck into unexpected offices and ears, and there had been times when she was glad it had.

She remembered how comforting seeing Dr. Waxman had been. Now the children saw rotating doctors in a large practice a town away. Was that really better for them? It was clearly better for the doctors, who were earning more money and seeing more patients. But if patients saw a different doctor every other visit, did they ever establish the same comfort and relationships she had enjoyed with Dr. Waxman? How could they? The doctors were at least a town away, some even farther. They couldn't possibly know if a child won a spelling bee or was a flower girl in a wedding. They would have no way of knowing if Mr. Mace was under stress because his crops weren't doing well, or if her father hadn't left his house in a month. They couldn't know if the library held a writing contest or which child won. Those were the types of things that could help them understand a patient's current emotional state and help in diagnosing as well as comforting the patient.

Dr. Waxman had encouraged her to look beyond the gossip and remain focused on her goals. She wondered if he'd have any sage advice for her now. Should she follow her heart or the best path for a strong career?

A knock on her door pulled her from her thoughts. She'd just seen Luke, and she already missed him. She pulled open the door and was surprised to find Janice, puffy eyed, dressed in clean clothing, her hair freshly brushed and styled, sans Michael attached to her hip.

"Janice. Is everything okay? Where's Michael?"

Janice barely managed a smile. "Hi, Daisy. He's

with my mom. Can I come in?"

"Of course." She stepped aside, steeling herself for another verbal bashing, even though Jerri assured her that Janice wasn't angry with her.

Old habits died hard.

"Can I get you a drink? I think I have some lemonade or iced tea."

"No, thanks. I just came to talk to you." Janice sat on the sofa and fiddled with the seam of her jeans.

Daisy sat beside her and tucked her hands under her thighs to try to ease her nerves.

"I...um. I wanted to thank you for helping me today."

"Of course. I was happy to." She noticed Janice's hand was trembling.

"Lynn said you cleaned up, too, and that you had Kevin and Luke with you." She dropped her gaze to her lap. "I'm so embarrassed. I don't even know what to say." Tears slipped down her cheeks.

Daisy didn't think as she drew Janice into her arms. At that moment, the pain of the past fell away completely, and all that remained was a woman whose life had been upended. A woman Daisy's age who had, and would continue to, face rumors about her husband, and in turn, herself. Michael was young, so he was protected from the ruthless rumors, but rumor mills ran like ghosts in the night, driven by jealousy or hatred, feeding off of the misfortune of others. Daisy couldn't stop that from happening any more than she could have stopped the rumors about herself years ago, but she could be there to help Janice through them. She could support her and remind her that alcoholism was a disease that needed to be handled by professionals. She could be her friend. Who could understand the pain rumors caused better than Daisy? Daisy had moved past the pain of it all, but the irony of the situation didn't evade her. *Forgiveness and community*. The two seem to be bonking her on the head these days. Maybe that was a good thing.

She stroked Janice's back. "You shouldn't be embarrassed. This is a chemical dependency that Darren has to deal with. You didn't cause it. This is *not* your fault."

Janice drew away and wiped her eyes. "Daisy, I'm sorry. I'm sorry for all those years I treated you badly, and I'm sorry for pulling you into this with Darren today. I just didn't know what else to do."

"It's okay." As she said it, she realized that everything was not okay. "Wait. Janice, all those years of gossip and rumors, that *wasn't* okay, but this...Coming to me and asking me to help with Darren? That's all okay. I'm glad I could help, and I owe you an apology, too. I said horrible things to you at the clinic the other day. I was angry, and hurt, and...I'm sorry."

"I deserved it. I was kind of a bitch." Janice dried her eyes and fiddled with the edge of her jeans again. "I'm sorry."

"Let's just consider it water under the bridge and try to move forward. Are you really staying with your mom?" God, she hoped so.

Janice nodded. "I can't let Michael be around anything like what happened today."

Daisy breathed a sigh of relief. "Good. I'm glad to

hear that. I like Darren, but he needs help."

"I know, and I love him. I can't help it. I've always loved him." A tentative smile lifted her lips. "I'm going to try to get him to seek help, but I'm staying with Mom until he does."

Daisy looked at the boxes stacked against the wall in the living room. Four boxes labeled MEDICAL BOOKS. Medicine was about so much more than science. It was about personal connections and caring about the patients. Daisy realized that she wanted to know her patients as more than charts and names, and that those bonds were far more important than being in the thick of diversity and cutting-edge research.

Her cell phone rang. "I'm sorry, Janice. Do you mind if I get that?"

Janice rose to her feet. "It's okay. I should go anyway." She moved to hug Daisy, and they ended up in an awkward semi-embrace. "Well, thanks for being there, Daisy. I know Darren was lucky that you were here and willing to help."

"Hold on one sec." She answered Luke's call. "Luke, can you hold on a sec?"

"Sure," Luke said.

"Thanks." She lowered the phone. "Janice, what would you have done if you hadn't found me?"

Janice pressed her lips together and shrugged. "I'm just glad I did. Tell Luke I said thanks. I'm really sorry I dragged you guys into this mess."

"If you ever need anything, I'm here, Janice."

She watched Janice leave and then went back to her call. "Sorry, Luke."

"Everything okay? Was that Janice?"

"Yeah. Everything's more than okay. She apologized, and so did I." Daisy exhaled loudly. "How are your girls?"

"Well, my best girl sounds like she's pretty good, but my littlest girl has a gash on her leg."

"Oh no. Shaley?" Daisy's heart ached at the thought of it.

"Yeah. I just cleaned it up. It's not too bad, but—"

"I'll get my stuff and we can stay there. I know you can't leave her."

"Dais..."

I love you. He didn't say it, and neither did she, but she wanted to so badly, it practically burst from her lungs.

"Bring enough clothes so you never have to leave."

She closed her eyes, absorbing the meaning behind the words.

"I'll be right over."

Daisy called Alice on the way to Luke's.

"Hello?" Alice's voice was heavy with sleep.

"I'm so sorry, Alice. This is Daisy Honey. I didn't realize it was so late. I can call back tomorrow."

"Don't be silly. I'm up now. I heard that Darren was pretty bad off. You did good, Daisy."

"Thank you. I was wondering if you were serious about letting me use the space at the library for the physicals."

Daisy heard Alice breathing louder, and she made a noise in her throat, as if she were sitting up in bed. When she spoke, Alice's voice was strong and excited, fully awake. They scheduled the clinic for a week from Saturday from eight to eight. It would be a long, grueling day, but Alice said that Betty already had more than thirty families who were interested, and Daisy agreed to hold the clinic during the same hours the following weekend as well, to see anyone who wasn't able to make it to the first one. Kevin would help her see patients. They would be busy, but it would be worth it.

Chapter Sixteen

LUKE HOVERED OVER his older brother Ross's shoulder as Ross examined Shaley's leg. Ross was five years older than Luke and he had a veterinary practice in town.

"Mind giving me a little space?" Ross looked over his shoulder at Luke. "You're like a mother hen."

"I can't stand that she's hurt." Luke stepped from the stall to give Ross space.

"She'll be fine. It's a fresh wound. You caught it early, Luke. That's a good thing. I can't tell you how many clients don't check their horses closely enough at night and wonder how bacteria can settle in overnight. You did good. It's a three-inch gash, and it's not too deep. I cleaned it up and put salve on it. You'll have to check the dressing to make sure it doesn't get too tight and change it twice a day."

Luke heard Daisy's car in the driveway. "I'll be right back." He met her on the path to the barn and wrapped her in his arms. "I'm so glad you're here."

"Is Shaley okay? I saw the Braden Veterinary truck. Is Ross here? I haven't seen him in years."

"Yeah. He's checking her out. He thinks she's okay."

"Hey, are *you* okay? You look really worried." She stroked his cheek, and he pressed his hand to hers and held it there.

"I'm worried. I hate that she's hurt, but I'm okay. I'm better now that you're here. I missed you." He kissed her as they walked into the barn.

Ross came out of Shaley's stall and wiped his hands on a rag. "She'll be okay, but, Luke, you need to keep an eye on it. You know the drill. If she gets feverish or the skin gets hot—any signs of infection, call me." He smiled at Daisy. "Daisy Honey, I haven't seen you in a hundred years. I think you were twelve or thirteen the last time I saw you."

"Hi, Ross." Daisy's eyes jumped between the two men. "Wow, you guys could be twins."

"I'm much better looking." Ross rolled up his sleeve. "And my tattoo is much cooler than his." He flexed his biceps and the palm tree on his muscle wiggled.

Luke punched him in the arm.

"You're a doctor, right?" Ross asked. "What's your specialty?"

"Family medicine."

"Great. We need a new doc in town."

"Actually, Daisy's not sure she's going to practice here," Luke explained.

"I haven't decided." She looked at Luke, and he could tell she was wrestling with the decision.

His gut clenched tight at the reality that she was still considering leaving.

"I know you're the town vet, but do you mainly handle large animals, or do you see small animals, too?" Daisy asked.

"Both. Like a small-town doc, I do whatever the good old Trusty residents need, but I'm sort of known for doing regenerative therapy in horses. I do state-of-the-art stem cell and platelet-rich-plasma therapy to enhance the healing and quality of repair of tendon and ligament injuries."

"You do PRP. That's fascinating."

Luke stole into Shaley's stall while they talked. It killed him to see Shaley's leg wrapped up.

"I have to take off, Luke. Keep it clean and change the dressing twice a day."

Luke rose to his feet and embraced Ross. "Love you, bro. Thanks for coming out."

"Anytime." Ross opened his arms to Daisy. "We're huggers, so you might as well get used to it." He folded her into his arms. "Take care of Luke tonight. He's a big baby where his girls are concerned. He'll need pampering."

Luke loved seeing Ross welcome Daisy so warmly, and when Daisy met Luke's gaze over his brother's shoulder, he could feel the love she felt for him.

"I think I can handle that."

After Ross left the barn, Luke drew Daisy into a deep kiss.

"You guys look so much alike, it's scary."

He kissed her again. "Don't get any ideas. I'm a much better kisser than him." He nuzzled against her neck. "Did you bring your closet?"

"Just about. I've got my bag in the car." She knelt by Shaley and stroked her belly. "How are you, sweet baby girl?"

Luke joined her, and they sat in the stall with Shaley. "Are you sure you don't mind being here instead of your place?"

"I want to be wherever you are, and now I want to be wherever she is. Poor girl." Daisy's eyes filled with compassion. She scooted closer to Luke, and he draped his arm around her. "You know you treat your girls like they're your children."

"I do?"

"Yeah. It's really cute. I love it, actually."

"Before my cousin Treat and his wife, Max, had their baby, Adriana, it had been ages since I'd been around a baby. One thing's for sure. You can't be in a bad mood with a baby around. You should see Treat with her. He's six foot six, and she's so tiny. One smile does him in."

"My mom always says babies turn grown men into melted butter." She smiled, he assumed, at the memory.

Luke kissed Daisy's cheek. "So do you."

"Do you ever think about having kids?"

He felt her tense a little against him as she asked the question. It struck him as a very big question, one that made him hope she was contemplating a future with him. Honesty rolled easily off his tongue. "Before I met you, I never thought about having a girlfriend, much less kids. Being with you has brought a lot of stuff to the surface. I've been thinking a lot about my dad. A few days ago, I asked Pierce to help me track him down. He called earlier and said he's got the information. Pierce is visiting my uncle in Weston, so I'm meeting him there on Friday. I won't be gone long, just a few hours."

"Wow. Is that...Wow. You've never met your father, right?" She looked up at him with an assessing, and compassionate, gaze.

"Nope. I'm not sure if I want to now, but I want answers. I don't really know why he left, or why he never got in touch with me to, I don't know, get to meet his son. He left before I was born. I'm the only one he's never met."

"Oh, Luke. I hadn't thought about that. That has to hurt. I'm so sorry." She squeezed his hand.

He shrugged. "It is what it is. I just...I want to move forward with you, but I feel like I need to have closure with my past before I can make a meaningful future."

"I'm sorry, Luke. You must have had this on your mind. I should have been more aware of your feelings."

"How could you? I wasn't even aware. I've never thought about family much. I sort of take them for granted, you know? But being with you has me thinking about all sorts of things." He lifted her hand to his lips and kissed it. "Enough about my father. Tell me what happened with Janice."

"Being with you has me thinking about things, too."

They held each other's gaze, the silence filled with unasked questions—*What things are you thinking about? Do you want more with me? Should we talk about it?* There were a million things Luke wanted to ask, and it was his fear of the answers that held him back. He knew what he wanted with Daisy—a future. Everything. And he could feel that she loved him. He didn't doubt that one bit, but what she had at stake was her entire future, the career she'd worked toward for eleven long years.

He saw questions and worry in her eyes, too. He loved her too much to force the issue. He held his tongue and let her lead their conversation in whatever direction she chose.

"Janice," she said quietly.

Disappointment hung over him like a cloud, but he didn't blame her for choosing that path. With Shaley hurt and their emotions so raw, she needed time.

When she continued, her voice was stronger. "She showed up at my apartment and thanked me for helping her and apologized. It was weird, but I'm glad she came over. It was nice to actually sit down and talk instead of just reacting to crazy situations, you know? She's staying with her mom, but she loves Darren. Gosh, I could see it in her eyes, Luke. She *really* loves him."

I know the feeling. "Hopefully, he'll get some help." Luke pulled her close. "Are you sure you're okay?"

"Yeah, just tired, and I'm trying to figure out my job situation. You know."

Boy, do I ever. His stomach clenched. "Want me to give you a rubdown?"

She narrowed her beautiful blue eyes. "Is that code for something dirty?"

Luke rose to his feet. "It wasn't, but I'll have to keep that in mind. I'll be right back." He went into the tack room and came back with a blanket, which he spread on the ground outside Shaley's stall. "Take your shirt off, lie on your stomach, and I'll help you relax."

She hooked her finger in his jeans with a flirtatious smile. "My shirt? This is definitely something dirty."

"You keep doing that and it will be something dirty." He lifted her shirt over her head, and the sight of her lacy pink bra drew a groan from him. "Okay, maybe that wasn't a good idea." He lowered his mouth to her bare shoulder and kissed his way to the crest of her breast.

"Or maybe it was a very good idea." She slid her hands beneath his shirt, and his body instantly reacted to her touch.

He drew back. "Jesus, Daisy, you get me hard so fast. This is not where I was headed." He guided her down to the blanket on her stomach. "You're way too sexy. You make it hard for me to think."

She stretched her arms above her head and closed her eyes. "Then don't think."

He came down on his knees beside her and kissed her cheek. "As much as I want to climb on top of you and love you until you scream out my name…" He kissed the back of her neck. He was so nervous about revealing his feelings that he was having trouble concentrating. "This is harder than I thought."

She opened her eyes and smiled. "Or *you're* harder than you thought."

"I'm stumbling over my own feet, Dais. I was hoping we could talk about things." He needed to talk to her, had to clear the air and see where they were heading. He forced himself to push aside his lust—if only for a little while. He placed his hands on her shoulders and her hot, silky skin had him even more befuddled.

"Things?" She smiled. "Like the weather?" She wiggled her hips.

"That is so unfair." He massaged her shoulders. "Like us and where we're headed." He felt her shoulders tense beneath his touch.

"Okay."

"That made you tense." He drew a deep breath. Somehow, thinking about and talking about the future were very different. He thought it would be easy, but now fear trickled in. What if she was dead set on going to New York or Chicago?

"Not tense, just nervous," she admitted.

"Me too." Luke worked his way down each arm, squeezing the muscles and kneading the tension away. "Does that help?"

"Tremendously."

She exhaled, and he felt her tension slip away, just as he had with the horses. Maybe he could connect on a deeper level. Wasn't that what his emotions had been driving him toward all along? It wasn't that he couldn't connect, he was realizing. It was partly that his past was holding him back, but now he realized that it was so much bigger than that. How could he bond with anyone on a deep, meaningful level without the base of love? The love he felt for Daisy was pure and real. Nothing in his life had ever come close. Even his love for his family and his love for his horses—all of whom he thought he loved with his entire being—was different. They'd scratched a deep groove into his soul—Daisy ripped it open and slipped straight through.

He drew the tension away from her spine, massaging outward with a firm, loving touch. He contemplated not revealing his feelings. Maybe she'd feel pressure to stay if he did, and that wouldn't be good. He took another deep breath.

"If you take one of those other jobs, when would you leave?" His stomach took a funky, nervous dive. He felt her holding her breath, which caused him to hold his, anticipating and fearing her answer. He moved his hands down to her leg and massaged her thigh.

"I'm not sure I can think with you doing that," Daisy said in a seductive voice.

"If I can think, and I'm the one touching you, then you can at least try." His thumb grazed the crease of her ass. He grit his teeth against the urge to follow that curve right up between her legs.

"I'll try." She exhaled loudly. "Trusty is the last place I wanted to settle down, but now that I'm here, it's hard to ignore how badly they need a doctor."

He was afraid to get his hopes up. He squeezed her leg as he moved down toward her calf. "And?"

"I don't know." She sucked in a breath when he moved his hands to the other leg. "If I was rubbing you like this, there's no way you'd be able to think."

"I can barely think now, Dais."

"Or you're trying to relax me into submission." She turned over onto her back. "Does this help relax *you* into submission?"

Luke's eyes took a slow stroll down her body, drinking in taut nipples pressed against her lacy bra and the swell of her hips above the waist of her low-riding cutoffs. His chest constricted so tight, he thought it might clamp down and his lungs would stop functioning if he didn't get it out right then.

"Daisy, I..." *Love you. Want to touch you. Need to touch you.* What he felt for her was so much bigger than three simple words. "You make my head spin." He inhaled deeply, trying to concentrate—which was becoming more and more difficult with every breath he took. He lay down beside her and brought his thigh over hers, then draped his arm across her stomach and leaned on one elbow. Daisy lay on her back, gazing up at him with so much love in her eyes it felt like an embrace.

"I've been restless my whole life, and I couldn't, or maybe I wouldn't, connect with anyone. I don't know why that was, but I've never felt anything like what I feel when I'm with you. When I think about sharing my thoughts, or sharing my bed, there's only you, Daisy." He cupped her cheek and gazed into her eyes. "I love who you are, and I want to *be* with you—when you want me and when you need me. I want to feel your body melt against me at the end of a hard day, and I want to help you hold down bloody, drunken guys in bathtubs."

"Luke," she said in a breathy whisper. She reached for him, and he took her hand in his and pressed a kiss to it.

"Let me finish." His pulse raced. He was powerless to stop the words from tumbling out. "I know you might not feel as strongly, and I know you have big plans for your career, and that you might leave Trusty and go to New York or Chicago, or someplace else altogether. I get that, and if that's where you're headed, then it is. I support whatever you want to do. But I want you to know that I want to be with you, Daisy." He brushed her hair from her face and cupped her cheeks. "I feel like I can't think beyond being with you."

Daisy put her hands on his wrists, and for a minute—which felt like a lifetime—she didn't say anything. Her eyes searched his; her luscious lips parted. He wanted to lean down and kiss her, but he was struck numb. Had he made a mistake? Had he totally misread her? He lowered his hands from her cheeks, and she blinked several times, as if she'd been struck as numb as he had.

When she finally spoke, her voice was a jagged thread. "I do feel just as strongly. I…" She lifted up on her elbow; her lips were a breath away.

"You do?" He could barely breathe.

"Yes. I love everything about you. I love the way you look at me and how when another guy walks by, you tighten your grip on me."

"I tighten my grip?"

She nodded, smiled. "Yeah. Just a little."

"I didn't even realize it."

"I know. I figured. But you don't do it around Kevin."

"No? I guess coming from a big family, I understand that no one person can be everything to the person they love. Friends have a valuable place in everyone's life." Luke's siblings had always filled the roles that friends filled for others. "Kevin was there for you when you needed him most, and I expect he'll be there for you forever. Or at least I hope so. That's a good thing, Dais. I'm glad you have him. He loves you and cares about you like you're his sister…or at least that's how it seems to me."

She shook her head. "I love that about you. Some boyfriends would be jealous of Kevin."

Boyfriend. He loved that.

"Know what else I love about you?" She continued. "That you care enough about people to step in and stand up for them when they're too weak to stand up for themselves. I love that you wanted to stay with Shaley tonight. I love that you're close to your family and that you care enough about me to help my dad. But mostly, I just love being with you. It doesn't matter if we're kissing, talking, cutting hay, or holding down a drunken, bloody guy in a bathtub. My heart is full when we're together, and when we're not, it's the emptiest feeling in the world."

Luke's world stilled as her words sank in, and when he lowered his mouth to kiss her, more words tumbled free.

"I love you, Daisy."

Her eyes dampened. "Oh, Luke. I was afraid to say it, because it's all so fast, and I thought I must have been fooling myself or something, but I trust my feelings, and I love you, too."

Their lips met with a tender, loving kiss that sealed their words.

Chapter Seventeen

THEY SPENT THE night wrapped in each other's arms on the blanket in the barn. Daisy had awoken several times to find Luke checking on Shaley. She loved how attentive he was toward her. She'd seen the pain in his eyes and the tension in his jaw and mouth, similar to what she'd seen on the faces of parents of ailing children. When her phone alarm went off, Luke was out in the pasture with the other horses. She'd joined him for a few minutes, and Chelsea and Rose had nuzzled right into her chest and followed along the fence line as she'd headed into the house. She could see why Luke bonded so easily with the horses—especially his horses. They were so easy to fall in love with, and she found herself recognizing certain identifying sounds of each of them, like how Chelsea's whinnying was an octave higher than Rose's and how Rose walked a little slower, remaining closer to the younger horses as they came to greet them.

She turned on the shower, watching Luke walk

shirtless up the hill toward the house. The sun glistened off of his tanned, hard muscles. She could still feel those muscles wrapped around her body like they were last night as he buried himself deep inside her and loved her until she could barely think. The same powerful muscles that had worked to help her father and had stood sentinel between Darren and Janice.

God, she loved him.

She heard the back door open, then close. The bathroom filled with steam, and she stepped into the shower, hoping, praying, he'd join her. She heard his footsteps in the bedroom, and her nipples hardened in anticipation.

He loved her. He loved her! Her head was still spinning with their admission. It was so right, so real and true. She could feel it down to her core. She never would have believed she'd find love in Trusty, Colorado, and here she was, watching the man she'd fallen for slither out of his jeans and step into the shower with the most alluring look in his dark eyes.

Thoughts of the job offers skittered through her mind. How could she ever consider leaving him? Luke placed his hands on her hips beneath the warm spray of the shower, and thoughts of her job offers slid from her mind and followed the trail of water right down the drain.

"Hi," he whispered as he drew her close and kissed her.

Oh Lord. She had no idea that Luke's kisses, which made her knees weak and her belly shift and flutter, could be even more delicious with water seeping between their hungry lips. When he drew back, she was panting—literally. She needed him. He had become her drug of choice.

He gathered her hair over one shoulder and pressed his stubbly cheek to hers. "Do you expect me to behave?"

Hell no. Please, no. Hearing the insinuation in his gravelly voice made her quiver. She shook her head, and a slow smile spread his delicious, full lips as he took her breasts in his hands and lowered his mouth to her neck. He brushed his thumbs over her nipples; then he slid one hand between her legs, and—Oh God—she was already halfway to the moon. He met her gaze, and his eyes were nearly black.

"Oh, baby, you're so ready."

She closed her eyes as he stroked her, teasing her until she felt herself swell with desire. He pressed his cheek to hers again. His hot breath sent a shiver of heat through her.

"I love how you want me." He pressed his body against her. "Do you feel how much I want you?"

She couldn't have answered if her life depended on it.

Luke backed her gently against the cold tile wall and spread her legs with his feet. She closed her eyes again, feeling his tongue drag down her shivering stomach. He grabbed her hip with one hand, his other still working its magic, taking her right to the edge. She could feel the taunt of an orgasm, just out of reach. Then his hot breath spread across her thigh. His tongue blazed a path to her center, and he hovered above her sex, breathing. Teasing.

Take me. Touch me.

He used his hands to spread her legs further, then licked the insides of her thighs, her hips, above her wet curls. Every goddamn place except where she needed him most, driving her out of her ever-loving mind.

Oh God. Please. She tangled her hands in his hair, unable to hear past the stream of the water and the rush of blood in her ears. He slid his fingers deep inside her, and she moaned at the blissful sensation. He stroked her, licked her, then rose to his full height. She could feel his breath on her mouth, smell her arousal on his lips. She opened her eyes, and he pressed one hand to the wall and leaned his chest in to her; his other hand glistened with her juices. He sucked his fingers, and her entire body flamed with heat. She closed her eyes and he pressed his mouth to hers again, taking her tongue into his mouth and sucking, then laving it with his before he dropped back down to his knees, his hands on her thighs, drawing her trembling legs apart again. He licked, loved, devoured her, using his fingers and tongue to bring her to the edge again. She slammed her palms against the tiles and flexed her thighs, grasping for the orgasm that was still just beyond her reach.

"Luke. Please, Luke."

He thrust his tongue into her and—*Oh God*—expertly took her over the edge, filling her body with heat and ice at the same time. She panted, trying to bring her brain back to some modicum of functionality, but her eyes wouldn't open. Couldn't open, and when he used his hand to bring her up, up, up again, she cried out his name, and he captured it in his mouth and kissed her as her body pulsed with need.

"I love when you come apart."

Oh dear God. Hearing him talk like that made her legs weaken. When she opened her eyes, his were filled with desire, his body swollen and ready. She looked down at his erection, and she wanted him. She wanted it. She splayed her hands on his chest, dragged them down his hot, wet body, and then took his hard length in her mouth beneath the warm spray of the shower pounding her shoulders and back.

"Daisy, you don't...Jesus..."

She couldn't get enough of him, and as she stroked and sucked, he swelled within her hands.

"Daisy...I'm gonna..." He picked her up effortlessly and slid her down upon his hard shaft, then kissed her as his muscles flexed, and he thrust inside her again and again, taking her up over the edge again. She felt every pulse of his carnal release as he filled her with his love.

He drew back, panting. "Holy...Christ."

He took her in another mind-blowing kiss, breathing air into her lungs, and when he drew back again, his lips grazed hers. "I want everything with you, Daisy. I want you in my life."

She was the luckiest girl on the planet—almost. Her job offers still loomed like the apple in *Snow White.* They looked almost too enticing to forgo, held so many promises of greatness, but from what she'd seen and heard about the impersonal gap between doctors in larger practices and their patients, Daisy was beginning to sense the poison within those offers.

EVEN THE CHAOTIC afternoon at the clinic hadn't been able to distract Daisy from what Luke had said in the shower. She wasn't one of those girls who dreamed about her wedding or who planned her looks around catching a man. She was focused, determined. She knew what she wanted—a medical career—and she'd known she'd wanted to leave Trusty since she was fourteen years old. How could her heart betray her carefully constructed career plan?

"Hey, lover girl." Kevin handed her another chart. "Last one before you leave. It's Mr. Mace, room four."

"Oh no. Didn't he get checked out at his doctor's office?" Daisy didn't wait for an answer as she stalked down the hall toward exam room four. She pushed open the door and found Mr. and Mrs. Mace standing in the center of the room. Mr. Mace held a gift-wrapped box.

"There she is." Mrs. Mace wore a blue knee-length dress. Her gray hair still held the fresh curl of a new haircut that framed her round, friendly face.

"Mr. and Mrs. Mace." Daisy closed the door and did a quick visual assessment of him. His color was good. He wasn't sweating. His breathing appeared normal. "How are you feeling today?"

Mrs. Mace touched his back. "Thanks to you, Daisy, he's feeling much better. We're not here for a medical visit. We're here to say thank you. We did go back to see our doctor, and as you said he would, he gave us a diet plan and medications. I think Harv is on the right track now."

"That's a big relief. I'm so glad you followed up with your doctor." Maybe they didn't need her here as much as she'd thought.

"Eve made you these cookies." Mr. Mace handed her the box.

"You didn't have to do that. Thank you." She reached for the box, and Mr. Mace held on tight.

"Daisy, my doc helped me tremendously, but he's still forty-five minutes away. And he's not you. He helps, but it's quick and impersonal, like I'm the words on the chart, not the person sitting in the room." He glanced at his wife, still holding tightly to the gift; then he drew his eyes back to Daisy. "This box is a thank-you, but if you would consider staying in Trusty, Eve will make you cookies every week. Won't you, Eve?" He looked at his wife, and her eyes widened.

"Harv, I told you not to try to bribe her. I'm sorry, Daisy. He's relentless." She took the box from her husband and handed it to Daisy. "Your mother said you have offers in Chicago and New York. Have you made a decision where you're going to practice?"

She'd thought of nothing else—except Luke, of course—and the most surprising things had been going through her mind. Working in a larger metropolis would offer her hands-on experience with a wider variety of illnesses, and she could learn from some of most prestigious specialists in her field, but what was pushing its way to the forefront of her mind were the things that she couldn't get in those cities. A sense of community. History. Family.

Luke.

"I haven't made my decision yet." Daisy set the

box of cookies on the counter behind her. "I appreciate the gift very much, and it means the world to me that you want me to stay."

"If you change your mind, you've got two patients right here waiting for you." Mr. Mace patted his stomach. "And I promise to try to eat healthier and to come see you regularly."

She could tell by the sincerity in his gray-blue eyes that he meant it. As they walked out the door, Mr. Mace paused.

"Oh, Doc?"

Doc. She remembered how he'd called Dr. Waxman, *Old Doc Waxman*, and *Doc* didn't sound too bad to her. It was a step in the right direction. "Yes?"

"What you did for Darren Treelong? No big-city doc would ever do that, so when you move to the highfalutin city, don't lose that personal touch." With a nod and a smile he left the office.

She knew that if she worked in a big city, she wouldn't have time to breathe, much less make a house call.

ON HER WAY to her parents' house, Daisy called Luke.

"How's my beautiful girlfriend?"

Daisy smiled. "What? You have another girlfriend? Who is this beautiful girlfriend? I'll take her down."

Luke laughed. "Never, babe. There's only you."

"And your girls. How's Shaley?" She wished she could go straight home and be with Luke and Shaley, but she hadn't seen her parents in days, and she wanted to see if her father was making any progress. *Home to Luke and Shaley.* That feels so natural and so right.

"She's doing great. Her skin is clear and, so far, no infection."

"Oh, thank goodness. How many times did you comb the pasture today?" He'd gone out in the pasture multiple times, looking for the source of Shaley's injury, even though everyone who owned horses knew that most of the time the source of an injury like hers would never be found.

"Not many. I don't know how she got the cut. I'll probably never know. It's part of ranch life, but it still sucks."

"Yeah, I know. But at least she's got you taking care of her." She loved that he cared about his horses so much, and the more she got to know them, the more attached she became, too.

"I'm heading to Dad's and then I'll be home. *Over.* Sorry." She winced at her mistake.

"Home. It's okay, Dais. It is home."

Her heart couldn't open more than it had. She'd fully embraced Luke, their love, and even the life they'd developed so quickly together. If she could only embrace Trusty.

She pulled up in front of her parents' house and spotted them walking across the field toward the house. Her father hadn't ventured far from the front porch in weeks. Hope swelled in her chest as she ran across the field to join them.

Her father's color was good; his gait was stilted but stable. Her mother walked beside him wearing a yellow skirt, white blouse, and a smile on her face.

"Dad, look at you! How does your back feel? How

far did you walk?" She walked beside him, thrilled to see him up and about again. She hadn't realized how his not leaving the house brought a repressed, heavy feel to being home. Seeing him in the fields, the place he was the happiest, made everything feel lighter. Better.

He stopped walking and nodded. "I feel pretty damn good. Your mother forced me to get out here, and you know, Daisy, it was a good thing. Maybe you two weren't so wrong after all."

"You think?" She shared a knowing look with her mother.

"Don't get too high and mighty, Daisy Lee."

"Don't worry Dad. I'd never even think of being high or mighty. But I might think of being a good doctor who knows what the hell she's talking about."

"He walked across the whole field, Daisy," her mother said proudly. "And he promised to try to do it every day."

"That's great. It's good for your brain, Dad. And if you feel uncomfortable, skip a day, but there's nothing worse than locking yourself inside. Your body will expect to be sedentary."

Her father sighed. "We've been talking about the farm and what to do with it."

Daisy's nerves tightened. "And?"

Her father began walking toward the house again. "We're thinking about hiring a manager. I think that's a better option than selling. The land's been in our family for too long to let it go."

"But, Dad, you're not exactly good at letting other people take over."

He narrowed his eyes, then shifted them to the house. "Maybe not, but I think it's about time I learned. What are your plans, darlin'? Are you moving away again the minute I figure this out?"

She wasn't expecting the question, and she hesitated.

"I take it that means you're still seriously considering it?"

Her mother took her father's hand in hers. "Give her time to speak, David."

"I'm still deciding, but I have to admit that I'm seriously considering staying." She *was* seriously considering staying, she realized. It surprised her as much as it surprised them. The idea had been floating around in her mind, but she hadn't realized it had taken root. How could she not? she wondered. The idea of leaving Luke made her stomach hurt, so much so that whenever she started to think about it, she pushed it away.

"Daisy? Really?" Her mother's eyes widened. "Oh, David, did you hear that?"

"Yes, I heard it." He kept his eyes trained on the house.

Daisy watched him closely. She could only assume he didn't want to believe her, but as they came to the porch and her father held on to the railing, drawing in a few deep breaths, she feared it was something worse.

"Dad? Are you okay?" Suddenly, Daisy saw her parents with clearer, less self-centered eyes. They were aging. Today her father's back was injured, but what if it was his heart next? What if her mother fell and hurt herself? Could she leave a busy practice and be here for them if they needed her? If she moved away, how often could she come back to visit? Every few months? Once or twice a year?

"I'm fine." He looked away. "It's a harsh reality to leave a lifetime behind."

"You're not leaving it behind, Dad. You're moving on to a different part of your life. You'll never leave the farm behind." Could she leave the farm—and her family—for good? *Really* leave them behind and start a life elsewhere? Not just for three-quarters of the year for school, knowing she would be home during summer breaks, but forever? She'd changed so much over the past couple weeks. She knew her eyes had been opened, but she felt ashamed, or maybe just selfish, for not thinking about what it would really mean to leave her family and start a life elsewhere on a permanent basis.

Her father lowered himself to the porch step and patted the space on either side. "I suppose you're right, darlin'. I'll never leave the farm behind, and I guess I always hoped that you might not be able to, either."

A lump lodged in Daisy's throat.

"Sit here with me a minute." Her father looked up at her mother. "Sit down, Susie."

Daisy sat beside him, thinking about her family. She'd gone eleven years rarely seeing them, getting by with phone calls and quick visits. She'd been so busy with her own schedules, her plans, building the legwork for her medical career, that she hadn't realized how much time had passed. Eleven years was a damn long time. She thought of Janice and Michael and of Lynn and the girls coming to the house to pack up their things. Who would she have in New York or Chicago? If she was working full-time, wouldn't the people she became friends with be people she met through work? Wouldn't they be working as well? Who could she call and know, with one hundred percent certainty, that they'd drop everything and rush to her side?

Would she ever find the support of a community in a large city?

Her father draped his arm around her shoulder, a rare and welcome affection. "You know, Daisy, I can remember when you were just a baby. You'd get yourself all worked up into a tizzy, and the only thing that would calm you was when I'd lay you across my chest and rock you out here on the porch. You'd listen to the crickets or my breathing, or whatever babies focused on, and you'd quiet right down."

"Really?"

He smiled, a rare, warm sight. "It soothed whatever had you tied in knots. And when you were a toddler, you were just an itty-bitty little thing. You'd come out at night in your pj's and rock your baby dolls like we used to rock you."

"Oh, David. She was so sweet." Her mother rested her hand on his leg.

"I don't remember any of that." *But I wish I did.*

"You were too little to remember, but here's a memory I'm sure you haven't forgotten. When those girls used to make fun of you in high school, you'd come out at night and stalk off to the creek. You'd sit there for hours, all by yourself with your face all pinched tight, and when you'd finally come back inside, you'd left all that angst by the water."

"Dad, you knew?" She got chills remembering the nights she'd forced herself to forget. It didn't matter if it was freezing cold, raining, or a warm, starry night; she found solace at the creek.

"There isn't much I don't know, darlin'." He sighed. "It pained me to know what was going on, but I'd spoken with their fathers, and, well, you know teenage girls. Their claws aren't easily retracted."

A lump had lodged in Daisy's throat. "You...talked to their fathers?"

"Of course. You're my girl." He put his arm around her and pulled her close. He smelled of Old Spice, the same cologne he'd always worn. "I only wish I could have gone into school where it was all taking place and knock some sense into those fools." He glanced at her mother.

"He tried, but I stopped him. I was worried that if your father showed up at school, you'd be teased for that." Her mother's hand clutched her father's leg tighter.

Daisy shook her head. "You never said anything to me."

"Those rumors were not kind, Daisy, and they were about a subject that I'm not real comfortable talking about. Your mother talked with you, and I thought it would just be uncomfortable for both of us if I brought it up. I knew what kind of girl you were. What kind of woman you are. I've always been proud of you, Daisy."

Daisy's eyes filled with tears. She'd been so emotional lately, and for a woman who prided herself on never shedding a tear, she was getting pretty good at the whole teary-eyed thing.

"I was proud of how you handled things back then. It would have been easy to name call right back, but you never stooped to their level." He pulled her against his side again and kissed her forehead. "I only wish you never had to go through it at all. It made you stronger, but I fear it's driven you away from your home, and, darlin', that's something I'll always regret."

"Daddy..." She didn't know what else to say. It had been her past that had driven her away, but it was the apologies, and talks like these, that were tethering her here now.

Chapter Eighteen

WHEN LUKE'S ALARM went off at four thirty Friday morning, he'd already been awake for an hour, thinking about meeting Pierce later that morning. This was it. He was going to make a decision about meeting his father today, and while he should feel relieved, he was going back and forth over the issue from a million different angles. Daisy stirred beside him and draped her arm over his chest. He hoped he'd never have to know what it felt like to wake up without her.

Daisy lifted her head and looked at him through heavy lids. "Hey."

"Hey, babe. Sorry if I woke you."

"You didn't." She pushed up onto her elbow. Her hair tumbled over the thin strap of her cami as her fingers traveled along his abs. "Nervous about talking with Pierce?"

"A little."

She ran her hand over his chest and kissed him above his nipple. "Whatever you decide is okay, Luke.

You'll know the right thing to do when you get there. Are you sure you don't want me to take off work and go with you?"

He kissed her forehead. "I love that you would, but I think I have to face this alone, and you're meeting with Kevin and the girls to coordinate the clinic at the library, aren't you?"

"Yeah, but if you need me, I'll cancel."

"Don't be silly." He loved that she'd put her own agenda aside for him, but he had no idea what he was going to find out today, or how he'd react. It would be safer for him to deal with it on his own, with Pierce.

He pulled Daisy onto his chest, and good Lord, she was soft and warm and inviting enough to be dangerous. She lowered her lips to his chin, then kissed his neck and wiggled her body down—making him hard as a rock—so she could kiss his chest again.

"Careful. I'm not very good at resisting you."

"Who says I want to be resisted?" Her hair tumbled in front of her eyes, and she bit her lower lip, looking seductive as hell.

Luke wrapped his arm around her waist and gently flipped her onto her back, settling his legs between hers. He brushed her hair from her face and gazed into her eyes. "Do you have any idea how much I love you?" A smile formed on her lips, and he kissed her softly. "I love that you help your family." He kissed her again. "I love that you take care of others." He kissed her neck and pressed his hips into hers, then whispered in her ear, "I love the way you feel beneath me."

Her fingers slipped beneath his briefs, and the feel

of her soft hands pressing on his ass as she rocked her hips sent a shudder through him. She tugged his briefs down and he made quick work of taking them off. He straddled her and came up on his knees.

"Now, this is a little unfair. I'm naked as a jaybird and you're dressed in your silky..." He drew her cami up and lowered his mouth to her breast. "Seductive top." He laved her breast, feeling her nipple pebble beneath his tongue as he pulled her top off and tossed it aside. "That's better." He took her other breast in his mouth and brushed his thumb over her other nipple.

"Oh God, Luke..."

He kissed his way down her body to her panties. "You're still way too clothed." He snagged the silky material with his teeth and dragged them down to her thighs; then he licked her sweet center. She breathed harder, and her thighs tensed as she rocked against his mouth. He loved how her body reacted to him. He slid his fingers inside of her, and she gripped his shoulders. He'd learned how to take her right up to the brink of release, and when she began sucking in halted gasps of air, he drew his mouth away and stroked her inner thighs with his tongue while he rubbed the sensitive nub that he knew would take her over the edge. She writhed beneath him, making sexy little noises that were driving him out of his mind. He came back to her center to taste her again as he reached up and squeezed her nipple.

She gasped a sharp breath.

Her body began to tremble, and her inner muscles clamped down, pulsating around his fingers as she rocked into him, panting with need. He moved up her body and took her in a deep, hard kiss. Jesus, he loved making love to her. Before she could come down from the peak, he drove into her. Her eyes flew open, and she sucked in a breath, clawing at his shoulders, his arms, wherever she could find purchase.

She bit down on his shoulder. He nearly came from the exquisite pain, sending him into a frantic frenzy of kissing, sucking, licking her neck, her shoulder, her cheek. He groped her breasts. She felt so damn good, he had to thrust harder, faster, deeper. Her head fell back, and she cried out a loud sound of pleasure. Her beauty was mesmerizing. Luke slowed his pace, wanting more of her, more time with her. He wanted to feel her body clamp down around him again, and he drew himself out, teasing her with the tip, until she opened her eyes wide and clenched her teeth.

"Un-fair." She rocked in to him.

The desire in her eyes made him shiver. Her fingers dug into his back in perfect sync to her inner muscles clenching around him, driving him to thrust in deep. Their heated bodies slicked with sweat as they stroked and loved, groped and caressed, and clung to each other as if their next breath depended on the strength from the other. Luke thrust in deep, again and again, taking them both over the edge until they fell to the mattress, their bodies pulsing with aftershocks.

Luke used to think sex was a great stress reliever, and as he reached for Daisy's hand, he realized that as close as he and Daisy had become, they weren't having sex at all—they were truly making love. Bringing their bodies as close together as their hearts, minds, and souls had already become. Like second skins.

Daisy laced her fingers with his, and as Luke brought it to his lips, he knew he could handle whatever he learned about his father, as long as he had Daisy to come home to.

Chapter Nineteen

AS LUKE BLEW past the WELCOME TO WESTON sign, the bone-shaking growl of his Harley vibrated through his body and his stomach tightened, taking his heart right along with it. He'd spent the first few years of his life in Weston before his mother bought her property in Trusty, Colorado. The rural back road gave way to slow-as-molasses Main Street, the center of Weston. Main Street had been built to replicate the Wild West, and like in Trusty, the people of Weston dressed the part, in jeans, cowboy boots, and Stetsons. Luke dressed the part, too, he realized, in his typical Levi's and T-shirt. His mind shifted to Daisy, and whether she wanted to admit it or not, the girl lived and breathed the West. No woman had ever looked finer in a pair of snug jeans and cowboy boots. *God, I hope she stays with me.*

He was still thinking about her as he pulled down his uncle Hal Braden's long driveway, five hundred acres sprawling before him, nestled against the

Colorado Mountains. Luke had spent much of his first six years hanging out with his cousins, Treat, Dane, Rex, Savannah, Josh, and Hugh, who were all either married or on their way to the altar. With the exception of a quick visit to meet Treat and his wife Max's daughter, Adriana, he hadn't seen them since he bought his own ranch two years earlier, and he missed the hell out of them.

Luke cut the engine, taking in the ranch that had been his home away from home for so long. *Good memories.*

Hal came through the front door and made his way slowly down the porch steps toward the circular drive. His long legs carried him across the walkway, and a slow smile crept across his sun-kissed, deeply lined face. Despite being in his early sixties, Hal's broad chest and thick arms told of his years toiling on his ranch. Luke's chest swelled with gratitude at the sight of the man who had been the driving force behind his love of ranching and horses. He stepped from his bike, and Hal folded him into his arms. At six foot six he had a few inches on Luke, and his bear of an embrace was strong and solid.

"I've missed you, son." Hal took a step. He was wearing a T-shirt and jeans, with the same cowboy boots that he always had. He'd always called Luke *son*, and when Luke was a boy, he'd wished for a father like Hal—brave, protective, wise, and loving beyond any man he'd ever known. Hal gave Luke a quick once-over with dark eyes that were common among the Braden men and nodded. "Glad you're here."

Over the years, seeing his uncle and cousins had

stirred all sorts of feelings that Luke would never admit to—jealousy, longing for a father he'd never have—but he was at a crossroad, ready to move forward with Daisy if she'd have him, and he needed to gain a foothold on the past to ensure he could leave those uneasy feelings behind. He could only imagine that Pierce wanted to meet him at his uncle's ranch because, as with most things, Hal Braden held the answers.

He spotted his cousin Rex heading up from the barn. His Stetson rode high on his head, his arms naturally arced away from his body, giving breadth to his massive biceps. Luke lifted his hand in greeting.

"Heard your motorcycle pull up. That's one loud hog." Rex pulled him into an embrace, another commonality among Bradens. Affection seemed to flow in their blood.

"She's got a sweet growl, that's for sure."

"How're your horses? How's the ranch?" Rex was a few years older than Luke and had helped run the Braden ranch since he graduated from college.

Luke's chest filled with pride. "My girls are great, and the ranch?" He inhaled deeply, thinking of the day they'd pulled out of Weston and the sinking feeling that had brought his head to rest against the window of his mother's car as they left behind the relatives and ranch he'd loved so much. "The ranch is everything I've ever hoped it would be."

Pierce's Land Rover pulled into the driveway. Pierce stepped from the truck, tall, dark, and eyes filled with wisdom.

"Should I tackle him?" Rex straightened his

Stetson and eyed Pierce.

Pierce and Rex were close in age, and the two used to challenge each other like two gorillas pounding their chests. Then they'd roll around on the ground in an endless wrestling match until they were covered in dirt and sweat. *Good times.*

Pierce came around the truck, wearing a pair of jeans and a black polo shirt. His dark hair was as sleek as Luke's was coarse, and like his younger brother, he wore it short on the sides and longer on top. He, like all of the Braden men, was a few inches over six feet tall with broad shoulders and dark brown eyes.

"Bro!" Pierce opened his arms and embraced Luke. "Damn, it's good to see you."

"You too."

Pierce narrowed his eyes at Rex. "Do I need to take this guy down?" He and Rex danced around each other with fists in the air, feigning and dodging punches.

"Shit. You wish." Rex slapped Luke's back again. "I've got to get back to the horses. Good to see you, Luke."

Pierce and Hal exchanged a quick glance. "So, little brother. You sure you want to go down this road?"

"Yeah, I think so." *I need to.*

"In that case..." Pierce handed him an envelope, and when Luke took it, Pierce held on tight. His voice grew serious. "Hal and I want to take you for a ride and show you something. It's your choice, but my advice is that you wait to open this until afterward."

Luke wanted to tear the envelope open and devour the information it contained, but the serious look in his brother's and uncle's eyes, held him back.

"Sure. Okay."

He followed them into Pierce's SUV. They passed through town and continued toward the mountains. Luke gazed out the window at the familiar scenery, acres upon acres of fields and pastures. When Pierce turned off the main road and the pavement turned to dirt, Luke felt his gut clench. The SUV ambled along the rutted road that led to his childhood home. Just as the old farmhouse came into view in the distance, Pierce cut to the left down a dirt road. They drove for a mile or more before coming to a huddle of trees, out of place in the open field.

Pierce parked beneath the trees, and the three of them stepped from the SUV.

"Are we burying bodies out here?" Luke felt a tug of familiarity but could not grasp it.

"Sort of." Pierce threw an arm around Luke. "Does this look familiar?"

Luke's nerves prickled. "I don't know. Should it?"

"I wish I could say no." Pierce walked over to the tree and opened his arms. "Look around, Luke. Does any of it feel like you've been here before?"

A memory tugged at Luke's mind, just out of reach, like a ghost waiting in the shadows. The hair on the back of his neck stood on end.

"Maybe you should clue me in." Luke ran his eyes between his uncle and his brother.

Hal rubbed his chin. "Son, there's no easy way to talk about all of this. I expect it'll come back to you, and I expect you're not going to feel very good about it. The last time you saw your father was right here."

Luke's chest constricted. "Saw him?" He shot a look at Pierce, who nodded. "I saw him? When? Here?"

Hal closed the distance between them. "You were five."

Pierce touched Hal's shoulder. "Let me." He set his eyes on Luke. "After Buddy left, he came around to the house. He'd come by drunk and cause all sorts of hell for Mom. You were just a baby, which is why you don't remember, and then he disappeared with that other woman for years. But he came back twice."

Luke felt the air leave his lungs. "Twice?" It was barely a whisper. "Did he come to see me?"

Pierce didn't answer.

Luke took a step forward. Breathing hard, he locked eyes with Pierce. "Did he come to see me?" His hands fisted at his sides.

Pierce ran his hand through his hair and exhaled loudly, flashing a quick glance at Hal, who stood by silently, giving Pierce the chance to explain, as he'd requested.

"Damn it, Pierce." If Pierce hadn't been his brother, if he hadn't seen the tortured look in his eyes, he would have grabbed him by the collar and shaken the shit out of him.

"No. He didn't come to see you, Luke. And he didn't come to see me, or Ross, or Wes, or any of the others."

"He came to see Mom." Luke crossed his arms against the truth, huffing each breath. *He didn't come to see me.* He'd known it his whole life, and the truth was still a bullet to his chest.

"No." Pierce's eyes glazed over with anger. "He

didn't come to see Mom. He came to get Mom's money." Like their uncle, all of his siblings and their cousins, their mother had inherited the Braden family wealth.

Luke felt Hal's heavy hand on his shoulder. His nerves were on fire, muscles corded tight. He shrugged him off. "What the hell are you talking about?"

"Son, this is going to be painful to hear." Hal looked down at Luke. He was so close that Luke could see the veins in his neck pulsing. "Your father wanted your mother's trust fund. He didn't want to be a parent."

Hal's tone was calm, even, terrifyingly prepared, unlike Luke, who felt like he'd run headfirst into a bullet train. Luke tried to process the information. "So…he was a greedy bastard. Did she give him money?"

"She did," Hal answered. "Until I found out what was going on."

Luke paced. "I don't understand. I thought he left with some other woman."

"He did," Pierce explained. "He left with a woman from another town, but he came back. Twice. He signed away his parental rights when he left, but something must have changed. He told Mom that if she didn't give him money, he'd take her back to court and get us back." Pierce drew in a long breath and blew it out slowly. When he continued, his voice was calmer, quieter. "The problem was, Luke, he didn't want us. If he had taken Mom to court, he probably wouldn't have won anything more than visitation, but Mom wasn't going to take that chance. She knew he didn't want anything to do with us."

He didn't want anything to do with us. Why did he think he wanted to know this pig of a man? What the hell was he thinking? "If that's the way it went down, and Mom paid him off, then why did he come back the second time? And why did he stop coming by? And what the hell does this place have to do with any of it?"

"Let's walk." Hal walked down the road.

Luke reluctantly followed, shaking his head.

Pierce walked beside him, steady as a rock, as he'd always been. "Listen, Luke, this is not easy shit. You sure you want the details?"

"Fuck yes. Why the hell didn't you tell me ages ago?"

"I didn't know it all, not really. I was a kid. I didn't remember. When you asked me to track him down, I asked Hal about it," Pierce explained. "It sucks man. You're sure?"

"I want to know so I can put it away, Pierce. Don't you get that? Right now Buddy's a fucking skeleton in my closet."

"Fine. But don't go apeshit on me," Pierce warned.

Hal's deep voice silenced them. "The first time Buddy showed up, your mother gave him twenty-five thousand dollars. She thought that would be the end of it, that she'd be able to move on with her life, and that you and your siblings wouldn't have to deal with him showing up anymore."

"Was he that much of an ass?" Luke wished like hell he could remember.

"Worse," Pierce answered. "I remember what it

was like when he lived with us, and he was demeaning and nasty to Mom day in and day out."

"I can't see her taking that kind of shit from anyone."

Hal answered. "Your mother loved him like no other, Luke. Love's not something you can turn on or off. It sneaks up on you and wraps itself around your nerves. It seeps into your soul, and it infiltrates all the crevices of your mind so you can't think past it."

Luke knew that all too well by the all-consuming love he had for Daisy.

"Once he left and your mother had space and time without him, she reclaimed her mind and her heart." Hal stopped walking and faced Luke. "She realized what he'd been like, and she's never let anyone else get that close to her again."

Pierce slid his eyes to Hal, then back to Luke. "I heard Mom talking to Buddy on the phone before school one morning, and when I got to school, I told the nurse I forgot my homework so I could call home, but I called Uncle Hal. We all had school, but you had a doctor's appointment, so you stayed home."

Hal ran his hand down his face, then crossed his arms across his broad chest. "I called Catherine, but she refused to let me step in. I did something I don't regret, Luke, but you're not going to like hearing it." He paused just long enough for Luke to cross his own arms over his chest, steeling himself for whatever was to come. Hal's brows knitted together. His solemn stare was locked on Luke, and when he continued, though his voice was even, his chest rose and fell with the ache of his confession.

"I followed your mother here, where she met Buddy. You were in your car seat in the backseat of your mother's car. I heard him hollering at her from way down the road. He didn't touch her. He wasn't a violent man, but he was mean as a snake."

Shivering began in Luke's limbs and an icy rush filled his chest. "Wait." Bits and pieces of the memory slammed into his mind. "He...He was hollering. The window was down a few inches, and I heard him. I can't remember what he said, but..." He paced, kicking up dirt beneath his feet. "I struggled to get out of the stupid booster seat. The seatbelt was stuck. I had to wrench my neck to see above the headrest. She was yelling, too. I...I saw your truck at the same time that I got out of my car seat, but the doors had those stupid child-safety locks. I couldn't get out."

Hal nodded. "You banged on the window, hollering and crying your eyes out."

Luke met his gaze. "I saw you. You stepped between him and Mom. Mom grabbed your arm." He fisted his hands. "Damn it."

"She insisted she could handle him." Hal's voice remained calm. "But I was done with it, Luke. I was not going to let some cretin treat my sister and her children like pawns. I sent your mother away with you. I didn't want you to see any more than you already had."

"Pierce, did you know all of this?" Luke met his brother's gaze.

Pierce shook his head. "Not until recently. I only knew that he stopped coming around after that last time. I sort of knew Hal was involved, but I was a kid,

Luke. I didn't want to know. I was just glad he wasn't making Mom upset anymore. I know Buddy's a mystery to you. To me he's a nightmare I can't forget fast enough." Pierce shrugged.

"Uncle Hal, what happened next?"

Hal held his gaze. "I ended it."

"How?"

"That's not important. I did what I had to do to keep you kids and my sister safe. Buddy left, and no one's heard from him since." Hal's eyes never wavered from Luke's.

How he did it wasn't important, whether by fists, money, or words alone, Hal had done the right thing—probably the only thing—that would have allowed Luke and his siblings, and their mother, to have normal lives. Luke would probably never know if Hal had beaten Buddy up, threatened him, or paid him off, and frankly, he didn't give a rat's ass. *Family knows no boundaries.* He'd heard it a million times, and until this moment it hadn't clicked so clearly into place.

"I'm sorry that he wasn't a better man, Luke." Hal continued. "It pains me that you kids didn't have a better father, but you had a damn good mother."

Luke nodded. "Apparently, too good. Sounds like she should have dumped his ass before she had any of us."

"Don't you ever say that." Hal's voice turned stern. "The only good thing that man did was to give you kids life. Don't you ever regret that. Your mother sure as hell doesn't."

The pieces of Luke's memory were finally falling into place. He'd been locked in the car. Even at five years old, he'd known that the way his father had been shouting at his mother hadn't been right. He'd carried that with him for twenty-five years.

"That's why I do it." Luke said more to himself than to them.

"What?" Pierce leaned in close.

"That's why I step in." He met Pierce's dark gaze. "That's why I react so viscerally to guys treating women like shit. I can't ever let it go. Christ, Pierce. In my head, those guys are *him*. Those women are Mom. He did fuck me up." No wonder Pierce had watched over him with the eagle eyes of a parent. *A missing parent.*

Pierce laid a hand on his shoulder. "No. He made you a better man than the likes of his sorry ass."

Luke needed to climb onto his motorcycle, race down the highway, and let the wind drive away the memories and the ghost that he still felt clinging to his back.

No, that's not what I need at all.

I need Daisy.

He needed to see her, feel her in his arms. He wanted to help her realize her dreams and treat her like she deserved to be treated, love her like she deserved to be loved, by a man who no longer had the cloud of his past hovering over him.

Luke took one last glance behind him as they drove away from the huddle of trees. The ache in his gut and the emptiness that his father's leaving had left in his wake was gone. Left in the dust. *Buried.*

He rolled down the window and let the crisp summer air whisk him clean of any remnants of the past. When they reached Hal's ranch and his motorcycle came into view, more puzzle pieces fell into place.

My bike. No locked doors.

Luke waited for the pain to grip him. He waited for the ache that he thought he'd just left behind. He stepped from the SUV and was surprised to feel lighter, more in control than ever before. He embraced Hal and Pierce, thanked them, and still…no pain.

Buddy. My father. He taunted the pain. Still no reaction.

A smile formed on his lips.

He was ready to move forward. *Damn ready.*

Chapter Twenty

DAISY FOUND ROSS in the barn with Shaley.

"Hey, Daisy." He finished dressing Shaley's leg. "I just gave her a chance to nurse and brought her back in. I wanted to check for infection since Luke was in Weston." Ross picked up his supplies and came out of the stall. "She's doing great. Her wound looks clean, no signs of infection. She can go back in the pasture tomorrow."

"That's great. She's such a sweet girl, and Luke worries so much about her." She walked with Ross back out toward his truck.

"Luke said you were thinking about practicing in New York or Chicago. Have you decided where you'll go?" Ross put his supplies in the back of his truck.

"Not yet." She looked out over the pasture. This was her favorite time of day, when darkness hasn't quite settled in and the heat of the afternoon had lifted. "It'll be hard to leave if I decide to. I mean, look around. You can't get this in a city."

Ross smiled as he climbed into his truck. "That's why I'm here. Tell Luke to call if he needs me. Good to see you."

Daisy headed back down to the barn to see Shaley, comforted that Ross had already checked on her and that she'd already nursed. Support seemed to be popping up everywhere in Trusty. Her mind traveled to her afternoon. The meeting at the library had gone well, and as promised, Kevin, Kari, Lynn, Jerri, and Tracie had all shown up. Betty and Alice were prepared with lists of parents who had asked for appointments. After working her way through the PTA membership to enlist the help of others—the generosity of her time and energy totally blew Daisy away—Betty had prepared a newsletter for Daisy to review. Tomorrow she would distribute it through each of the school's email lists. They developed a system for the clinic to ensure it would run as smoothly and efficiently as possible. They'd worked together like friends. A team. *A community*.

Daisy was still reeling from their support when she heard Luke's bike rumble down the driveway. She closed Shaley's stall and went to meet him. He stepped from the bike and whipped off his helmet. Her breath caught in her throat—would that ever stop? The man literally took her breath away. A wide smile lit up his face and when it reached his eyes it took her by surprise. She thought he'd be solemn, maybe even angry, after an afternoon spent learning about the man who had abandoned him. She ran the last few feet and jumped into his arms. He held her close and pressed fast, loving kisses to her cheeks, lips, and chin.

Magical kisses. He lowered her to the ground, held tight, and kept her close.

"I say it every time I see you, but God, I missed you." He kissed her again.

"Me too, you." Everything felt different. It wasn't just his eyes. *He* felt different. "How did it go?"

Luke cupped her cheeks with his big hands and tilted her back, so their eyes locked. He didn't speak, or move to kiss her, but as she searched his eyes, she saw emotions moving, changing, passing. Love, sadness, hope. Daisy tightened her grip on his waist and she felt his muscles shift against her fingers.

He nodded, and his glassy eyes told her that it had gone well. He cleared his throat and pressed his lips together. He pulled his shoulders back, stood up taller. The rawness of his emotions told her he needed time. A need Daisy understood well.

She took his hand. "Ross was here. He took Shaley out to nurse, and he checked her wound. He said she's doing great."

He nodded and they walked silently down to the barn. He sat with Shaley for a few minutes, kissed the foal's head; then he looked seriously at the door that led to the apartment above the barn. He pulled his phone from his pocket.

"I'm texting Emily and telling her that I'm done with changes. She can move forward with the apartment." He sent a text, then shoved the phone back in his pocket.

"Done? What about the alcove you wanted her to design?"

He reached for Daisy's hand. "I must have been

filling a gap. It's like today took that last inkling of restlessness away." He shrugged as they walked toward the stone fire pit on his back patio, where he set to work building a small fire.

"Today cleared up so many things for me, Dais." With the fire lit, he drew her to his side. "I was trying to figure out how to put it all into words. I didn't mean to shut you out." He kissed her temple and she snuggled against his side.

"I know. I didn't feel shut out."

He withdrew an envelope from his back pocket and held it up. "This has Buddy's info in it."

"But it's sealed."

Luke nodded. "That, it is. I haven't opened it." He looked out over the mountains and exhaled, a long, low breath. The fire glistened in his eyes. "He was a greedy man." He shrugged. "My brothers were right. I know enough about him now, and honestly, his leaving should have told me everything I needed to know." He ran his fingers over the envelope. "I've always believed that I could figure out a person by their actions. That knowledge has always been right there before my eyes, and I've lived by it. Except where Buddy was concerned. He was a mystery to me. He's no longer a mystery. He was a thief, a rotten man. He's in the past now, Daisy. Done. Buried." He looked at her and his eyes grew serious. "It just dawned on me that you might worry that I'll turn out like him. *Huh*." He shrugged. "I think—"

She placed her hand on his cheek and drew his eyes to hers. "No, Luke. I don't think you could be a rotten man if you tried. You're loving. So loving, it blows me away. You're kind, generous, protective. You're...Oh, Luke, you're the best man I know, and I love everything about you. It wouldn't matter who your father was. You see, that thing you said about how you know who someone is by how they treat others? That's all I ever needed to know who you were. But are you okay?" she asked in a tender, thin voice.

"More than okay." He kissed her softly. "I understand more about myself than I ever have, and I'm at peace with who he was and that he left." He searched her eyes, and the hope and surety in his drew her in. "Daisy, do you believe in fate?"

"I..." *Oh God*. Did she? "I don't know. Maybe. Kind of." Daisy was a doctor. She worked on tangible evidence, facts. Scientific evidence, if possible. Not hopes and dreams and cosmic forces. She was there in Trusty by coincidence. *Coincidence*. Not fate. Wasn't she? Luke's eyes were dark tunnels that led right to his emotions, his fears, his soul, and, God, she loved him. Was that fate?

He placed the envelope in the fire. The edges of the thick paper sizzled red, then flamed orange and yellow. Thick black smoke rose in fluid waves and dissipated into the night sky. It was all Daisy could do to watch the evidence he'd chased go up in flames.

"I believe in fate, Dais." He took her hand and led her to the wooden bench. "I never did, until you came along. I've been thinking about it. I love my ranch, and honestly, I love it here in Trusty. I love you, and when I see my future, I can't imagine it without you."

Daisy's stomach twisted. *But...*

"But I'm not sure I'm a big-city type of guy."

Her entire body went numb. She couldn't feel her legs, and she was sure she'd stopped breathing. She couldn't even shift her eyes to look into his. This was the end. The ultimatum. The *live here or lose me* moment.

She felt his hand on her leg, but was unable to reach out and touch it. Her brain wasn't working. Her heart was crumbling inside her chest, and she was afraid to try to move for fear of falling over. She felt his arm wrap around her shoulder as he scooted closer, his side pressed against hers. Tears filled her eyes and she tried to blink them away.

"So I was thinking..."

Thinking.

"You probably aren't sure if you're a small-town girl anymore, either, so..."

Oh God. Just say it! So we should break up. Say it quick so my heart can fall apart all at once and I don't have to die a slow, painful death.

"Dais, you're shaking." He pulled her closer. "Are you okay?"

Not even close. "Mm-hm," she managed.

"I was thinking that if you want to stay together, which I hope you do, then maybe there is a way we could find a middle ground, you know? Like if you take one of those jobs, we could live outside of the city. Close enough for you to commute and far enough for me to run some kind of ranch."

What...what are you saying? She tried to concentrate, but she was stuck in heartbreak mode.

"Dais?" He lifted her chin so she was looking into

his serious, dark eyes. "What's wrong?"

Nothing. Everything. "What...? You...You would move with me?"

"Isn't that what I just said?"

"I don't..." She was breathing so hard she had to hold on to his shirt just to remain upright. "Yes?"

A smile spread across his handsome face. "Yes. Yes, Daisy."

"But...You might hate it there." *I might hate it there.* As surprising as it was to her, Daisy was coming to feel at home at Trusty.

"We could live in Alaska, and as long as we were together, I would find a way to love Alaska." He wrapped his hand around the back of her neck and rested his forehead against hers. "I love you, Daisy, and people who love each other do whatever it takes to help each other be the best they can be and achieve their dreams. If your dream is to be a big-city doctor, then that's what you need to be."

"Oh God, Luke." She let out a breath and wiped her eyes. "I thought you were breaking up with me."

He drew back, his brows knitted together. "Have a little faith, Dais." He pulled her close again.

"What about your family? You'd be so far away."

"I love my family, Daisy, but when you start your own family, you do what's best for them. You've worked too hard to leave your dreams behind."

Best for them? Was it best to be far from family? If they married and had children, would it be best for them not to grow up knowing her father's farm the way she did?

"And what about your dreams?"

His face grew serious. "Until I met you, I didn't have dreams. I love my girls, and I love my ranch, but they're not dreams, Daisy. They're what I do for work, and if we move, my girls—our girls—come with us. You're my dream, Daisy. I can buy a ranch anywhere you want to live."

"And what if I want to stay in Trusty?" Daisy was afraid to give him hope that she'd decide to stay, but she felt herself pulled in that direction with every passing hour.

"Do you?" he asked hopefully.

She wished she had an answer, but this was too big of a decision to jump into without being one hundred percent sure. Knowing Luke was willing to move with her took the pressure off. *Now I can make a decision based on where I want to work instead of where the man I love wants to live.*

The selfishness of that thought settled heavily around her. How was she ever going to make this decision?

Chapter Twenty-One

DAISY USUALLY SLEPT for another hour, but the clinic for the children's physicals opened at eight, and the deadline for her job offers was upon her. Her mind ran in circles and every nerve in her body prickled her awake. More than a week had passed since Luke said he would move wherever Daisy decided to accept a job. Daisy lay in the crook of Luke's arm the following Saturday morning, listening to the even, peaceful cadence of his breathing and the sounds of the horses filtering in through the open window. Her eyes skittered over her perfume bottle, hairbrush, and earring tree, all lined up next to his cologne and a photograph of his girls on his dresser. Her eyes settled on the two thick envelopes beside the picture frame. Her offer letters. Cuddled up with Luke, in his house that had somehow become her home, she was having trouble remembering what had seemed so enticing about living in a busy city and working a million hours a week.

Her mind drifted to her parents. She and Luke had helped her father by delivering hay the other evening, and when they'd arrived at the farm, he was just coming in from what had become his nightly walk. Her father had surprised her again when he'd asked Luke's advice about the crops for next year. She'd never seen her father ask *anyone* for advice about farming. Progress. He was up and around, and he'd decided to hire a manager for the farm. He was fairly settled, or at least he had a plan in place. She was free to leave. Then again, hadn't she always been?

She anticipated the alarm and turned it off. In a few minutes, Luke would wake, shower, and head out to care for the girls. God, she loved those horses. Horses weren't like cars or clothing. They had feelings, too. How could she ask Luke to uproot them and start over? Shaley was just beginning to trust her surroundings, and she knew trust was everything when it came to training horses. The thought of moving them brought a lump to her throat.

She kissed Luke's cheek to wake him, and he reflexively pulled her closer. She stroked his unshaven cheek—God, she loved his face—and kissed him again, drawing a sensual moan, followed by a sigh as he opened his eyes.

"Today's your big day," he said in a sleepy, sexy voice. "Are you nervous or excited?"

Scared shitless. "Both. Still in shock that Lynn, Jerri, and Tracie are really going to help." She'd expected Kari and Kevin to be on board, but the girls who'd made her life hell? No way.

"I told you—that was ages ago. Life has a funny

way of making people grow up." He sat up and pulled her against his bare chest.

She murmured against his pecs. She was a doctor, and she knew that with age his muscles would atrophy and his skin would wrinkle like leather from years spent in the sun. And when that happened, she knew her love would remain as strong. Those features were just the sexy packaging that initially drew her in, but it was Luke—loving, compassionate, protective, intelligent, fiercely loyal Luke—who made her melt in his arms. Those traits were more beautiful and seductive than all of the rest put together. And that would never change.

While Luke was in the shower, his phone vibrated with a text. She reached for his phone without thinking and read the text from Emily. *Tell Daisy I said good luck today! She'll do great! Xox.*

It struck her that she'd just read a text meant for him—and she hadn't hesitated. What did that mean? It felt natural. Would he have done it? Was their relationship strong enough for her to feel that way? She listened to the shower water running for a minute as she thought about it. She glanced at her personal things on the dresser and knew she had clothes hanging in his closet, her razor in his shower. With a sigh, she clutched the phone to her chest.

Yeah, it's strong enough, and it feels good. How could she move away from *this*?

She read the text again. *How can I move away from that?* A woman who was quickly becoming a friend who cared enough to wish her luck at five in the morning, and the sister of the man she loved, to boot?

She buried her face in the pillow and groaned.

EVERY CHAIR IN the library was full. Kids read books while their parents filled out the necessary medical forms. They were using two rooms at the library as exam rooms, and she and Kevin were more than ready to begin handling physicals. Daisy took a deep breath. Her phone vibrated with a text from Luke. It was a picture of him at arm's length, standing in front of the girls. His eyes were bright, and his smile warmed her all over. The caption read, *We're so proud of you! Love you!* God, she loved him. She'd thought it a million times, and she'd probably think it a million times more—this hour.

She wanted to remember this moment forever. She wished Dr. Waxman were there. Oh, what she'd give to see his face on the first day of the very first clinic she would ever manage. She surveyed the people out front again, and her stomach flipped and twisted. She was surrounded by at least a dozen people she'd gone to high school with, most of whom had either teased her or done nothing to deflate the rumors that had circulated about her.

Things really could change. People could change.

She touched her dark hair, and for the first time in several years, considered going back to her natural white-blond shade.

Tracie sat at the registration desk of the library with a sign-in sheet, handing out medical forms to the parents for completion. They had a system in place, and Daisy realized that she couldn't have made this work without the help of the other women. Lynn was taking the completed forms and preparing charts for each patient, and in a few minutes, Jerri would bring the patients and their charts back and keep the process moving efficiently, fitting in as many physicals as they were able. Kari was in charge of keeping shots and medical supplies stocked in each room. They were working together. A team.

A community.

My community.

"Can you believe you're doing this with their support?" Kevin asked, nodding toward the women who had come to help.

"There are so many things about being here that have taken me by surprise, but yeah. I'm starting to believe in miracles." She touched his arm, and the thought of leaving their friendship behind again was too painful to consider. They'd burned the cell phone lines up while they were in college and when she was in medical school and during her residency. She'd never had girlfriends, but she'd had Kevin, and that was enough for her.

"Kev, thanks for always being there."

"I'm still counting on you to find me a sexy stranger to fall in love with." He took a deep breath. "You ready to take this show on the road?"

Kitty Carlington, who owned the florist shop in town, came through the front door, carrying an enormous vase of red roses.

"Lover boy strikes again," Kevin said.

"No way. Luke's not a roses type of guy. Daisies or wildflowers, maybe." Daisy stepped forward to greet Kitty.

"Darlin' these are for you." Kitty was plump, forty-something, with a dark bob and pink cheeks. She smiled as she waddled across the floor and handed Daisy the vase. "Three dozen," she whispered.

"Wow. Thank you." She looked for a card. "Who are they from?"

"Oh gosh. I was afraid the card would fall." Kitty pulled a card from her back pocket. "Here you are, Daisy. Um...*Dr. Honey*." Kitty scrunched her shoulders up and smiled. "Wow, little Daisy Honey is a doctor. So hard to believe. Funny how you got older and I stayed the same age." Kitty laughed at her own joke on the way out the door.

Dr. Honey. Things really had changed.

"So? Who're they from? My bet is on Luke." Kevin peered over her shoulder.

Daisy read the card.

Daisy—

Success is always the best retaliation. Heard you came back to help the very people who drove you away. That's the mark of a good woman and a great doctor. I always knew you had it in you.

Love, Doc W.

IT WAS NEARLY eight o'clock in the evening when Kari pulled Daisy aside between what was supposed to be the last of her patients, but she was running behind.

"We have a problem." A few tendrils of hair had come loose from Kari's ponytail, framing her face.

"What is it?" Daisy signed off on the file she'd been holding.

"Look in the waiting room. I mean the front of the library."

Daisy hadn't gone out front since they began. She peered around the corner and saw a handful of people milling about. Elderly couples she recognized and mothers holding infants, who were definitely *not* there for school physicals.

"What are they doing here?"

"They figured that you could fit them in. Winona Wade's baby has a cough. Mr. Jacob hurt his leg. He thinks it's just a pulled muscle or something. The list goes on seven patients deep. What do you want me to do?"

"We can't see everyone. We're supposed to be closing, and I still have two physicals to do. So does Kevin." She felt awful. A sick baby? A hurt leg? How could she turn them away?

"That's what I thought. In fact, that's what Tracie has been telling them, that you had no free slots and the clinic was just for school physicals." She lowered her voice to a whisper. "But they're still here." When she continued, she spoke normally again. "Winona brought you one of her dried flower arrangements as a thank-you. Oh, and your dad came by about an hour ago. He said not to tell you, but, Daisy, he was so proud. I swear he had tears in his eyes. Don't tell him I said that."

Daisy looked up at the ceiling to quell her own tears. *Dad*. "Oh my God. What am I going to do?" She peered around front again. "I can't just turn them away."

"Well, think of it this way. One way or another you're leaving in a week or so, right? So they'll be upset for a little while; then you won't have to see them again until the holidays when you come back to visit your family." Kari shrugged. "And if you plan it right, you'll be in and out of Trusty over a weekend. You probably won't have time to see anyone anyway. I'll get rid of them."

Daisy grabbed her arm. "Wait." She couldn't turn them away. How could she? Mr. Jacob had been her sixth-grade teacher. He'd stayed after school to help her with a science project for a full week, and she'd gone on to win the science fair competition, which might not have happened if he hadn't helped her. And Winona's baby? No, she couldn't walk away and leave her in need. Winona had been teased in high school, too. *More common ground.* She was beginning to see that she'd been so wrapped up in how much she loathed the small town because of what had happened during high school that she had forgotten the good parts. *The community.*

They saw their last patients at ten o'clock, and by ten fifteen Daisy had sent everyone home. Kevin fought her on it, wanting to stay to help organize the charts, but Daisy needed time to think. They'd seen forty-three people today. She was exhausted—and completely, one hundred percent fulfilled. And she hadn't seen any unusual diseases. She hadn't met with specialists to learn about a new procedure. Heck, she hadn't even done the physicals in an actual medical office. But she'd seen neighbors and friends. She'd helped parents gain their own peace of mind about their children, and she'd saved them having to drive forty-five minutes for a physical. It wasn't rocket science, but it was every bit as important.

After organizing the day's charts and double-checking signatures, Daisy finally headed out to her car. She locked the library doors, and when she turned around, she found Luke standing against the light post, ankles crossed. He pushed from the post and opened his arms. Daisy fell willingly, blissfully, into them.

"What are you doing here?" He felt so good she didn't want to move.

"I missed you." He kissed the top of her head. "How did it go?"

"Amazing. Sorry I'm so late. I would imagine next weekend will be just as bad. People are showing up with sick babies and aches and pains that have nothing to do with school physicals."

"And you saw them all." He kissed her, and Daisy relaxed against him. "I'm so proud of you, Dais."

She looked up at him, thinking of the emotional ride they'd both gone through over the last week. "How was your day?"

He smiled. "Great. Shaley's back out in the pasture, and...I missed you."

It was a balmy, starry night, and as Luke took her hand, Daisy couldn't think of anything she'd rather do than take a walk with him...well...almost anything. She could kiss Luke all night long, but that could wait.

"I know it's late, but can we take a walk?" They walked down Main Street beneath the streetlights. The shops were closed, and the sleepy town was quiet and peaceful. She'd forgotten how serene the town felt at night, and how pretty Main Street was with the old-fashioned streetlights illuminating the sidewalks.

"You know, without the veil of rumors clouding my vision, Trusty isn't such a bad place." She loved the crinkles that formed at the corner of Luke's eyes when he smiled and the way he exhaled a breath as his lips spread.

"It grows on you." Luke pulled her against him. "I know you don't have much time to decide about where you want to live, but have you given it any further thought?"

They came to the corner of Main Street and Old West Court and turned onto Old West. Brick office buildings with big-lettered signs hanging above green awnings lined the right side of the street. At the end of the cul-de-sac, set against the backdrop of Trusty Town Park and with a glorious view of the mountains, was Dr. Waxman's vacant home. It looked out of place, but it was another hallmark of Trusty, and Daisy was glad it had never been torn down or renovated into a brick office building.

"What do you think of this place?" The idea had come to her as they were walking, and standing before Dr. Waxman's office with Luke, she knew exactly what she wanted to do.

"This particular piece of sidewalk, or Trusty in general?"

She turned to him, her hands pressed flat against his chest. She felt his heart beating evenly, and when he gazed into her eyes, it kicked up a notch.

"If you had your choice of living anywhere, where

would it be?"

"Wherever you are." His answer came easily, and she could see in his eyes that it came honestly, too.

"Would you want to go to New York or Chicago? Or would you want to stay here?" She could envision herself walking into Dr. Waxman's office as her own. Stopping in at the diner for lunch, walking through the park with Luke at the end of a long day, before returning home. Together.

"If you chose to work in those places, sure."

She noticed a difference in his voice as he answered. "I'm asking about you, Luke. Not where I'll work. If you had your druthers."

"Dais, none of that matters, because what matters to me is being with you, and you've put years into your career, far more years than I've put into mine." He ran his hand through his hair and began to pace the sidewalk.

"Talk to me, Luke. Because I love that you're supportive of me and my career, but I also feel something else, and whatever that is, hesitancy or something else, I think I feel it, too."

Luke took her hands in his. His eyes grew serious, then softened. "Babe, I love you, and I want to support you, but honestly, I'm having trouble thinking about moving so far away from family."

"Me too." She exhaled and swore an invisible elephant had just jumped from her shoulders.

"You too?" He searched her eyes, and as he did, his lips curved up into a smile. "You're thinking of staying?"

She couldn't help but smile and hold his surprised

stare. "Once I let myself see past the old stuff, I started seeing things more clearly, and when I think about pouring my heart and soul into a business..." She shrugged, that good old universal shrug that she knew he understood. "I want to do it here, where I'm caring for the people I know and the people I love, and if I ever start a family, I know that my mom and dad are nearby."

"But you said you wanted to be on the cutting edge of medicine, and...you're working in a library. Not exactly cutting-edge." He wrapped his arms around her again. "Daisy, this is why I didn't say anything. I don't want you to make your decision because I want to be close to my family. This is *your* life. I'll stand behind you, and if you're saying all of this because of what happened with my dad—"

"I'm not. I'm saying it because of what's happened with *my dad*, and with Janice, and Mr. Mace, and Winona Wade's baby, and Dr. Waxman, and...yes, because of you, too. I love you, Luke, and I want to be with you. But I want to be with you in a community where I know if you get hurt, or I need help, people who care will be there for us. And if I need to make a house call, I won't have red tape and guidelines holding me back. I want to know that in May there's a stupid parade through the center of town, and at Christmas everyone sings around the tree in front of the library. I want to trick-or-treat with my kids on the same streets I grew up on. I want to know that if Shaley gets hurt, Ross is nearby, or if you want to change your mind about a renovation, your sister will yell at you and do it anyway. I want to know that you can zip to your uncle's ranch for an afternoon and that I can walk out my back door and inhale crisp, clean mountain air."

He brushed her hair from her face and pressed his hands to her cheeks. "Daisy Honey, look me in the eye and tell me you're not doing this just because of me."

She stared into his dark, serious eyes. "Luke Braden, I am not doing this because of you."

He searched her eyes, and as understanding dawned, his eyes widened. "Babe. You're really thinking about this."

"I'm really thinking about this."

He looked at Dr. Waxman's house. "You want to be the next Trusty doc? Jesus, Daisy. Really? You're sure?"

She laughed a little. "Yeah. I am. I feel like it's the right thing to do."

"Do you want to sleep on it? Think it through and see how you feel in a few days? Giving up those positions is a big deal."

"I've made my decision, and as far as sleeping goes, it's totally not what I had in mind to celebrate."

He lowered his mouth to hers, and she closed her eyes, letting the concerns fall away for a few precious moments. His body was warm and hard—oh, so gloriously hard. When his hand slid to the small of her back and he pressed his hips to hers, she wasn't thinking about offices or job offers. There was only now, this moment, and the love that carried them back toward home. *Together.*

Chapter Twenty-Two

Five months later...

DAISY STOOD IN the lobby of her new medical office. Dr. Waxman's placard above the door had been replaced with a wooden sign in the front yard that read, DR. DAISY HONEY, FAMILY PRACTICE. She'd finally unpacked her boxes when she'd moved in with Luke, and the shelves in Dr. Waxman's old office held her medical books. It was a good feeling. The renovations had taken time, but Emily had handled the whole process, making the living areas into exam rooms and offices, and Daisy was pleased as punch with the outcome.

Daisy smoothed her lavender dress and looked at her reflection in the window. The street and sidewalk were packed with residents. Even the local news team had come out to cover the grand opening of her practice. The residents had begged, pleaded, and practically insisted on a ribbon-cutting ceremony, a small-town tradition Daisy used to roll her eyes at and now welcomed. Luke had strung a giant yellow ribbon across the yard, and in a few minutes, she would cut the ribbon and officially open the practice. Her practice—in her community.

Luke wrapped his arms around her waist from behind and kissed her cheek.

"You look gorgeous."

"I'm so nervous." She turned and clutched his T-shirt, drawing strength from his ever-present calm and confident demeanor. They'd been living together for months, and she still fell deeper in love with him every day.

"Let me kiss that nervousness away."

He lowered his lips to hers—and sure enough, even after months of kissing his delicious lips several times a day, he still had the ability to turn her brain cells to mush. And she loved it.

"Better?"

"Much. But now my knees are weak."

Emily came through the front door wearing a black shift and heels. "Okay, lovebirds. You've got a ribbon ceremony waiting to happen out there, and I've got a meeting to get to." She put her hands on her hips and sighed. "Wow, Daisy, with your hair blond again, you're even prettier than before. That's not really fair you know." Emily placed her hand on Daisy's arm and led her toward the door. "I can't believe my baby brother fell in love before I did. I swear, life is looking super unfair on so many levels right now."

"Em, give her a minute." Luke blocked the door. "Dais? Are you sure you're ready?"

Daisy's heart squeezed. Luke was so protective of

her feelings. How did she get lucky enough to fall in love with the best man on earth? She took a deep breath and blew it out slowly. "I think so."

"I'm right here, okay? If you get nervous, just find my eyes."

"Yeah, and then my knees will go weak again." She touched his chest. "I love you, but as much as you make me stronger, you also turn me to Jell-O."

"I want to turn to Jell-O." Emily pouted.

Luke shook his head, murmuring something about women, and opened the front door. Applause sent Daisy's stomach into a tumble and drew her through the doors to the wide porch, where Kevin, Kari, and the girls who had helped them at the clinic had tied balloons to the railings and the limbs of the tree in the center of the yard and hung a banner that read, CONGRATULATIONS, DR. DAISY HONEY!. Daisy's father stood front and center beside her mother. He was up and around, out of the house, and though he wasn't back on his tractor, he was managing the farm with the same firm hand Daisy had always remembered. Her mother waved with a cheesy, proud mother's smile and tears in her bright blue eyes.

Luke and Emily descended the porch steps and stood with Catherine, their mother, and Wes, Ross, and Pierce. Jake, one of Luke's older brother's who was a stuntman in Los Angeles, had Skyped earlier in the day to congratulate them, but he was on a movie shoot and unable to come home for the event.

The crowd filled the street, and Daisy lifted a hand to wave at Alice, Margie, Betty, and Kari. Lynn and Jerri waved with wide smiles, and Tracie and her daughter clapped and smiled, their matching red hair blowing gently in the fall breeze.

Kevin gave Daisy a thumbs-up. She drew in another deep breath as she slid her gaze to Janice, holding a healthy and smiling Michael. Darren stood beside them looking clear-eyed and sober. He'd spent two months in a rehab facility in Denver and was attending weekly AA meetings. Daisy was glad for them.

She looked over the community from which she'd once felt miles apart, and she swelled with love for it. It had become her community. The people had become her friends, and among the transition from Dr. Honey, big-city girl, to Dr. Honey, Trusty family doctor, she'd managed to find love and become part of Luke's family. The whole turn of events still stunned her, though she'd become a believer in fate. Yes, even without scientific evidence.

"Speech!" Kevin yelled, reminding her she was supposed to do more than just look dumbfounded.

She smiled and cleared her throat in an effort to gain control of her nerves.

"Thank you for coming out in support of my grand opening. I grew up with most of you, and..." *Oh boy, here comes the honesty.* "And it wasn't always easy." She met Janice's gaze, then shifted her eyes to Lynn, Jerri, and Tracie, and finally, she met Luke's soulful, confident eyes. True to his word, it was his strength that found her and spurred her on. She looked at her parents, and the words came easily.

"I had almost forgotten how wonderful Trusty was, but I learned and I remembered. There's a reason people tend to stay in Trusty. Trusty is the sheer definition of small-town living. We have hay farms and horse ranches. Everyone knows where to go for the best iced tea in town." She smiled at Margie. "We have silly parades and gossip that runs thick as rivers. But to those who really know Trusty, they realize that this small town is also known for forgiveness, and community, and I'm proud to be back and part of such a wonderful town. Thank you."

She descended the steps, and Luke handed her a pair of giant scissors. With his arm protectively on her lower back, she cut the ribbon, and the crowd cheered. In the next breath, Daisy was passed from one person's arms to the next.

Her father held her close in a tight hug that brought a tear to her eye. "I'm so proud of you, darlin'."

"Thank you, Dad. I'm proud of you, too." She was proud of him. Over the past few months, he'd taken an active part of his own recovery, and she knew it wasn't easy.

"Sweetheart." Her mother held her close; then she touched the ends of Daisy's newly blond hair. "I missed this. I missed you." She hugged her again.

"Me too, Mom. I'm here to stay, and I think the blond is, too."

She was passed from Kevin to Alice, to Janice and Margie, and when she finally found a gap in awaiting arms, she took a deep breath. She turned around and nearly ran into Wes.

"I think I might need to make an appointment." Wes wore a bright green button-down shirt streaked with dirt. He had a towel wrapped around his hand. Over the past few weeks, she'd bandaged, stitched, and splinted Wes's injuries.

Daisy shook her head. "Stitches?"

"Maybe just glue?" Wes shrugged.

"Wesley Braden, what have you done now?" Catherine, Luke's mother, grabbed his arm. She was a few inches taller than Daisy, with intelligent eyes and thick brown hair she wore with a side part that hung past her shoulders in natural waves. She had the same wide smile as each of her children, and she radiated positivity.

"Crap. I was hoping you wouldn't see this." Wes disappeared into the crowd.

Daisy loved the way Luke's family teased and loved so easily.

Catherine embraced Daisy. "I'm proud of you, Daisy, and so happy you and Luke have come together." She and Daisy had become close over the past few months, and it was easy to see how Luke had turned out to be such a loving and generous man. Catherine was those things and more. She was a positive light that glowed like the sun. "I guess you've figured out that my boys are all brawn on the outside, but sweet as kittens on the inside."

"Mom," Luke complained.

"Tigers, maybe," Pierce said.

"Meow," Emily teased Pierce, and he swatted her.

Luke caught Daisy's eye, and the right side of his lips lifted in the most alluring little smile. She made her way toward him, her stomach fluttering like a schoolgirl again. He was talking with Wes. She hooked her finger into the waist of his jeans and felt his muscles shudder against it.

"Wes..." He glanced at Daisy, and she moved closer, pressing the side of her hip to his. She loved teasing him, seeing him struggling to keep focused on his conversation. "Um...did you ever fill that...position?" Luke asked.

"Not yet." Wes narrowed his eyes, having clearly noticed Luke's discomfort, and a grin spread across his face as he ran his eyes between them. "I've got a few interviews coming up. Believe it or not, five out of six are chicks."

"Hey, girls can run cattle and ride horses." Emily pushed her way between her brothers with a feigned scowl on her face.

Luke took the opportunity to draw Daisy against him, press his hips to hers, and whisper in her ear, "So unfair. Feel what you do to me."

Ross sidled up to them. "Glad you stuck around, Daisy. I'd hate to have to wipe Luke's tears."

Luke shook his head, locking his dark, sensuous eyes on Daisy. "I would have followed her anywhere."

She knew he would have, and when Luke leaned down and kissed her, she had a hard time keeping the smile from her lips.

"Sweet Lord, Dr. Daisy Honey," Luke whispered. "What is that look in your eyes?"

"Love. Happiness." She pressed her cheek to his and whispered, "With a hint of lust."

The End

Please enjoy a preview of the next
Love in Bloom novel

Fated for Love

The Bradens

Love in Bloom Series

Melissa Foster

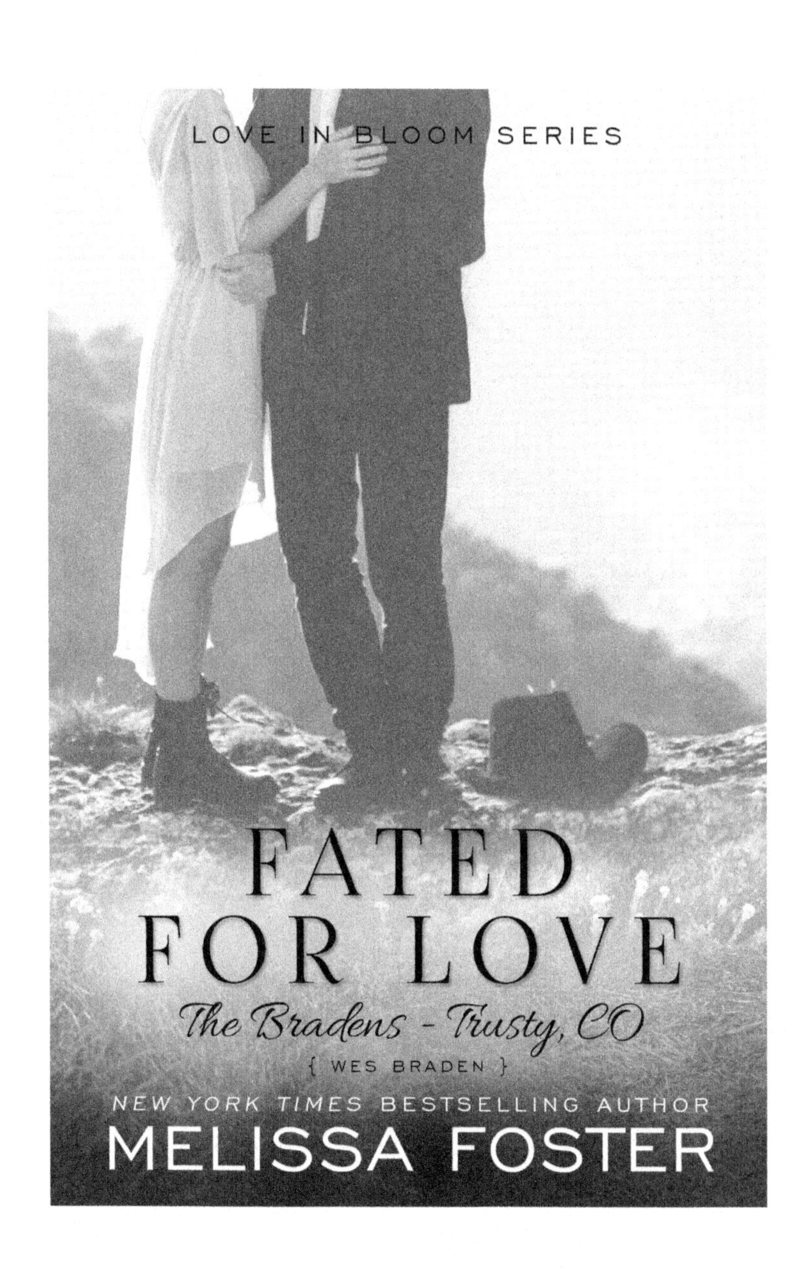
LOVE IN BLOOM SERIES
FATED
FOR LOVE
The Bradens - Trusty, CO
{ WES BRADEN }
NEW YORK TIMES BESTSELLING AUTHOR
MELISSA FOSTER

Chapter One

CALLIE BARNES PICKED through the new releases in the Trusty Town Library, where she'd worked as the assistant librarian for the last four weeks. She snagged the last copy of Kurt Remington's newest thriller, *Dark Times,* and put it on top of the two others she was carrying. The cover depicted the silhouette of a man at the edge of a cliff, holding a bloody knife that glistened in the eerie moonlight. She turned the book over. She couldn't even *think* about those types of situations, much less read about them. Callie's first love was fairy tales. She loved the idea of knights on white horses and happiness coming when a person least expected it. Fairy tales were safe, and the princesses were always loved for who they were, flaws and all. Her second secret love was women's fiction, specifically, chick lit and light romances, where the worst thing that a character encountered was a broken heel during an interview and all the sex scenes were left up to the reader's imagination, *as they should be.* She didn't need to read about some hunky hero touching a woman's thigh...with his tongue. She felt her cheeks flush at the thought and wished she hadn't worn her hair pinned up in a bun so she could hide behind it. She hugged the books to her chest, closed her eyes, and inhaled deeply. *Puppies. Kittens. Ice Cream. Brownies. Chocolate syrup...oh yes...all over his—*

"Hey, Callie. You okay?"

Cripes! She clenched her eyes shut. Wes Braden's voice sent a shudder through her entire body. Of course he'd come in when she was thinking about chocolate syrup all over...*Stop, stop, stop!* This was the best—and the worst—part of Thursdays. She mustered a smile and turned around. He stood a few inches away, which brought her face oh so close to his broad, muscular chest. She could press her cheek to it and hear that big heart of his pounding beneath all those layers of muscle.

Holy cow.

She lifted her gaze and met his slightly amused dark eyes.

"Hey." His eyes landed on the books she was still clutching against her chest. "Those for me?" Wes came into the library every Thursday to pick up the latest thrillers and an occasional biography.

Callie's body pulsed with anticipation over the few minutes they shared each week—so much anticipation that when she was alone in bed in the dark of night, it was Wes's face that appeared in her mind and his voice that whispered in her ear. It was his full lips and his piercing dark eyes that made her heart race and her body so hot she couldn't help but satisfy the urges he stirred deep within her.

Callie opened her mouth to answer, but his masculine scent surrounded her dirty thoughts, shooting her hormones into overdrive and gluing her tongue to the roof of her mouth, which she was pretty sure was a godsend, because otherwise she might have drooled all over him. She shoved the books into his hands and was rewarded with a grateful smile that made her legs turn to wet noodles.

Wes's eyes lingered on her high-collared blouse, which was buttoned up to her neck; then he lifted his eyes to hers again.

She felt her nipples harden under his hot stare, and of course her cheeks flushed again. She wished she could disappear into one of those books right there and then.

"Thanks, Callie. Any interesting plans this week?" He'd asked the same question every week for the past four, and each week she answered with the titles of the books she was reading, which was not only all she could manage, but it was also the truth.

There were no two ways about it. Callie's life was boring. She heard it from her girlfriends all the time; of course, that was because none of them lived in the tiny town of Trusty, Colorado, where she'd moved to take her dream job of working in a library. They still lived in Denver, where Callie and her friends had grown up and gone to college, but after four years of working in jobs she didn't enjoy, the assistant librarian position opened up in Trusty, and she'd jumped at it. And while it might be miles away from her real-life friends and family, at least she was surrounded by more fictional friends than she could ever hope for. Besides, when Alice Shalmer, the head librarian, finally retired, she'd be next in line for the position. She hadn't expected the added weekly bonus of being able to ogle all six foot something of delicious Wes Braden, the hottest man she'd ever set eyes on.

Totally worth being away from my friends.

Finally she was in a position to give Wes a more exciting answer.

"My friends are taking me to a spa for a few days." She bit her lower lip to keep from grinning like a kid going to Disney World. She couldn't wait to spend a few days with her friends, where being pampered meant plenty of reading time. It would be a perfect long weekend.

Wes arched a thick, dark brow, leaned one hand on the bookshelves beside her head, and gazed down at her with a sexy, dark stare. "A spa? Now, that does sound interesting. Which one?"

She could barely breathe with him leaning in like that, bringing his clean-shaven, chiseled face, full lips, and...Her heart went a little crazy.

"Yeah," she whispered. Callie's stomach fluttered, and she realized she must be gazing at him with a horrifyingly dreamy look in her eyes. She turned back to the books—and away from the badass guy who taught hunting and fishing and made her sharp mind numb.

"Um." She tried to remember what the question was. *Spa. Which spa?* "I'm not sure which one, or even where it is. They're surprising me." Her girlfriends had scheduled this trip before she began working for the library, and Alice was kind enough to give her the time off even though she'd been there for only a month.

"What do girls do at a spa for a long weekend?" he asked over her shoulder.

Did he really expect her to think with him standing so close? She could feel his hot breath on the back of her neck. "Um...Massages." *Jeez! I might as well have said,* Have strangers touch us all over! She took a deep breath, which helped exactly none since his scent took shelter in her nose and lungs.

She forced herself to finish answering. "Uh...read, take walks." She stumbled back a step and knocked a book from the shelf. When she bent to pick it up, her darn too-tight pencil skirt trapped her knees together halfway to the floor. She made a mental note to stop eating ice cream as a replacement for those dirty things she was trying not to think about.

Wes retrieved the book, and their eyes met and held for a long, hot beat. He handed it to her and rose to his full height again. "Well, that sounds a lot more relaxing than spending a week with a group of people who are probably afraid of heights, spiders, and snakes." He tucked the books she'd given him under his arm, ran his hand through his short, dark hair, and shrugged, causing all those hard muscles in his shoulders to flex beneath his tight shirt.

"If you add *deep water* to that list, you've described me perfectly." Callie didn't know much about Wes, other than he liked thrillers and biographies, he turned the heads of every female in the library, and he taught alpha male stuff, like hunting, fishing, and...She had no idea what else, but the thought of guns and deep water made her dizzy. Or maybe that was a side effect of being around him. She wasn't sure.

"Wes?" Tiffany Dempsey ran her eyes up and down Wes's body with an appreciative smile, like a mountaineer revisiting a familiar peak.

It had taken Callie a week to realize why Tiffany appeared in the library every Thursday but never took home a single book or said a word to Callie.

Wes smiled at Tiffany in a way that made Callie blush. His eyes were as seductive as his voice. "Hey, Tiff."

Tiffany flipped her long blond hair over her shoulder and ran her finger down his forearm. "How's it going? Oh, I see Callie picked out some good books for you again."

Callie was surprised that she knew her name.

"Callie knows her books." Wes smiled down at Callie.

Knows her books. Callie watched him walk away with Tiffany, then banged her forehead against the bookshelf, wishing she could be anyone but the girl who *knew her books.* No, that wasn't really true. She loved books—everything about them, from the weight of them in her hands to the smell of the pages and the worlds they held between their covers. The world she loved to climb into, live vicariously through, and where she hid away from the world. She had no idea *what* to wish for. She was who she was and she liked who she was, even if she'd never be the type of woman a guy like Wes Braden would be interested in. She glanced around the quiet library. There were two women sitting at a table staring at Wes like he was made of gold. In the reference aisle, she noticed another woman, who, she realized, also came in only on Thursdays. She was peering out of the aisle at Wes, too. And then there was Tiffany, stealing every ounce of Wes's attention in three seconds flat. Callie sighed. She'd never be like Tiffany. Callie sucked at the whole one-touch-turn-on thing that Tiffany had down pat. Tiffany was tall and lean, and every outfit she wore was tight and revealing in the all the *right* ways. Callie would feel silly in the tight, black minidress Tiffany wore like a second skin. She somehow managed to look sexy *and* strong, which was probably nothing more than her brazen personality. Callie was petite and far from athletic. Even though she did her Jillian Michaels DVD religiously, she could never do the things she imagined Wes doing, like wrangling cattle or riding bulls.

Though, I wouldn't mind riding him.

She shivered with the painfully unrealistic thought. She needed that damn massage, and she hoped the masseuse was tall, dark, and handsome. Maybe she'd throw caution to the wind and do all those behind-closed-doors dirty things she wished she could do with Wes and had been trying not to fantasize about.

Her damn cheeks flushed again.

She looked up at the ceiling and wondered if there was a handbook for nerdy girls who fantasized about badass men to learn to take the reins and land their men.

Stick to fairy tales, Callie.

WES SHOVED A stack of papers to the side of his desk, yanked open the file drawer, and weeded through the hanging file folders. *Shit. Where are they?* He didn't have time for this. Wes and his partner, Chip Shelton, owned The Woodlands, a dude ranch about an hour outside of Trusty, in the Colorado Mountains, and he was meeting a group there just before dinnertime. If he could only find the itineraries he'd put together, he could get on the damn road so he wouldn't be late.

He moved around the desk and looked down at the fifteen-week-old bloodhound sleeping soundly beneath his desk. "Hey, Sweets. Any idea where I put those itineraries?" He hoped he hadn't left them at his house. Wes split his time between his house in Trusty and his cabin at The Woodlands, and the last thing he needed was to make an additional trip before getting on the road to the ranch.

Sweets turned sad eyes up at him and yawned, then laid her head back down on her cushy bed. Wes had found Sweets a few weeks earlier on the side of a remote mountain trail, all skin and bones and sick with distemper. With the help of his brother Ross, the Trusty veterinarian, he nursed her back to health and fell in love with probably the only bloodhound on earth that had no sense of smell. Zero. None. A bloodhound that couldn't track a lost person would be of little use if a client turned up missing, but he loved her so damn much that even her missing sense didn't make her any less amazing.

Wes leaned down and loved up Sweets; he

scratched her belly and pressed a kiss to her forehead. Then he sat in his chair and rubbed his eyes with his forefinger and thumb.

"What's that piss-ass look for?" Chip stood in the doorway, his shaggy blond hair hanging in his eyes. He'd been Wes's business partner since they opened the dude ranch doors eight years ago, and Wes's best buddy since second grade.

Wes sighed and set a dark stare on Chip's annoyingly amused baby blues. They were two peas in a pod—no risk was too big, no job was too difficult, and no woman was worth more than a night or two. Chip knew as much about Wes as his own five siblings did, and Wes loved him like a brother, but love wasn't the emotion that was currently brewing in his gut.

"Have you seen my itineraries for the new group?"

Chip flopped into the chair across from Wes's desk, the amused look in his eyes now coupled with a smirk. He stretched his long legs and clasped his hands behind his head. "How can a guy who's overprepared for anything outdoors be so frickin' unorganized with paperwork?"

"Either tell me where they are or get out." Wes went to the file cabinet near the window and tugged the top drawer open.

"Dude, you do this every other week. Just admit it: You have an aversion to paperwork."

"Shut up." Wes slammed the file cabinet closed. He peered out of his office door and hollered down the hall. "Clarissa?"

"I don't have them!" Clarissa Simmons, their secretary and bookkeeper of three years, hollered.

Chip laughed.

Wes slid him another narrow stare. "If you're not going to help me look for the damn things, get out."

Chip pushed to his feet. "Did you look in your put-off-until-later pile? That would be my guess." Chip lifted his chin toward a pile of papers currently holding down the edges of an open map on top of a table in the opposite corner of Wes's office.

Wes stalked across the floor and snagged the top file in the stack. The itineraries.

"I'll refrain from telling you I told you so." Chip snickered as he glanced over the map, checking out Wes's trail for the overnight with his group. "You're all set for your days in female hell?"

"Yeah. You want to take them?" Wes loved running the dude ranch and he enjoyed taking charge of the outings, but they'd recently lost Ray Mulligan, a key employee who ran a third of the overnight trips, which left Wes and Chip to pick up the slack until the position was filled. They had flipped for the lead on this group, and Wes had lost.

Chip held his hands up in surrender. "I'm taking the day trips, remember?" He tapped his finger on his chin. "I'm thinking big burly broads who are out to show you how little you know." He shrugged. "You know, out for a week of fun."

"Or four women who think that I'm part of the package." As much as Wes loved women, fending them off during the outings had lost its charm about two months after they opened The Woodlands. He realized exactly what women must feel like when guys like him sized them up for a quick lay.

Wes slapped his leg twice, and Sweets lazily stretched, then scampered out from under the desk and came loyally to his side. She tried to climb up Wes's legs.

"Down, Sweets." Wes placed the pup's paws on the floor and loved her up again. "See you up there," he said to Chip.

He stopped by Clarissa's desk on his way out.

Sweets's nails clicked on the hardwood floors as she walked around Clarissa's desk. Clarissa glanced up from the spreadsheets she was studying and eyed the file in Wes's hand. Her dark hair curtained her serious eyes. Though she was seven years younger than Wes's thirty-two and probably weighed about a hundred pounds soaking wet, she ran the administrative side of The Woodlands with an efficient iron fist.

"Found them, I see." She bent to kiss Sweets.

Sweets tried to scale her legs and climb into her lap.

"No, Sweets." Wes shook his head. "I found the file in my procrastination pile."

Sweets whimpered, then sat at Clarissa's feet while she petted her.

Clarissa sighed and leaned back in her chair. She was smart as a whip and cute as hell, with long dark hair and a slim figure. More important, she was organized and efficient, and though Wes's siblings thought they'd hook up—given his penchant for cute females—she was a little too tough for his liking, and he'd never seen her in an amorous way. Not to mention that she seemed to have eyes only for his anally efficient partner, who happened to saunter into the room as if on cue.

"You're still here?" Chip sat on the edge of Clarissa's desk, and her eyes took a slow roll down his torso.

"Heading out in a sec."

Chip glanced at Clarissa, and their eyes held for a split second too long.

Clarissa lowered her eyes and began shuffling papers on her desk. "All set for the group?"

"As ready as I'll ever be." Wes ran his eyes between Clarissa and Chip. The air practically sizzled between them, but every time Wes brought up the possibility of Chip going out with Clarissa, Chip refused to acknowledge there was even a spark of interest. "Do you have my cheat sheet?"

Clarissa grabbed a piece of paper from the corner of the desk and pushed it across to Wes.

"Kathie Sharp, Bonnie Young, Christine Anderson, and Calliope Barnes, midtwenties, three married, one single, all experienced with high school sports and hiking, yada, yada. No medical concerns, no worries." She looked up at him from beneath her long bangs. "You're doing the overnight, right?"

"Yeah."

Her eyes widened. "Four twenty-something women and one hot wrangler, tents, moonlight, margaritas..."

Wes didn't live by many rules. And though it wasn't an official rule, he refrained from hooking up with Woodland guests, much to several sexy guests' dismay. He slapped his thigh, and Sweets came to his side again. "Have a little faith. The last thing I need is some woman suing me for my trust fund, my resort, *and* my dignity. No, thanks."

She rolled her eyes and pointed her pencil at him. "Wes, what if one of them is your soul mate? I wish you'd at least leave that door open a crack."

"Colorado's a big state. Too many pretty horses in the corral to be roped to just one." Wes turned and headed for the door with Sweets on his heels.

Sweets jumped onto the front seat of Wes's pickup truck and settled onto the plaid blanket he'd bought the first night after he'd found her. She rested her head on the books he'd gotten from Callie and looked up at Wes with another yawn. Wes picked up the book on the top of the stack. *Dark Times*. He ran his hand over the cover, thinking of Callie and knowing he'd never have time to read three books with the busy days ahead of him. He usually got through at least one of the books she chose for him. She had good taste, and even if he didn't get through a single book, he couldn't stop himself from going back for more. He smiled as he set the book back down, thinking of her curvy little body in that tight black skirt and how flustered she became every time she saw him. She was sweet and proper and nothing like the women he was usually attracted to, and as he drove out of Trusty and headed into the mountains, he couldn't help but wonder what it might be like to take her hair down and run his fingers through it—and he was powerless to quell his desire to climb beneath her conservative facade and help her move from women's fiction to erotica.

(End of Sneak Peek)

To continue reading, be sure to pick up the next LOVE IN BLOOM release:

FATED FOR LOVE, *The Bradens*, Book Eight
Love in Bloom series, Book Sixteen

Please enjoy a preview of the next
Love in Bloom novel

SEASIDE DREAMS

Seaside Summers, Book One

Love in Bloom Series

Melissa Foster

NEW YORK TIMES BESTSELLING AUTHOR

MELISSA FOSTER

Seaside Dreams

Love in Bloom: Seaside Summers
Contemporary Romance

Chapter One

BELLA ABBASCIA STRUGGLED to keep her grip on a ceramic toilet as she crossed the gravel road in Seaside, the community where she spent her summers. It was one o'clock in the morning, and Bella had a prank in store for Theresa Ottoline, a straitlaced Seaside resident and the elected property manager for the community. Bella and two of her besties, Amy Maples and Jenna Ward, had polished off two bottles of Middle Sister wine while they waited for the other cottage owners to turn in for the night. Now, dressed in their nighties and a bit tipsy, they struggled to keep their grip on a toilet that Bella had spent two days painting bright blue, planting flowers in, and adorning with seashells. They were carrying the toilet to Theresa's driveway to break rule number fourteen of the Community Homeowners Association Guidelines: *No tacky displays allowed in the front of the cottages.*

"You're sure she's asleep?" Bella asked as they came to the grass in front of the cottage of their fourth bestie, Leanna Bray.

"Yes. She turned off her lights at eleven. We should have hidden it someplace other than my backyard. It's so far. Can we stop for a minute? This sucker is heavy." Amy drew her thinly manicured brows together.

"Oh, come on. Really? We only have a little ways to go." Bella nodded toward Theresa's driveway, which was across the road from her cottage, about a hundred feet away.

Amy glanced at Jenna for support. Jenna nodded, and the two lowered their end to the ground, causing Bella to nearly drop hers.

"That's so much better." Jenna tucked her stick-straight brown hair behind her ear and shook her arms out to her sides. "Not all of us lift weights for breakfast."

"Oh, please. The most exercise I get during the summer is lifting a bottle of wine," Bella said. "Carrying around those boobs of yours is more of a workout."

Jenna was just under five feet tall with breasts the size of bowling balls and a tiny waist. She could have been the model for the modern-day Barbie doll, while Bella's figure was more typical for an almost thirty-year-old woman. Although she was tall, strong, and relatively lean, she refused to give up her comfort foods, which left her a little soft in places, with a figure similar to Julia Roberts or Jennifer Lawrence.

"I don't carry them with my arms." Jenna looked down at her chest and cupped a breast in each hand. "But yeah, that would be great exercise."

Amy rolled her eyes. Pin-thin and nearly flat chested, Amy was the most modest of the group, and in her long T-shirt and underwear, she looked like a teenager next to curvy Jenna. "We only need a sec, Bella."

They turned at the sound of a passionate moan coming from Leanna's cottage.

"She forgot to close the window again," Jenna whispered as she tiptoed around the side of Leanna's cottage. "Typical Leanna. I'm just going to close it."

Leanna had fallen in love with bestselling author Kurt Remington the previous summer, and although they had a house on the bay, they often stayed in the two-bedroom cottage so Leanna could enjoy her summer friends. The Seaside cottages in Wellfleet, Massachusetts, had been in the girls' families for years, and they had spent summers together since they were kids.

"Wait, Jenna. Let's get the toilet to Theresa's first." Bella placed her hands on her hips so they knew she meant business. Jenna stopped before she reached for the window, and Bella realized it would have been a futile effort anyway. Jenna would need a stepstool to pull that window down.

"Oh...Kurt." Leanna's voice split the night air.

Amy covered her mouth to stifle a laugh. "Fine, but let's hurry. Poor Leanna will be mortified to find out she left the window open again."

"I'm the last one who wants to hear her having sex. I'm done with men, or at least with commitments, until my life is back on track." Ever since last summer, when Leanna had met Kurt, started her own jam-making business, and moved to the Cape full-time, Bella had been thinking of making a change of her own. Leanna's success had inspired her to finally go for it. Well, that and the fact that she'd made the mistake of dating a fellow teacher, Jay Cook. It had been months since they broke up, but they'd taught at the same Connecticut high school, and until she left for the summer, she couldn't avoid running in to him on a daily basis. It was just the nudge she needed to take the plunge and finally quit her job and start over. *New job, new life, new location.* She just hadn't told her friends yet. She'd thought she would tell them the minute she arrived at Seaside and they were all together, maybe over a bottle of wine or on the beach. But Leanna had been spending a lot of time with Kurt, and every time it was just the four of them, she hadn't been ready to come clean. She knew they'd worry and ask questions, and she wanted to have some of the transition sorted out before answering them.

"Bella, you can't give up on men. Jay was just a jerk." Amy touched her arm.

She really needed to fill them in on the whole Jay and quitting her job thing. She was beyond over Jay, but they knew Bella to be the stable one of the group, and learning of her sudden change was a conversation that needed to be handled when they weren't wrestling a fifty-pound toilet.

"Fine. You're right. But I'm going to make all of my future decisions separate from any man. So...until my life is in order, no commitments for me."

"Not me. I'd give anything to have what Kurt and Leanna have," Amy said.

Bella lifted her end of the toilet easily as Jenna and Amy struggled to lift theirs. "Got it?"

"Yeah. Go quick. This damn thing is heavy," Jenna said as they shuffled along the grass.

"More…" Leanna pleaded.

Amy stumbled and lost her grip. The toilet dropped to the ground, and Jenna yelped.

"Shh. You're going to wake up the whole complex!" Bella stalked over to them.

"Oh, Kurt!" Jenna rocked her hips. "More, baby, more!"

"Really?" Bella tried to keep a straight face, but when Leanna cried out again, she doubled over with laughter.

Amy, always the voice of reason, whispered, "Come on. We *need* to close her window."

"Yes!" Leanna cried.

They fell against one another in a fit of laughter, stumbling beside Leanna's cottage.

"I could make popcorn." Jenna said, struggling to keep a straight face.

Amy scowled at her. "She got pissed the last time you did that." She grabbed Bella's hand and whispered through gritted teeth, "Take out the screen so you can shut the window, please."

"I told you we should have put a lock on the outside of her window," Jenna reminded them. Last summer, when Leanna and Kurt had first begun dating, they often forgot to close the window. To save Leanna embarrassment, Jenna had offered to be on sex-noise mission control and close the window if Leanna ever forgot to. A few drinks later, she'd mistakenly abandoned the idea for the summer.

"While you close the window, I'll get the sign for the toilet." Amy hurried back toward Bella's deck in her boy-shorts underwear and a T-shirt.

Bella tossed the screen to the side so she could reach inside and close the window. The side of Leanna's cottage was on a slight incline, and although Bella was tall, she needed to stand on her tiptoes to get a good grip on the window. The hem of the nightie caught on her underwear, exposing her ample derriere.

"Cute satin skivvies." Jenna reached out to tug Bella's shirt down and Bella swatted her.

Bella pushed as hard as she could on the top of the window, trying to ignore the sensuous moans and the creaking of bedsprings coming from inside the cottage.

"The darn thing's stuck," she whispered.

Jenna moved beside her and reached for the window. Her fingertips barely grazed the bottom edge.

Amy ran toward them, waving a long stick with a paper sign taped to the top that read, WELCOME BACK.

Leanna moaned, and Jenna laughed and lost her footing. Bella reached for her, and the window slammed shut, catching Bella's hair. Leanna's dog, Pepper, barked, sending Amy and Jenna into more fits of laughter.

With her hair caught in the window and her head plastered to the sill, Bella put a finger to her lips. "Shh!"

Headlights flashed across Leanna's cottage as a car turned up the gravel road.

"Shit!" Bella went up on her toes, struggled to lift

the window and free her hair, which felt like it was being ripped from her skull. The curtains flew open and Leanna peered through the glass. Bella lifted a hand and waved. *Crap.* She heard Leanna's front door open, and Pepper bolted around the corner, barking a blue streak and knocking Jenna to the ground just as a police car rolled up next to them and shined a spotlight on Bella's ass.

CADEN GRANT HAD been with the Wellfleet Police Department for only three months, having moved after his partner of nine years was killed in the line of duty. He'd relocated to the small town with his teenage son, Evan, in hopes of working in a safer location. So far, he'd found the people of Wellfleet to be respectful and thankful for the efforts of the local law enforcement officers, a welcome change after dealing with rebellion on every corner in Boston. Wellfleet had recently experienced a rash of small thefts—cars being broken into, cottages being ransacked, and the police had begun patrolling the private communities along Route 6, communities that in the past had taken care of their own security. Caden rolled up the gravel road in the Seaside cottage community and spotted a dog running circles around a person rolling on the ground.

He flicked on the spotlight as he rolled to a stop. *Holy Christ. What is going on?* He quickly assessed the situation. A blond woman was banging on a window with both hands. Her shirt was bunched at her waist, and a pair of black satin panties barely covered the most magnificent ass he'd seen in a long time.

"Open the effing window!" she hollered.

Caden stepped from the car. "What's going on here?" He walked around the dark-haired woman, who was rolling from side to side on the ground while laughing hysterically, and the fluffy white dog, who was barking as though his life depended on it, and he quickly realized that the blond woman's hair was caught in the window. Behind him another blonde crouched on the ground, laughing so hard she kept snorting. *Why the hell aren't any of you wearing pants?*

"Leanna! I'm stuck!" the blonde by the window yelled.

"Officer, we're sorry." The blonde behind him rose to her feet, tugging her shirt down to cover her underwear; then she covered her mouth with her hand as more laughter escaped. The dog barked and clawed at Caden's shoes.

"Someone want to tell me what's going on here?" Caden didn't even want to try to guess.

"We're..." The brunette laughed again as she rose to her knees and tried to straighten her camisole, which barely contained her enormous breasts. She ran her eyes down Caden's body. "Well, *hello* there, handsome." She fell backward, laughing again.

Christ. Just what he needed, three drunk women.

The brunette inside the cottage lifted the window, freeing the blonde's hair, which sent her stumbling backward and crashing into his chest. There was no ignoring the feel of her seductive curves beneath the thin layer of fabric. Her hair was a thick, tangled mess. She looked up at him with eyes the color of rich cocoa and lips sweet enough to taste. The air around them pulsed with heat. Christ, she was beautiful.

"Whoa. You okay?" he asked. He told his arms to let her go, but there was a disconnect, and his hands remained stuck to her waist.

"It's...It's not what it looks like." She dropped her eyes to her hands, clutching his forearms, and she released him fast, as if she'd been burned. She took a step back and helped the brunette to her feet. "We were..."

"They were trying to close our window, Officer." A tall, dark-haired man came around the side of the cottage, wearing a pair of jeans and no shirt. "Kurt Remington." He held a hand out in greeting and shook his head at the women, now holding on to each other, giggling and whispering.

"Officer Caden Grant." He shook Kurt's hand. "We've had some trouble with break-ins lately. Do you know these women?" His eyes swept over the tall blonde. He followed the curve of her thighs to where they disappeared beneath her nightshirt, then drifted up to her full breasts, finally coming to rest on her beautiful dark eyes. It had been a damn long time since he'd been this attracted to a woman.

"Of course he knows us." The hot blonde stepped forward, arms crossed, eyes no longer wide and warm, but narrow and angry.

He hated men who leered at women, but he was powerless to refrain from drinking her in for one last second. The other two women were lovely in their own right, but they didn't compare to the tall blonde with fire in her eyes and a body made for loving.

Kurt nodded. "Yes, Officer. We know them."

"God, you guys. What the heck?" the dark-haired woman asked through the open window.

"You were waking the dead," the tall blonde answered.

"Oh, gosh. I'm sorry, Officer," the brunette said through the window. Her cheeks flushed, and she slipped back inside and closed the window.

"I assure you, everything is okay here." Kurt glared at the hot blonde.

"Okay, well, if you see any suspicious activity, we're only a phone call away." He took a step toward his car.

The tall blonde hurried into his path. "Did someone from Seaside call the police?"

"No. I was just patrolling the area."

She held his gaze. "Just patrolling the area? No one *patrols* Seaside."

"Bella," the other blonde hissed.

Bella.

"Seriously. No one patrols our community. They never have." She lifted her chin in a way that he assumed was meant as a challenge, but it had the opposite effect. She looked cuter than hell.

Caden stepped closer and tried to keep a straight face. "Your name is Bella?"

"Maybe."

Feisty, too. He liked that. "Well, Maybe Bella, you're right. We haven't patrolled your community in the past, but things have changed. We'll be patrolling more often to keep you safe until we catch the people who have been burglarizing the area." He leaned in close and whispered, "But you might consider wearing pants for your window-closing evening strolls. Never know who's traipsing around out here."

(End of Sneak Peek)

Check online retailers for the Seaside Summers series

Coming Late Summer 2014

SEASIDE DREAMS, Seaside Summers, Book One
Love in Bloom Series

Complete LOVE IN BLOOM Series

For more enjoyment, read the Love in Bloom novels in series order.

Characters from each series carry forward to the next.

SNOW SISTERS

Sisters in Love
Sisters in Bloom
Sisters in White

THE BRADENS

Lovers at Heart
Destined for Love
Friendship on Fire
Sea of Love
Bursting with Love
Hearts at Play

THE REMINGTONS

Game of Love
Stroke of Love
Flames of Love
Slope of Love
Read, Write, Love

THE BRADENS (coming soon)

Taken by Love
Fated for Love
Romancing my Love
Flirting with Love
Dreaming of Love
Crashing into Love

SEASIDE SUMMERS (coming soon)

Seaside Dreams
Seaside Hearts
Seaside Sunsets
Seaside Secrets

Acknowledgments

The Bradens are a joy for me to write, and every email I receive from fans spurs me on to write more and to bring you new and different journeys toward love featuring fun, sexy, and flawed characters with whom you can laugh, cry, and, of course, swoon over.

Taken by Love takes place on a breeding horse ranch, and I am grateful to Shanyn and Earl Silinski, who have answered my endless questions with patience and humor. I've taken creative liberties in my writing. Any and all errors are my own and are not a reflection on the Silinskis. Kathie Shoop, my friend and go-to person to help me bang my ideas loose, your friendship is a gift to me. Thank you for being who you are and welcoming me into your circle.

The support of the members of Team Pay-It-Forward, the blogging community, and my sisters at heart, the volunteers of the World Literary Café, is endless. Stacy, Amy, Bonnie, Christine, Tasha, Clare, Rhea, Wendy, Emerald, Amy, and Gerria, thank you all for embracing me and enabling my obsession for romance.

My editorial team deserves a standing ovation for their meticulous and experienced skills. Thank you, Kristen Weber, Penina Lopez, Jenna Bagnini, Juliette Hill, and Marlene Engel. Special thanks to Lynn Mullan, one of my early readers. My amazing cover designer, Natasha Brown, and my formatter, Clare Ayala, are not only talented, but able to put up with me and my endless tweaks. That speaks volumes about you both.

Thank you for allowing me to take advantage of your mad skills.

To my husband, Les, who listens to me read chapter after endless chapter, remembers each character, and fleshes out plot lines without complaint, you are my world. Thank you.

Melissa Foster is a *New York Times* and *USA Today* bestselling and award-winning author. Her books have been recommended by *USA Today's* book blog, *Hagerstown* magazine, *The Patriot,* and several other print venues. She is the founder of the Women's Nest, a social and support community for women, and the World Literary Café. When she's not writing, Melissa helps authors navigate the publishing industry through her author training programs on Fostering Success. Melissa also hosts Aspiring Authors contests for children, and has painted and donated several murals to the Hospital for Sick Children in Washington, DC.

Visit Melissa on her website or chat with her on The Women's Nest or social media. Melissa enjoys discussing her books with book clubs and reader groups and welcomes an invitation to your event.

www.MelissaFoster.com

CPSIA information can be obtained
at www.ICGtesting.com
Printed in the USA
BVOW04s2348060617
486153BV00022B/7/P